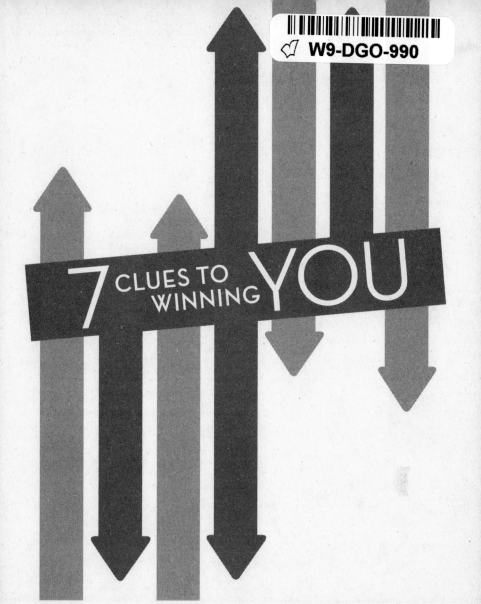

7 CLUES TO WINNING YOU

7 CLUES TO WINNING YOU

Kristin Walker

razOr
bill

An Imprint of Penguin Group (USA) Inc.

Seven Clues to Winning You

RAZORBILL

Published by the Penguin Group
Penguin Young Readers Group
345 Hudson Street, New York, New York 10014, U.S.A.
Penguin Group (USA) Inc., 375 Hudson Street, New York, New York 10014, U.S.A.
Penguin Group (Canada), 90 Eglinton Avenue East, Suite 700, Toronto, Ontario,
Canada M4P 2Y3 (a division of Pearson Penguin Canada Inc.)
Penguin Books Ltd, 80 Strand, London WC2R 0RL, England
Penguin Ireland, 25 St Stephen's Green, Dublin 2, Ireland
(a division of Penguin Books Ltd)
Penguin Group (Australia), 250 Camberwell Road, Camberwell, Victoria 3124,
Australia (a division of Pearson Australia Group Pty Ltd)
Penguin Books India Pvt Ltd, 11 Community Centre,
Panchsheel Park, New Delhi — 110 017, India
Penguin Group (NZ), 67 Apollo Drive, Mairangi Bay, Auckland 1311, New Zealand
(a division of Pearson New Zealand Ltd)
Penguin Books (South Africa) (Pty) Ltd, 24 Sturdee Avenue,
Rosebank, Johannesburg 2196, South Africa

Penguin Books Ltd, Registered Offices: 80 Strand, London WC2R 0RL, England

10 9 8 7 6 5 4 3 2 1

ISBN 978-1-59514-414-0

Library of Congress Cataloging-in-Publication Data is available

Printed in the United States of America

For Mom and Dad

CHAPTER 1

THE PROBLEM WITH SOME OF THE STEAMIEST romances in Shakespeare is that everyone ends up dead. I never saw the point of going through all that anguish and passion and sneaking around just to end up with a pile of corpses. It didn't seem right. So whenever my dad picked *Romeo and Juliet* for one of our family Shakespeare readings when I was a little kid, I always changed the ending so Juliet woke up in time. It drove Dad nuts, but I just couldn't help it. I'm a girl who likes happy endings.

Family Shakespeare readings were just one of the by-products of having an English teacher for a father. I'm pretty sure I was the only eight-year-old who could recite Sonnet 29. That was years ago, though, long before Dad got promoted to principal of Ash Grove High School, over in the next school district. I wasn't too thrilled that he was the principal of our rival school, but at least he wasn't principal here at Meriton. Can you imagine how horrifying that would be? Talk about a tragedy.

But like I said, I'm a firm believer in happy endings. I wanted my own happily ever after, but I wasn't about to leave it up to chance. I had everything planned out, step by step.

I'd graduate from Meriton High in the top of my class, get into Bryn Mawr (majoring in literature with a minor in classics), and marry a man from Haverford. My wedding dress would be a strapless ivory silk-satin ball gown with a beaded shrug and birdcage veil, the reception would be held in the Rittenhouse Hotel in early June, and we'd live in Swarthmore: north of Yale Road, but east of Chester. I'd get my master's degree in education and then teach at Swarthmore College, getting tenure in record time, while my husband commuted to the city for his upper-level corporate job.

We'd enjoy cozy holidays snug in our warm restored historic house. We'd host engaging dinner parties with the university elite. I'd do charity work with underprivileged orphans. We'd be blessed with four darling children of our own (boy–boy–twin girls . . . but of course I would be happy no matter what we got) who would go to the finest private schools (my husband would come from old Philadelphia money, of course). There would be flowers in the garden, stars at night, and undying love from my handsome husband. We would live happily ever after.

Everything was right on track by the last half of my junior year at Meriton. I was getting top marks in my honors classes and had an impressive list of extracurricular activities that would demonstrate well roundedness on my college applications. I was also well liked and well dressed. In fact, it was just as I was swapping out my winter wardrobe for spring when things in my plan started to slip a little sideways.

"Blythe?" Dad called up to me from downstairs. "Can you come down for a minute?"

"Be right there!" I shouted. I stood in front of my closet, satisfied. "Perfect." My wardrobe was the last stop on my room organization blitz for spring. "Oops, hold up . . ." I reached in and plucked a pale aquamarine cami from the line of hangers and moved it to the other side of the nearly identically colored tank top next to it. "Now it's perfect." I trailed my fingers down the line of garments precisely organized by color. Spring clothes. Lovely, bright spring clothes. Gauzy chiffons and crisp linens. Pinks and yellows, prints and polka dots. I was so glad to be finished with my heavy winter wardrobe for the year. If I'd had to wear another ribbed cable-neck sweater, I was going to drop dead from asphyxiation. It was time to break out the cap sleeves and capris. Okay, sure, maybe it was only early March, but it was the beginning of spring break, and spring break was when I always organized my room and switched out my wardrobe. Come hell or high necklines.

I shut the closet doors and headed downstairs, making a mental list of my plans for the week. Shopping with Tara and the girls. Studying for the SATs. Hanging out with Tara and the girls. My weekly volunteer time at Shady Acres Nursing Home. Movie night with Tara and the girls. Sleeping late. Stalking the captain of the basketball team with Tara and the girls (her crush, not mine). And general relaxation.

When I got to the living room, I could tell something was up. Evidently, it was a Family Meeting. It didn't look good. Everyone was there, including Zach, my twelve-year-old brother, who almost never shows up for anything family-oriented if he can help it. He was stretched out on the floor playing a game on his PSP. As I stepped over his legs, he yelled, "DIE, YOU MUTANT SCUM!" and bent one leg just enough to trip me. I stumbled over him, and Zach cringed. He'd been talking to his game. "Oops, my bad!" he said as he returned to playing. "Sorry."

Dad stood with his back to us, staring out at the damp front yard through the bay window. There was definitely a weird vibe in the room. Zach let out a huge belch and said, "Ooh, that's better." Then the vibe became revolting.

Dad turned around and saw me. He motioned for me to sit on the couch, which I did. I searched my mom's face for some clue to what was happening. To my horror, she had on her lady look. The lady look was this expression of placid friendliness and utmost composure that Mom put on her face whenever she was in an uncomfortable situation. Picture the queen of England getting a wedgie, and that's the lady look. A lady never shows displeasure on her face, Mom always said. She'd been making that face for so long, I don't think she even realized when she did it. She'd learned it from her mother and passed it along to me. I'd found the lady look very useful for smoothing over sticky situations. Not that the situations I got in were ever terribly sticky.

When I saw the lady look on my mother's face as she perched on the edge of one of the matching sage-green wingback chairs, I knew that the situation was about to go nuclear.

Dad clasped his hands behind his back and rocked back and forth on his heels. I knew that move too. It was his "I'm about to do something that's going to make your life miserable, but first I'll pretend I'm on the fence about doing it" maneuver. He used it regularly as principal at Ash Grove. I knew Zach and I were in for it before Dad even said a word.

Dad cleared his throat. "Well. We weren't planning on telling you kids this for a few months, but circumstances have dictated an acceleration in the schedule."

"Dumb it down. Please. *Principal Mac*," Zach said without looking up from his game. "Try talking like a damn father." Zach loved to call Dad out for treating us like we were his students or worse—his faculty. Not that I understand why he'd talk like that over there. Ash Grove isn't exactly the kind of school that Rhodes scholars come from. More like Rhode-side garbage pickers. It may be a neighboring district to Meriton, but it's on the other side of the academic tracks, if you know what I mean. That's one of the sources of fuel for our rivalry.

"Do not swear in this house, young man," Dad said. Zach started to get to his feet and Dad barked, "Where do you think you're going?"

"Outside. To swear," Zack said. "Just like you ordered."

Dad pointed to the floor. "Park it." Zach plopped back onto the carpet and went back to his game. He always seems to know just how far to go to annoy our parents without getting in trouble.

Dad closed his eyes and inhaled deeply and dramatically. "You know how we talked about moving over to the Ash Grove school district after you graduated, Blythe, so that I would have a better shot at becoming superintendent when Hank Bascomb retires?"

"Yes," I said tentatively.

"Well, there's been a little change in those plans."

I lit up. "We're not moving? Oh thank GOD. The thought of coming back from college to some weird house makes me want to puke."

Dad didn't nod. Instead, he glanced at Mom and they locked eyes for an instant. Uh-oh. I froze, suddenly aware that I'd instinctively put on the lady look.

Dad cleared his throat again and said, "Well, last month, I got word that Superintendent Bascomb is retiring this year. So if I truly want a shot at his position, I . . . I mean, *we* . . . need to be living in the Ash Grove school district."

As he spoke, my stomach tightened and tightened until I found myself struggling to breathe. My fingers were curled into knobs pressing hard into the tops of my thighs. My toes burrowed into the carpet.

"So we're moving," Dad said. "Immediately."

Zach looked up from his game *without even pausing it*. That was serious.

My head buzzed. "But I'll get to stay at Meriton, right? I won't have to switch schools for my senior year, RIGHT?"

Dad rocked back and forth on his heels again. "Unfortunately not. In fact, you're going to have to switch to Ash Grove even earlier."

"Like how early?" I cried. "What's earlier than senior year?" Inside, I already knew what he was going to say, but I couldn't bring myself to admit it, let alone to say it.

"Junior year. Now. Directly after spring break, that is. I think the best time for you to transition is right at the start of the spring quarter. Luckily, our calendar at Ash Grove coincides with Meriton's, so you'll still have your vacation." He winked at me as though he'd done me some kind of favor on the sly.

My mother finally chimed in with, "If you think about it, sweetie, this is actually good news." She raised her eyebrows and tipped her Barbie-doll face to the side. "You'll have a chance to make some friends before senior year."

"That does not qualify as *good news*," I said, jumping up. "No, no, no. This isn't happening. I go to Meriton. All my friends are at Meriton. Meriton is a top school. I can't graduate from *Ash Grove*! Ash Grove graduates do NOT get into Bryn Mawr!"

Dad wagged his finger in the air. "Pardon me, young lady, but many Ash Grove graduates go on to top-rated universities."

"Not like Meriton grads!"

"Well, then you'll be at the top of the class, won't you?" Mom chirped.

"Ooh, that'll make her popular," Zach muttered.

"Hold on. Hold on," I said, struggling to come up with a solution. A resolution. Some kind of detour that would lead me back on the path to my happy ending. "I know! What if I live with Tara until graduation?"

Mom shook her head. "Blythe, sweetie, we can't possibly impose on Tara's family like that. It's out of the question."

Blood flushed up into my face and my fingers tingled. "I can't go to Ash Grove! Have you forgotten what happened to me there?"

Dad chuckled. "Honey, that was a year ago. I'm sure no one remembers it."

"Oh, really? Are you sure? Because I remember it. I remember it perfectly. The humiliation. The giggling. Even from a few Meriton kids who saw that awful picture. I can't imagine facing an entire school that did. Please, Daddy, you can't do this to me!" I knew that pleading as daddy's little girl was probably futile or at best a long shot, but I was determined to pluck his heartstrings as hard as I could.

"I'm not doing this to hurt you, pumpkin. This is my shot. My one shot. I have to take it. I promise the move will be easy, and I'll make sure things go well at school."

It was only really at that exact moment that the full trauma of this horrific ordeal hit me. I'd been focused merely on academic insufficiencies and the lingering humiliation of a bad viral photo of me from last year. But that wasn't all of it. "Oh my God," I said. "I'm going to be the principal's kid. Unbelievable. I might as well start planning a funeral for my social life right now."

CHAPTER 2

AFTER THE FAMILY FIREBOMB FEST, I TOOK OFF TO
meet Tara and the rest of my girls for some serious consola-
tion. There were five of us. Four of us had been really tight
ever since first grade. You know, like we knew every tiny
detail of each other's dream guy, dream date, dream wedding,
dream honeymoon, dream celebrity hottie who we'd secretly
make out with if he showed up on our honeymoon. Tara was
the kind of girl who didn't even care about getting married.
She hated the idea of being anchored to anything. If I ever
said, "Wouldn't it be cool to do such and such?" Tara would
say, "So, duh, let's go do it." I swear, if the electric company
could tap into Tara, she could power the entire East Coast.

Cerise and Veronica were tight with each other too. So tight
that they could've been twins. They even finished each other's
sentences and sometimes coordinated their outfits. They were
always jockeying for head of the class and had a running bet
that whoever made valedictorian senior year would get to decide where they'd spend the summer after graduation. Cerise
wanted to go to Montreal, but Veronica wanted to go to Palm
Beach. It was one of the few things they disagreed on.

Melissa was our new number five. She'd only been at

Meriton since the beginning of the school year, but she'd slid right into place like Cinderella's foot into the glass slipper. She was the one in our group who, if you were just casually checking us out, you might think was the cling-on. She dressed conservatively and didn't say much. She never tried to impress anyone, but that's because she didn't need to. Melissa was literally a descendant of royalty in some small European country. Okay, so she was the end of a long, twisty branch of the family tree, but related was related. Melissa's great-grandmother had had an affair with one of the nephews and got pregnant with Melissa's grandfather. The royal family flipped out and the nephew eventually sent great-grandma packing to the U.S. with the baby and a wad of cash. The money was gone long ago (thus public school for Melissa), but the lineage was still there. I mean, wow, to know you're a member of a royal family? How cool would that be? Yeah, Melissa was no cling-on.

Whenever one of us was having a crap day, we'd meet at the coffee shop in Meriton for large doses of caffeine, sugar, and chocolate or at the mall for some shopping therapy. A problem like switching schools definitely called for the mall. But shopping didn't make a dent this time. In fact, I pretty much just wandered from store to store in tears.

"I'm telling you, my mom would totally let you live with us," Tara said for the fifth time. She gave me a one-armed sideways squeeze and touched her head to mine.

"I wish," I said. "My parents would never let it happen, though. Besides, we'd probably start killing each other within weeks." I forced a hollow laugh.

"Yeah, most likely," Tara agreed.

"You should just emancipate yourself," Veronica chirped.

"Divorce your parents," Cerise added.

"Then you could do what you wanted," Veronica concluded.

"There's no time," I said. I'd already considered this option on the ride over here. "I start school right after break."

"Well, we'll just have to have a blowout spring break, then," Tara said. She hooked one arm through mine and the other through Melissa's. "Come on, ladies. Let's buy our girl here a giganto-sized caramel macchiato or three."

I dragged the sides of my index fingers along my bottom lash line to wipe off any smudged mascara and put on what I hoped was a convincing lady look. "Sounds great," I said.

We headed over to the food court and got our caramel macchiatos. Tara also got a handful of chocolate biscotti and passed them around at the table.

"My parents are actually meeting with a real estate agent as we speak," I said, dunking my biscotti, "to look for a new house and put ours up for sale, which seems totally surreal. I can't imagine not living there. I just . . . I can't believe it. I can't believe he's being so selfish." I chomped down on the dripping end of the biscotti.

"I know! What is his deal?" Veronica said, stirring a third packet of sugar into her coffee.

I swallowed. "All he cares about is his career. Making more money. Getting a higher position. I mean, he didn't even ask any of us what we thought. It's like we didn't even matter." Tears filled my eyes again. I started dunking violently. Tara passed me a napkin, and I dabbed the corners of my eyes so that whatever was left of my mascara would be spared.

"I felt the same way about my dad moving us here," Melissa said. "He got a promotion, so it was like, no question that we'd move. Meriton's not bad, though. I miss my old friends, but it's actually kind of cool to start with a completely clean slate, you know? Someplace where you have no history to live down."

"Except that she does," Tara muttered to her cup.

Melissa eyed us one by one. "So what did happen, anyway? I never heard."

I swallowed the last lump of biscotti, and it tried its best to lodge in my throat. I guess I was taking too long to respond, because Cerise jumped in and started babbling.

"Okay. Well. Over at Ash Grove, they have this yearly tradition where the seniors put on a scavenger hunt for the juniors in spring term. It's a kind of a race, where they have to find each object and turn it in to hear what the next object will be. Whoever turns in the final scavenger hunt object first wins some huge mystery prize." As Cerise spoke, Veronica made hand gestures as if she were the one talking. It was one of the more creepy things the pair of them did.

"Like impossible-to-get concert tickets and a limo," Veronica said. "Or a weekend at the shore."

"Something awesome, you know?" Cerise continued. "So last year, since Blythe's dad is the principal, one of the clues was to get a picture of him in his regular home life. Doing anything."

"Mowing the lawn, getting the mail, whatever," Veronica added.

"The stuff they have to find is all goofy," Tara interjected. "Enema bags, a case of fortune cookies, that kind of thing."

Melissa nodded and stirred her coffee methodically.

Veronica piped up. "So this one kid actually crept up to Blythe's kitchen window and snapped a picture of her dad inside."

"Which, I think, is illegal or should be, and that kid should've been charged," Cerise added. Veronica nodded vehemently.

I stepped in. "Well, my dad would never press charges and alienate his precious student body, but whatever. The kid took the picture. The problem was, I was in the picture too." I held up my foamy stir stick. "Now listen. Let me explain something first. I was just getting over a cold and my nose was super sore from blowing it. And I had a tissue right there in my hand, but it was hurting to try to use it, so . . ."

Tara jumped in. "She picked her nose! Right when he took the picture!"

"My nose was sore," I cried. "And it was only my pinky, which is barely even a real finger! So yes, kill me, I picked my nose, and everyone does it so whatever."

Tara was cracking up so hard that she hugged herself in pain. I shoved her, and she held up her hands in surrender. "I know! I know. It was totally scarring for you. And completely unfair." She snorted. "But it was kind of funny." She looked to the other girls for affirmation, then turned back to me. "You have to admit it," she continued. "I mean, it's not like it was a picture of you naked or making out with your cat."

"I don't have a cat."

"Well, if you did have a cat."

"It was bad enough," I said.

She gave me a soft grin and ran her hand across her short, razor-cut hair. "I know it was. I was right there with you the whole time, remember? I'd have taken that bullet for you in a second, and you know it."

I made little rips around the rim of my cup. "I know . . ."

"Okay, so someone took a picture," Melissa said as a puzzled look spread across her face. "How does that translate into some major history you have to live down?"

I inhaled, preparing to answer, but Veronica beat me to it. "It went viral. As soon as this kid turned it in for the scavenger hunt, some senior jerk noticed Blythe mining for gold in the background. He cropped and magnified the picture and e-mailed it to all his friends."

I shook my head at the memory. "Every time I think of Ash Grove, I think of that picture, and this flood of embarrassment and humiliation rushes through me all over again. How am I going to go to school there every day?"

"It's so old news," Cerise added. "Nobody's going to remember."

"I remember," I said.

"Oh my God, you have got to get over it," Tara said. She reached across the table and gave my hand a squeeze. "Seriously, Blythe. You're making it worse for yourself. Just let it go."

"I know, I know," I said. I tipped my cup way back and tapped the bottom, but the last dollop of foam wouldn't slip down. I gave up and set my cup down hard on the table.

"The picture even ended up in the Ash Grove school newspaper," Veronica whispered to Melissa.

"Hello?" Cerise cried at Veronica. "Not helping!"

Melissa's eyebrows knitted together. "Wasn't there a staff adviser? How could they allow that?"

"It wasn't the real school newspaper," I said, waving the air like the newspaper was nothing more than a bad smell. "There's this unofficial online student newspaper that supposedly tells the truth about all the hush-hush things that happen in school. You know, like which teacher got a DUI or how some study group turned into a drunken orgy . . . . That's where the picture was posted. I guess they were making fun of the principal's kid. Hilarious."

"Wow," Melissa said. "There's no way that kind of bullying would have been tolerated at my old school. Those kids would be expelled."

Bullying?

To be honest, I'd never thought of it as bullying. I'm not sure why. I guess I never considered myself as the victim type. All along, I figured that the whole fiasco was partly my fault because I did, in fact, pick my nose. And it's not like it was a sexting picture. Was it bullying?

"So wait," Veronica said, "you start right after spring break? So you'll be there for this year's scavenger hunt, right?"

"And you're a junior," Cerise said.

My stomach slipped to the floor. My jaw followed. "I hadn't thought of that," I said.

"But wait, this could be good," Tara said. "This could be your chance to get back at them. You could sabotage the scavenger hunt. Bring it down from the inside." She was grinning a bit too enthusiastically.

I sat in silence. Revenge was never my thing. Just the opposite, in fact. I was all about charity. Charity made for a much more appealing personality. Plus, it comes across super in college interviews. Nevertheless, Tara had a good point. The question was, was I willing to risk my social life and reputation to make their lives miserable? The answer became obvious. I couldn't care less about having a social life at Ash Grove. Between the viral picture and Principal Daddy, my reputation was already toast before I walked in the door. It really couldn't get much worse.

CHAPTER 3

LEGALLY, IN ORDER FOR ZACH AND ME TO REGISTER in Ash Grove schools, our parents had to prove that we were residents of the Ash Grove school district. To do that, we had to have a contract on some kind of home. So instead of spending spring break actually relaxing and enjoying my remaining days with my friends, I got dragged around on a hurricane house hunt. We must have seen thirty properties that week. Our real estate agent, Marjorie, took us to see one stories, two stories, raised bungalows, tri-levels. They had big lots, corner lots, walk-out basements, new roofs, replacement windows, upgraded kitchens . . . but no matter what we saw, nothing was good enough for Mom. It was too small. Too old. Too much work. Too sketchy a neighborhood. Too high property taxes. Too expensive (those two were Dad, really).

Finally, this traditional two story came on the market in a decent neighborhood not far from the town center of Ash Grove. It was "three-years new!" (perky agent-speak), bank-owned, and vacant. Some victim of a foreclosure, Marjorie surmised. At any rate, it was move-in ready (which you don't find with foreclosures normally, so this was sure to be a hot property, said Marjorie, and if we were interested, we should move on it *right away*).

It was actually bigger and nicer than our house in Meriton. I guess better school districts like Meriton drive house prices higher there. This place had a big front porch that wrapped around one side of the house, landscaped gardens with paver walkways, and a huge backyard. Mom couldn't find anything to object to, other than the tacky wallpaper. Dad promised to get it professionally removed and repainted before we moved in, if that would make her happy. So she agreed. I didn't hate the place. Zach was fine with it. Frankly, if a house had a toilet, electricity, and a basketball hoop, Zach was happy.

We put in an offer on the house and it was accepted. So, as soon as we sold our Meriton house, we could start our thrilling new lives as Ash Grove inmates. Excuse me, residents. My darling, sweet mother kindly counseled me by saying, "Blythe dear, we must maintain an open mind and attitude about this change in our lives. Each one of us has to make . . . adjustments to this new situation. Instead of focusing on the negative things, list the positives."

List? I couldn't come up with one positive, let alone a list.

Of course, the flip side to buying a house is that you have to sell the one you already own. Which means you have to fix all the broken, chipped, dirty, worn parts that you've managed to live with contentedly for years. Then you have to clean the places in the house that you've never cleaned— or even knew you should clean.

Who knew you were supposed to climb up onto your kitchen counter and scrub the tops of the cabinets? Who knew that all this time, you should have been cleaning the lint out of the exhaust tube in the back of the dryer? Who ever could have guessed that you're expected to purge and organize every closet, cupboard, shelf, and drawer? And I don't mean only the built-in ones, either. I mean all of them. Even the ones in your own personal furniture that you'll be taking with you and that the buyer has no business poking around in. Because buyers will look everywhere, Marjorie instructed us. *Everywhere.*

When your house is for sale, you may no longer have a junk drawer in the kitchen or that one closet where you throw the old shoes and broom handles and dirty buckets and broken things that you were going to fix one day and anything else you don't want to look at or deal with or smell. You may not leave a single family picture anywhere, no matter how expensive the frame was or how important that dead relative is to you. You may no longer let a load of laundry sit in the dryer for a moment after it's finished. Please, people, do not leave the toilet plunger sitting right there next to the toilet, out in the open like that . . . what are you thinking? And for the love of all things holy, never, *ever* forget to make the beds!

Throughout the massive cleanup, Dad would make these observations that he probably thought were deeply philosophical but actually were just complaints. "Does it strike anyone as ironic," he'd call out, "that we're making the house perfect just before we leave it?" And then, "How come we never could do this for ourselves, but we'll do it for someone else?" But the mantra he repeated again and again under his breath as he trudged from chore to chore was, "Eyes on the prize, Mac. Eyes on the prize."

The prize, of course, was not a good offer on the house; the prize was an appointment to superintendent. I didn't overlook that.

Zach and I had each been in charge of our own rooms. Mine wasn't too bad, since I'd just done my springtime organization. But Zach's looked like something from a show on hoarders. I wouldn't have been at all surprised if he uncovered a litter of desiccated baby raccoon carcasses. On the plus side, by the time he was done, he'd collected a small mountain of dirty odd socks.

By the end of spring "break," we were beyond exhausted. I momentarily slipped and caught myself looking forward to school on Monday. The sensation didn't last long, though. It was quickly replaced with dread. I tried to convince myself that I didn't care if people remembered the picture or not. I mean, it was a year ago. It had to be old news by now. Right?

So the next morning, I got up, made my bed, *of course*, and then did the one thing that helped me feel confident and together: I put on a new outfit. It was an adorable pink silk blouson top with a camel stretch pencil skirt that I'd gotten at the mall after my cry fest with the girls. I fixed my hair and makeup, slipped into a pair of pumps, and went downstairs to eat some cereal to settle my jumpy stomach. It was getting late, though, so after a couple of minutes, Dad and I headed out so I could follow him to school in my car. It's a gold 1995 Honda Civic in all its scratched and dented glory. It's not exactly a smokin' ride, but it's mine. It was a gift for my sixteenth birthday from Dad. My grandparents had wanted to get me an electric-blue Mini Cooper convertible, but Dad shut that down. He was adamant that the car should come from him and should be something that wouldn't crush like a soda can or eject me fifty feet if I happened to get into a fender bender. Hello, safe, reliable Honda.

When we got to Ash Grove, I parked in the student parking lot in one of the last free spaces, approximately 150 miles from the building. As I schlepped with my messenger bag across the enormous parking lot in heels, I kicked myself for not riding with Dad since he got the sweet principal's parking spot right beside the door.

No, I told myself. *It's better to distance myself from him. Better to be Blythe.*

When I got to the door, I paused to take a cleansing breath, straighten up, and arch my back slightly for good posture, as Mom always emphasized. This also was definitely a time for the lady look, so I put one on, opened the door, and walked inside.

The first thing that hit me was the smell of the place. It was a smell unlike anything at Meriton. In fact, Meriton didn't really have a smell at all, except after they polished the floors on the weekends. But Ash Grove smelled like ancient mildew and disinfectant mixed with bad cologne over BO.

It smelled like academic mediocrity.

I knew I had to go to the office first, and Dad had told me how to get there from the student parking entrance. But twenty seconds after I entered the building, all memory of his directions evaporated.

My heart was a madman pounding out of its cage of bones. Pinpricks of sweat bloomed on my upper lip. Why was I nervous? Surely I was at least as intelligent as these people. And . . . now, I'm not saying I was necessarily *better* than they were or of a higher ilk or anything . . . but let's just say there wasn't a tailored pant in sight. God, there wasn't even a belt. Meriton might not be a private school, but at least we dressed the part.

I tried to swallow, but my gummy throat stuck to itself. Bodies everywhere pushed around like refugees jostling for heels of bread. It was a rising tide of fake tans and bad fashion. I noticed that I'd started to draw some looks. Some at my face, some at points farther south. I was, in fact, the only girl wearing a skirt. The glimmering thought sped through my mind that maybe this was the only skirt they'd ever seen at school. *Okay, so they don't dress for school here,* I thought. *I can deal with that. I don't like it, but I can deal.*

I started to muscle my way through the crowd, trying to remember where Dad had said to go. Was it the second or third hall on the left? I finally broke into a clearing and knew I was lost. I picked out a fairly friendly-looking girl a few feet away and walked up to her. "Hi," I said. "Could you please tell me how to get to the main office?"

The girl looked at me for a few seconds, and then her over-tanned face lit up with a huge openmouthed grin. Her hand flew up and cupped her mouth as she took a step backward. Then she dropped her hand, pointed one of her bedazzled fake nails at me, and squealed, "Oh, my *gawd.* You're that booger girl!"

CHAPTER 4

FACES SPUN TOWARD ME AND MELTED INTO SNICKERS as I inched my way down the hall. This was insane! The picture wasn't that big a deal that they'd remember it so well a year later. How did they recognize me right away? I started walking faster past the smirks. One guy doubled over into that phony, exaggerated imitation of hysterics. Some trashy-looking girls eyeballed me up and down like I was a fungus, then giggled. What were those little kids over by the wall laughing at? Me? But they had to be freshmen. They weren't even here last year! What was going on?

In my mind, I could hear my mother's voice repeating, "Dignity, Blythe. Dignity." She would know how to handle this situation. She was unflappable. So I pretended to be her. I set my jaw like Mom would. I kept my line of vision just above everyone's head. Eye contact with no one. I pinned my shoulders back and strode like Moses parting the Red Sea. Only, this was a sea of synthetic fibers and cheap hair extensions.

Trying to dodge one particularly vocal jerk, I made a wrong turn into what must've been the senior wing and rammed into the back of this tall skinny guy with dirty-blond hair and glasses. I apologized and tried to leave, but he snapped his locker closed and snagged my elbow. "Hold on. Who are you? You look familiar." At which point I rolled my eyes and tugged my arm away. I turned to go, but he stepped in front of me. "Wait! Now I recognize you. You're McMussolini's daughter. Wow, shouldn't you be over in Meriton with the rest of the socialites? What brings you out here to the slums?"

Even though I knew I shouldn't acknowledge any of these baboons, this guy irked me. So I tried a different Mom technique where she turns someone's sarcastic comment on its head and makes the commenter look like an idiot.

I gave the tall guy with glasses an innocent look and said, "I'm here to be educated. And what an education it's been so far, let me tell you. The overwhelming reception I've received this morning has touched me in the most unexpected fashion. I especially appreciate the way you've welcomed me, how you've gone out of your way to treat a complete stranger as though you actually knew her. I'll be sure not to forget it. Ever."

I didn't wait for a response. I tossed my auburn hair and waltzed away without looking back. I kept going until I found the damnable office. I didn't stop at the counter, either. I stormed right past it, through the clutch of secretaries' desks, and straight into Dad's office. I shut the door behind me before he even thought to say "come in."

The way he looked at that moment spooked me, though. It was like he'd just been caught. Wide eyes. Fish mouth. Hands dangling at his sides like empty sleeves. That's when

I realized he knew something. He knew something I didn't know. Something bad.

He held both hands out in front of him to stop me. "I just found out," he said. "I didn't know before now. One of the secretaries only just told me."

"Told you what? Wait, let me guess," I said. I pointed in the direction of the hallway. "She told you that I didn't even make it twenty feet inside the door before some girl called me 'that booger girl' and people started laughing? Even freshmen! They couldn't have seen the picture. How would they know? How could everyone still remember it enough to recognize me?"

"It might have something to do with the yearbook," he said meekly.

I narrowed my eyes and glared at him through the slivered gaps. I tried to stop my hands from trembling by clutching the strap of my messenger bag in a death grip. "What about the yearbook?"

He said nothing.

"What about the yearbook, DAD?"

He patted the air with both hands to try to get me to calm down. It didn't work. "Everything's going to be fine," he said. I didn't believe him. He took a baby step toward me and spoke in a low, steady voice. "When I told Gladys— she's the head secretary out there—when I told her that I was registering you for school here, she looked surprised. I asked her why, and she said because of the yearbook. When I said I didn't know what she was talking about, she told me that one of the pictures in this year's yearbook is . . . you know . . . the picture . . . of you. From last year."

"WHAT?"

"Now, honey . . ." he started, but I didn't let him finish.

"You're the principal! You're my father! How could you let them do that?"

He shook his head frantically. "I didn't know. I'm sorry. I should have known, but I didn't. These things are delegated out to the faculty, and the teacher in charge is new and didn't catch it, and obviously nobody knew you'd be matriculating here. Gladys happened to notice the picture when she sent the proofs off to the printer, but she assumed I'd given it the go-ahead, which, of course, I never, ever would do, so . . ." He trailed off.

I stood there stunned. My body hummed like a super-charged electric coil. Full of useless, angry joules with no circuit to flow through. "But everyone knows," I said. My jaw was clenched so tight, it barely moved. "It wasn't just the yearbook committee. People everywhere were laughing at me."

Dad blinked a few times and his face went blank. "That I can't explain. I don't know how everyone knows. I'm sorry, honey. I think you should just go back out there and act as though everything is fine and dandy, and the whole picture thing is a funny joke. Soon enough it'll be yesterday's news."

I looked my dad straight in the eye and said, "The only place I'm going back to is Meriton."

He shook his head. "You can't."

I planted my hands on my hips and cocked one shoulder up. "Oh, really? Why?"

"Because I already pulled your registration from Meriton.

It's against the law to be registered in two different schools." He sighed deeply, puffing his cheeks out. Then he clasped his hands behind his back and started rocking on his heels. Whoa, bad sign.

"I know you're unhappy right now, Blythe, but Ash Grove is your school. You're just going to have to find some way to reconcile the conflicts presented to you. It's the kind of skill that will help you throughout your life. There's no way you can judge this school after having been here five minutes. We have a strong school. We have a fine student body. You're going to have to adapt, Blythe, and that's all there is to it." I couldn't believe all the principal-speak he was throwing at me. He motioned to the door to usher me out as if I were a total stranger. "Now let's get your registration papers signed, print out your schedule, and get you off to class."

My feet wouldn't move. Not that I wanted them to. I was stunned that my father had pulled his Principal Mac routine on me. Stunned *and hurt*, to be honest. This had been the closest thing we'd ever had to a fight. I guess it actually was one. Normally, here's how our disagreements went: I got upset and Dad caved. That was how it worked.

I never took advantage of the situation, though, because I knew that if I did, eventually it would stop working. And since I didn't abuse it, Dad didn't feel bad about caving. He knew that if I got upset over something, then it must be genuinely important to me, and I wasn't faking or manipulating him. What he and I had was a perfectly harmonious symbiosis. Or at least it had been up to that moment, when I realized I was just another student to him.

I got my schedule and one of the secretaries walked me to my homeroom so I wouldn't get lost and be late. That's the reason she gave, anyway. I suspected that my dad had asked her to escort me so I wouldn't take off.

Luckily, most of my classrooms were in the same hall as my homeroom, so I made it through the morning without running into any more skinny guys with glasses accusing me of being a fascist's daughter. I got a lot of stares and snickers, though. A few people (mostly guys, but not all, if you can believe it) dug their pinkies knuckle-deep into their nostrils and shouted, "Pick a winner!" at me.

When the morning finally ended and I headed for the cafeteria, my heart started pounding like a jackhammer. I knew lunch was going to be disastrous. Anyone who has ever eaten in a high school cafeteria can understand this. The only thing that governs the chaos of high school cafeterias is the law of the jungle. If you happen to be the proverbial gazelle in this horde of jackals, then prepare for the worst.

Every cafeteria smells the same, too. Why is that? I don't know. But I do know that the stench of old soup, used fryer oil, and vinegar seemed to hang in the cafeteria air like a fog. I made a quick mental sweep of the room and decided that my best course of action was to grab a strawberry yogurt and a bag of pretzels (rather than waiting in line for an entrée) and walk straight to the back corner of the room where a couple of emos or punks or possible heroin addicts were making out at an otherwise empty table. At Meriton, these two would be called wasteoids. Here, I didn't care what they were called. They were already isolated from the rest of the students, so I figured people would probably avoid that table. I made a beeline for it. Any port in a storm, right?

I plunked down in a seat at the table on the opposite end of the face-sucking emo/punk/addicts and peeled the lid off my yogurt. Out of the corner of my eye, I could see that the girl was sitting on the guy's lap with one arm around his neck and the other one clutching one of the chains looping through his black canvas jacket. The two of them were making out so hard that I could actually hear it. That's right; I could hear their slobbery kissing. Unfortunately, when I stirred my yogurt it made an uncannily similar slurping sound, so I set it right down and grabbed my bag of pretzels. Now, I must say that whoever produced these pretzels was clearly a jerk, because no matter what I did, I couldn't pull the bag open. I tried to be discreet about it, but it wasn't budging, even when I put more effort into it than dignity allowed. I got so frustrated that I ended up grunting and grimacing, and I could feel my face turning into a sweaty, puffy beet. Finally, I gave up and smacked the bag on the table.

"Want me to try?"

It was the wasteoid guy. He and his girlfriend were evidently taking an oxygen break. "Sure," I said, and shot the bag sliding down the table toward him. He snatched them up and tore the top open in one motion. "There's a little nick in the bag at the top," he said. "You tear, not pull." His girlfriend whispered something in his ear and then kissed him full on the mouth. Afterward—while still on his lap—she plucked the bag from his fingers and leaned down the length of the table to hand it to me. She had about eight chunky silver rings on each hand and black-tipped fingernails that made me think of a French manicure gone evil.

"Thanks," I tossed off. "I'll keep that in mind." I scooted over to take the pretzel bag and ended up a bit closer to them. I didn't want to scoot away, though, because I thought it would seem rude. Instead, I kept eye contact to a minimum. I focused very hard on the bag of pretzels, as though I'd never seen anything more captivating than packaged snack foods.

"I'm Jenna," the girl said. I broke my stare from the spellbinding pretzels to look at her. She tipped her head slightly. "This is Cy." Cy hitched his chin in an upward nod. I tried not to ogle the monster-sized pointed metal stud poking out of the skin below his bottom lip. Or the black disk gauges in his ears. Or the lethal-looking silver spike speared through the upper ridges of his left ear. I seriously thought he could take someone out with that thing if he felt like it.

Jenna, on the other hand, only had a barbell through one eyebrow, although I was pretty sure I'd caught a glimpse of a tongue piercing. Her hair was shaggy and dyed three different colors: black on top, hot pink in the middle, and bleach blond underneath. Sort of like furry Neapolitan ice cream. She was wearing a boat-neck, three-quarter-sleeve, black-and-white-striped top with black leggings with an oversized studded belt. Actually quite stylish in an edgy, French bohemian sort of way.

Both Cy's and Jenna's eyes were lined with heavy black eyeliner and were focused directly on mine. I managed a respectable lady look and said, "I'm Blythe."

Jenna's scarlet pouty lips curled into a sly smile. "We know who you are."

I sighed and set down my pretzels. Here we go. "Okay, let's have it," I said.

Neither one of them said a word. "What are you waiting for?" I said. "Go ahead. Call me the booger girl. Tell me I'm daddy's precious pet. Pretend to pick your nose and have a big ol' laugh. Can we just get this over with so I can eat my lu . . . lu . . ."

I couldn't finish. The corners of my eyes started stinging, and a second later, tears rolled down my face. I swiped them off with the back of my hand. I straightened up and inhaled deeply through my nose. But as I slowly let the breath whoosh out of my mouth, the tears let loose again. I sniffled and dove into my messenger bag for a tissue. Out of the corner of my eye, I saw Cy pull a napkin from the dispenser on the table and hand it to Jenna, who squirmed off his lap and handed it to me. "Why would we do that?" she asked.

I dabbed the napkin into the corner of my eyes and blew my nose. "Why wouldn't you? Everyone else is," I said, thankful that I had my back to the room at least, so no one but Cy and Jenna could see my micro-meltdown.

"I don't know if you can tell," Cy said, "but we're not really the type to do the same stupid shit that those freaks do." A lock of his messy black hair fell over one eye. Jenna swept it back and gently kissed his forehead.

I wiped my teary eyes carefully so my makeup didn't smudge. "I just don't understand how so many people know who I am. I mean, yeah, my picture went viral last year, and I know that"—I had to stop and take a staccato breath—"that it's going to be in the *yearbook*." Took another breath, peppering like a machine gun. "But how come it's not just the yearbook people who recognize me? It's like everyone's been staring at that picture for the past month."

"Yeah, well . . ." Cy pursed his lips and then said, "That's because they were."

I froze with the sodden napkin pressed to my nose. "What do you mean, 'they were'?"

Jenna crossed her arms and leaned over the table toward me. She kept her voice down, which I appreciated. "There was a caption contest," she said. "The yearbook snobs thought it would be funny to have a contest where people submitted witty—"

"But mostly insulting—" Cy interjected.

Jenna continued, "Mostly insulting sayings or captions for a few of the yearbook pictures."

Cy said, "Everyone voted on their favorite caption, and the winner is being printed with the picture in the yearbook."

Jenna gave me an almost apologetic look, which was a nice effort. "One of the pictures was yours. The contest ran for three weeks."

I squeezed my eyes shut and pinched the bridge of my swollen nose. This wasn't happening. There was just no way. "Where were the pictures and captions posted?" I already could guess the answer, but I was grasping at wisps of hope here.

Jenna shared a glance with Cy, and I knew I was right. She said, "On *Buried Ashes*. It's this online newspaper. I think that's where your picture got posted last year too. Anyway, that's where it was. I guess people thought it'd make sense to have the contest there since everybody already goes to the site."

Sometimes a bad situation will get worse and worse until it's so bad that it defies all odds and reason and therefore becomes ridiculous and actually funny.

This wasn't one of those times. I pretended it was, though. I drew my mouth up into a smile and forced a few raspy chuckles out of my throat. "Well. That's just fantastic. That sure explains it." I think I looked more deranged than anything. To Cy and Jenna's credit, even though it was obvious that I was faking, they didn't call me out on it.

"Let me guess," I said. "The winning caption was 'Pick a winner,' right?"

Jenna nodded.

"Don't feel bad," Cy said as he snagged one of my pretzels and popped it in his mouth. "It could be worse. The one that came in a close second was 'Boogers: the other white meat.'"

That was what did it. That was the thing that tipped the situation right over into funny. I pressed my lips together, but spurts of laughter kept bursting out. Watching Jenna and Cy try not to laugh was even funnier. Finally, I just let go and the three of us cracked up over in our own little corner of the jungle.

I laughed so hard my nose started running again. I blew it right there at the table, which would've horrified Mom. "Do either of you know whose brilliant idea it was to put the picture in the yearbook in the first place?"

They both shook their heads. Cy said, "No idea."

"Someone from the yearbook committee, I guess," Jenna added.

"You don't know any names?" I asked.

Cy snorted. "I try to know as little information about these people as possible."

Jenna shared an amused look with him. "We're not exactly joiners," she said.

I'd have to get the names from Dad. "What about that online newspaper?" I asked. "Do you know who runs that?"

"Yeah, that's Luke Pavel," Jenna said. "He's a senior. He started *Buried Ashes* his sophomore year. He thinks it's cutting-edge news that the administration doesn't want the students to know, but it's mostly just a tabloid."

Cy disagreed. "There's some decent information. He'll write about some issue or whatever that nobody knew anything about. Something substantial. He's a decent guy even if he does have a bit of a god complex. Like he answers to some higher power of integrity and has an obligation to *undermine authority and expose corruption*." Cy said the last bit in Superman's voice. Then he made a gesture indicating a certain sexual act performed on a man.

I blushed and glanced downward to hide it, digging my spork into my yogurt. "Oh, sure. He's chock-full of integrity. Posting embarrassing pictures of people he doesn't even know is so admirable. What a guy."

Jenna stared out the window. "It's easy to embarrass people you don't know."

Cy beamed at her. "Spoken like the true goddess you are.

A hot, sexy goddess." They kissed again with lots of tongue, so I politely pretended I was invisible.

When they came up for air again, I asked what Luke Pavel looked like.

"Tall guy. Glasses," Cy said.

"Blondish hair," Jenna added. "Kinda curly."

"Wait a sec. Is he skinny? Tall, skinny guy with wire-frame glasses?"

"I wouldn't call him skinny," Jenna said. "He's, like, lean. But in a cute way." Cy reared back and fake-gaped at her. She blushed.

"Oh, really?" Cy tickled her ribs. "Cute, eh?" Jenna giggled and squirmed. Cy laughed. "So you think Luke Pavel is cute, do you?"

"Yes!" Jenna gasped. "He's gorgeous!" Cy tickled harder and she squealed. "He's so sexy with those hot, hot"—more tickling, more squealing—"hot Harry Potter glasses!" Cy kept her in wriggling hysterics for a few more seconds before finally letting her go. She laid her head on the table and curled her arm around it, panting. With the other arm, she gave Cy a shove, and he winked at her.

"I think I might have met him," I said. "He called me 'McMussolini's daughter.'"

Cy huffed. "Yeah, that's gotta be Pavel. He likes to bitch about Principal Mac being a fascist and the school being a totalitarian state, blah blah, yadda yadda, and other equally boring things."

"As if that's breaking news," Jenna added.

A thought struck me that I hadn't considered before that

moment. "Can I ask you something? Is my dad an okay principal? I mean, is he a nice guy or a jerk or what? Do people generally like him?"

Jenna shrugged one shoulder. "He's not bad. I mean, Cy and I have . . . well, let's say we've met him a few times, even though Vice Principal Hinkler handles most of the discipline problems. She gets off on it. What a gigantic douche bag. Your dad doesn't treat people like crap the way *Finkler* does. But sometimes he's a bit, you know . . ." She tipped her head side to side and tried to find the right word on the ceiling.

Cy jumped in. "Like some psycho life coach robot spouting motivational sayings and cheering you on. Rah! Rah! You can do it! Keep a positive attitude and your problems will instantly disappear!"

Jenna drew figure eights on the table with her index finger. "He's a little out of touch. He doesn't really get where some of us are coming from. What we deal with day to day. But I mean, he's not a dick or anything. Just kind of clueless."

Cy hitched his chin at me. "What's he like as a dad?"

I considered it for a second. "Not a dick. Kind of clueless."

I almost said more. I very nearly told them how selfish my father was by moving us to Ash Grove just to advance his career, which wasn't even a sure thing. But I decided that I really didn't know anything about Cy and Jenna other than the fact that apparently they didn't eat lunch. The bell rang, anyway.

Out in the hallway, I checked my schedule for a computer class so I could Google *Buried Ashes*. Fifth period was Intro to Programming. I crossed my fingers that there'd be some free time at the end to mess around. Luckily, there was.

Intro to Programming seemed to stretch on forever. After we'd sat through a lukewarm instruction on how to make a batch file, we finally were turned loose to "work independently." That's teacher code for "If I have to teach you wretched sons of Satan one more minute, I'm going to self-combust. So, do whatever you turds want while I sit here contemplating suicide."

The second I got the chance, I went online and entered the web address. My intention was to go into the archives and look at the post about the caption contest, as well as the post from a year ago where Luke Pavel uploaded my picture and started this mess.

But I never made it past the homepage.

CHAPTER 5

BURIED ASHES

One-Stop Shopping for the Truth about Life at Ash Grove

Editor in Chief, Luke Pavel

Welcome back from spring break, groovy Grove-ies! The snow is melting and the sun is finally stepping up and getting the job done. Hopefully you juniors got a lot of rest because it's that time of year again. That's right—spring at Ash Grove means one thing:

THE SENIOR SCRAMBLE!

(Cue the hysterical screaming!)

This much revered rite of passage has initiated Ash Grove juniors into the senior class for decades. This year will be no exception, boys and girls. Right now, as you read this, the senior class is finalizing diabolical clues and assembling a mystery prize package that will blow your mind. Literally BLOW YOUR MIND. Wear a helmet.

For you newbies and freshmen who are scratching your butts right now wondering what the Senior Scramble is, here's the scoop:

Every spring, Ash Grove seniors compose a grueling scavenger hunt for the juniors to complete. But we're not talking about collecting paper clips and seashells, oh, no. The Senior Scramble is a hunt for insane, illogical, impossible-to-get things.

But there's a catch. (You didn't think it was going to be easy, did you?) The hunt is also a race. Each item must be turned in, one by one, before the next item is revealed. The first junior (or team of juniors) to turn in the final item wins the Senior Scramble and lives on in infamy.

So juniors, get ready to rock! Clear your calendars and jack up your caffeine addictions. Gird your loins or do whatever else your loins might need. Pick your teams if you're too chicken to go it alone, because . . .

The Ash Grove Senior Scramble starts in ONE WEEK!

JUST-POSTED UPDATE: You may have recognized a new student around school this morning. Will this fetching junior be participating in the Senior Scramble this year? After all, technically, it would be a *repeat appearance* from last year!

I stared at the screen for a moment and then read through the article again. Then once more. By the third time I'd read *"repeat appearance!"* I had pretty much hit my boiling point. How insulting was that? How dare he?

Oh, I'll be participating in the Senior Scramble, I thought. *I'll be participating in its demise. And who does he think he is, calling me fetching? As if I'd accept a compliment from him.*

I swear: those were the words ringing in my head. But I must admit that inside my body, something a little different happened. I couldn't help feeling a teeny flash of delight at having been called fetching. He called me fetching! He was still a jerk, though. No denying that.

But a girl likes a compliment.

I flicked that temporary insanity aside and resolved to have a little face-to-face with Editor Pavel ASAP and let him know he was in my crosshairs. I spotted him just after the last bell of the day, striding on those stork legs toward the school exit. A couple of his friends flanked him on either side. I trotted after him in baby steps, as fast as my pumps could take me. When I caught up with him, I grabbed the strap of the backpack on his shoulder. He turned around with a scowl that dissolved into a grin when he saw me.

"Is your name Luke Pavel?" I asked.

His blue eyes peered at me through those wire-frame glasses. "Guilty. So how was your first day? Make lots of friends?"

"Actually," I said, "I think it's you I have to thank for all the friends I made today. Or didn't make, rather."

One end of his mouth curled up like a dry worm. "I don't know what you're talking about."

"I'm talking about the way you've heartlessly humiliated me on your website. Numerous times. Even today."

Luke Pavel winked at me and half-shrugged. "It was news. I had to report it." He patted the side of my arm as if we were old pals. "Sorry, kid. Freedom of the press. What can I say? The First Amendment's a killer." He locked eyes with one of his buddies and they shared a conspiratorial chuckle. He turned to go, and I grabbed his backpack again.

"You know what else the First Amendment grants?" I

said. I didn't wait for him to answer. "The right to petition the government for a redress of grievances."

His eyes widened and he stuck out his chin, impressed.

"And you can be sure," I continued, "that I am going to petition the government of this school, and there will be a redress for my grievances."

He cocked his head. "I see. So basically, you're going to tattle on me to daddy. Is that what you mean?" He switched his backpack to his other shoulder and took a step away from me. "Go nuts. Herr McKenna can't touch me. I haven't done anything wrong."

"Illegal," I corrected him.

"What?"

"You haven't done anything *illegal*. You have done something wrong. Those two words are not synonymous."

Luke Pavel whistled high and long. It reminded me briefly of a missile in descent. "Wow," he said, "they sure do give you a good education over there in Meriton." He put on an exaggerated hillbilly voice. "We dun never seen such smarts an' words an' learnin' out here in the kern-fields of Redneckville." One of his buddies snorted. The other one laughed and made a lame attempt to cover it by coughing.

I cranked up the lady look and said, "NO KIDDING." I stiffened and walked past him, cutting just inside his personal space. Many times, Mom had advised me always to be the first to leave. Never be walked-out upon. That's how she said it, too. Walked-out *upon*. I didn't have the heart to tell her that it was tacky to end a sentence with a preposition. Mom came from old money and family breeding, but her formal education consisted largely of cotillions, lobster bakes, and cocktail parties. Her high school diploma and bachelor of arts degree were basically formalities purchased by my grandfather to ensure her attractiveness to men. His real hope for her future hung on his unfailing belief that she'd marry well.

Luke Pavel called after me, "If you hate it here so much, then why did you transfer?"

I stopped. Pivoted. Sauntered back to Luke Pavel. Made my eyes into slits and leaned toward his face. "I wasn't given a choice."

His expression blanked. Then his brows knitted like he was puzzling something out. I didn't stick around to hear his next witty comeback. I spun around and left. I couldn't help doing a bit of my supermodel runway walk to make sure that my pencil skirt looked good from behind. That was another trick of Mom's. *Way to go, Mom.* Who knew she'd come in so handy?

As I stalked away from Luke Pavel, generations of haughty women walked with me. They were in my DNA. Even though I tried to suppress the snobbery like Bruce Banner does to the Incredible Hulk, sometimes it just overtakes me. To be perfectly honest, there are also times it's pretty helpful. Just like the Hulk is for Bruce.

Only half of my DNA was upper class, though. The other half was blue collar. When Mom brought home a young high school English teacher who'd enchanted her with romantic lines lifted from Shelley, Keats, Browning (and of course Shakespeare), my grandparents freaked. When Mom told them that she and Dad were engaged, Gran threatened to cut her out of the will and Granddad actually got the key to the antique gun case. Then he said that Dad owed him for sixteen years of private school and university tuition, not counting the three years at the most exclusive preschool in Manhattan. To which my father said, "You put Anne in school when she was only two years old? What kind of father does that? No wonder she gravitated toward a teacher rather than some overbearing, alcoholic elitist who'd never done anything with his hands but count money." Dad was a bit of a radical at the time, and he had a big mouth. A freethinker leftover from the seventies. And also, to Granddad's horror, a Democrat.

It was only when they threatened to elope that Gran backed down. There was absolutely no way she'd allow it. Everyone would think that Mom was "in the family way" (which is the wealthy way to say preggers), and that simply could not be tolerated.

So they resigned themselves to having Dad for a son-in-law and threw an extravagant, black-tie New York wedding. My father's family drove in from New Jersey and were politely ignored for the evening. I've been told that they took ample advantage of the full bar, however.

After I came along, things smoothed out a bit between my parents and grandparents. Even more when Zach did. When Dad got the job as principal seven years ago and began hinting at something even higher, Granddad took it as an aspiration to politics and began slapping Dad on the back and shaking his hand and listening to Dad's conversation at the dinner table. When Dad registered as a Republican, I think Granddad nearly cried.

On my way to the main office, I composed my petition for redress. I made a list of reasons why Luke Pavel's online rag and the Senior Scramble should be given the ax. Posting the picture last year was nothing more than bullying. I knew for a fact that Dad had a zero-tolerance policy for that, so the bullying angle was probably my best bet. I would include the caption contest and yearbook picture in my bullying argument too. With any luck, I might be able to get him to recall the yearbook proofs.

As for the scavenger hunt, well, that was simply a bad idea. It had the potential to get out of hand. It was probably illegal, technically, even if it did just involve petty theft. It wasn't fair to expect the police to turn a blind eye to criminal mischief every year. Someone could easily get hurt. Someone *had* gotten hurt. And frankly, the scavenger hunt was tacky. I decided I'd save that last point in case I needed to appeal for my mother's help.

I would present my case in a sensible, logical fashion. I would not get upset. I would not play the crying card. There'd be no need to. Dad would see that I was right about the online newspaper, right about the Senior Scramble, even right about the yearbook. He would be taking a firm stance on bullying and sparing the junior class indignity and peer pressure.

It would make him look like a strong and responsible leader to the school board when the superintendent position opened up.

• • •

Just before the head secretary, Gladys, put on her official sec-
retarial smile, I caught a glimpse of burnt-out exhaustion on
her face. In that second, she'd looked ten years older than in
the next, when she blinked a few times and said cheerfully,
"Oh! How was your first day?"

Long ago, I had made two policies for myself: never complain to strangers, and never answer kindness with antago-
nism. So even though I wanted to tell her that it was terrible,
then brush by her without permission and barge into my
father's office, I didn't. I put my own official smile on my face
and said, "It was fine. Thank you for asking. I was hoping to
see my father for a minute. Is he available?" Dad's workday
didn't end until an hour and a half after school did.

Gladys glanced behind her at Dad's office door. It was
partially open, so she nodded and waved me by. I thanked
her and wished her a nice afternoon and then crossed to
Dad's door. I knocked softly and peered around the edge.
"It's me," I said.

Dad stood up quickly and motioned me inside. He
skirted around his desk and placed his hands on either side
of my shoulders. He gave them a squeeze and said, "So?
How'd it go?"

I opened my mouth to launch into my petition, but for
some reason, my brain did a quick run-down of the day like
a highlights clip. Actually, a lowlights clip would be more
accurate. I saw the girl who called me that first derogatory
name this morning. I saw my exchange with Luke Pavel
where he said my father was a fascist. I saw myself standing
in the lunchroom realizing that I'd have to sit alone. I saw

the issue of *Buried Ashes* on the computer screen. I saw Luke Pavel's smug expression from a few minutes ago.

And I started to cry.

No! I thought. *No crying! Not yet, anyway!* But it was no use. The tears kept spilling out like they'd escaped captivity. I inhaled in jerky gasps. My nose started to run. Dad shut the office door, pulled me to him, and wrapped his arms around me. I sank my face in his shoulder and sobbed.

Dad stroked the length of my hair and whispered, "Hey, hey. It couldn't have been that bad. What happened? Tell me what happened."

So I did. In between involuntary cry-hiccups, I gave him a detailed run-down of my lowlights. When I was done, he handed me a tissue from the box on his desk.

"I'm sorry, honey. Kids can be cruel." He'd said that like he was letting me in on a secret. Like he was imparting some ancient wisdom that I couldn't possibly have known and might not comprehend. Saying it with such condescension made the fact that he said it at all even more pathetic.

"Kids can be cruel? That's all you're going to say?"

He eased me off his shoulder and held me at arms' length. "Now, come on. Don't you think you're overreacting? Maybe just a little bit?"

I shrugged out of his grasp and crossed my arms. "Is that what you say to all the kids who tell you they're being bullied?"

Dad's eyes widened and he frowned. "Bullied? What do you mean bullied? Don't throw that term around lightly, Blythe. Bullying is a serious accusation."

"It's not an accusation, it's a fact," I shot back. "What would you call it when someone posts an inappropriate picture of one of your students on the Internet and the whole school joins in to make fun of her?"

Dad sighed. "The whole school did not join in to make fun of you last year, Blythe. Do you see how you're exaggerating the facts here?"

"I'm not talking about last year. I'm talking about the past month! The caption contest!"

Dad tipped his head like a dog hearing a high whistle. "Caption contest? What are you talking about?"

"There was a contest last month. On Luke Pavel's online newspaper. He posted a bunch of pictures that were slated to be in the yearbook and there was a contest for people to submit insulting captions that, for some perverse reason, they thought were funny. Everyone in school voted, and the winning captions got printed in the yearbook with the pictures. Guess what one of the pictures was?"

I knew Dad didn't need to be told. His face blanched and he leaned back against the edge of his desk. He opened his mouth but didn't say anything for a few seconds. "I wasn't aware of that," he finally murmured. He snapped into principal mode and stood up. He folded his arms and crossed back and forth in his office, just like he does when Zach's in trouble. He stopped in front of me and shook his head. "I'm sorry, honey. I didn't know about that. If I had, I would have stopped it. Who instigated the contest? Was it Luke Pavel or was it the yearbook committee?"

I gaped at him. "Do you know how absurd it is that

you're asking *me*? I've been here one day. You're the principal. Don't you think you're the one who should have that information?"

"I have a lot of things I'm responsible for, Blythe. Policing the student body is not one of them. I depend on the staff, students, and parents to keep me apprised of these situations."

"But you ARE my parent! How could you not have known about it?"

"I've been very busy lately, Blythe. You have no idea how many things require my attention."

"You mean like gunning for superintendent?"

He stuck a finger at me. "Now, that's not fair."

"Not fair? Not fair? You know what's not fair? Being torn away from your home and friends and a school where you were perfectly happy and never caused a minute of trouble to your ungrateful parents and being forced to endure humiliation and embarrassment with no friends, no future, and no escape! THAT'S not fair!"

"Spare me the dramatics, Blythe," he said in a low, firm voice. "Families are not democracies."

I shot back, "Then don't act so surprised to hear that it's all your fault!"

I never talked back to my parents. Ever. I don't think Dad knew how to react. I'd never blown up and lost my temper before, not even when I was a toddler. Mom always said that I didn't have terrible twos, I had tranquil twos. I just never got very upset about anything. Until then.

Dad glanced quickly over my shoulder, then stepped around me to shut his office door. "Blythe, I know you're upset," he said softly, "but becoming superintendent would benefit all of us, not just me. It comes with a forty percent increase in salary. Forty percent. I'm talking a whole different tax bracket here. That money would improve our lifestyle dramatically. Hell, we could actually afford to send you to Bryn Mawr."

I gaped. He'd never mentioned the cost of college before. I never thought it was something he had to consider. "Gran and Granddad are paying for college," I reminded him. "They've been saying that forever."

"I don't want them to!" Dad patted his chest. "*I* want to be the one sending you to college! Not them. I want to give my family everything they need." He turned away from me. His shoulders slumped. He watched his fingers lace and unlace. "I'm a grown man, Blythe. I'm done with taking handouts from them." His fingers curled into fists. "I have to be."

I wanted to go over and hug him. Then I remembered why I was there. I forced myself to bring him back on topic. "You don't have to be superintendent to give me what I need right now."

When he wheeled around to face me, he was Principal Mac again. Turns out, he was like the Incredible Hulk too. "What would you have me do, Blythe? Discipline the yearbook committee? Suspend Luke Pavel? Cancel the yearbook altogether?"

I knew he wanted me to react as though those punishments were ridiculous, but I didn't bite. "That's a start."

He wheezed a high, sarcastic laugh. "A start? What else did you have in mind, exactly?"

I drew myself up and set my shoulders back. I lifted my chin and said, "I think you should cancel the Senior Scramble."

It was Dad's turn to gape. "What? Are you kidding?"

"That's where it all started, Dad. If it wasn't for the Senior Scramble, that kid never would have taken my picture, and none of this would have happened. Look how easily the scavenger hunt can get out of hand. How mean-spirited the participants can become. Don't you think it's a bit heartless and irresponsible for you to let it continue? What will the school board think when they find out that your own daughter had been bullied at your school and you did nothing?" I was pretty sure that clinched it.

Dad drew in a long breath through his nose and exhaled vocally, puffing out his cheeks. "I see what you're saying . . . I just . . . it would totally alienate the student body. It's a tradition that's been around here a lot longer than I have. Some of those same school board members grew up here and took part in the Senior Scramble themselves."

"Yes, and that was back in the days before the Internet and before desensitization to violence. Back when bullying was written off with 'kids will be kids.' This is your chance to demonstrate the seriousness of your zero-tolerance policy. It would set a precedent. It would deter other would-be bullies. At the very least, it would send a message. In fact, it might send an even louder message if you *didn't* do anything. 'Ash Grove: where you can bully even the principal's daughter and not get in trouble.'"

I have to admit that I hadn't planned to spin my argument

quite that way. To make it such a big deal. To take a stand and challenge my father on such a serious point. The words had simply poured from my mouth, and I couldn't deny a certain truth in them. Neither could Dad.

He rubbed his hands up and down his grimacing face. "I need to think about this for a while." He turned away from me. Fiddled with some papers on his desk. "I need to think."

"Okay," I said contritely. Had I gone too far? If I was getting what I wanted, did it matter?

He sat down in his chair and squeaked it back and forth a few times. He laced his fingers across his lap. I felt like he was waiting for me to say something more.

"Are you going to Shady Acres today?" he asked.

I gladly went along with the subject change. "I'm heading there now."

"Okay. I'll see you later at home," he said. "Drive carefully."

"I always do."

I was nothing if not careful.

CHAPTER 6

I LEFT THE OFFICE FEELING DEFEATED. WHICH WAS odd, since I'd basically been victorious arguing my case. I needed to hear a friendly voice, so the second I was outside the school doors, I pulled out my iPhone and called Tara. She skipped the hello and got right to the point.

"Oh my God, are you alive?"

"Barely. It was brutal."

"I'm so sorry, B. I wish I was there. Imagine I'm giving you a big hug."

"I wish you were here too so you could give me a ride to my car. This parking lot is like five hundred square miles."

"Okay, now I know it's bad because you only exaggerate when you're upset. What happened?"

"Oh, you know. The usual new-kid bloodbath."

"They were mean to you?"

"Only when they weren't ignoring my existence," I said.

"Those little white-trash bastards. Ugh, I can't believe you have to go to school there! It's like a bad dream."

"Tell me about it. Listen, T, I have to go volunteer. Want to get together later and I'll give you all the gory details?"

"Sure. Food court?"

"Sure."

We set a time to meet at the mall and hung up. I climbed into my car and made my way over to Shady Acres. I'd been volunteering at the nursing home since I was a freshman. At first I did it because I knew it would look good on my college applications one day. And Shady Acres wasn't too bad, once you got used to the pervasive odor of antiseptic and stale urine. My job was to talk to the residents or play cards with them, call bingo, wheel them around outside for a while, whatever. It was actually kind of fun.

But the real reasons I kept volunteering all these years were Ms. Franny and Ms. Eulalie. Frances Calhoun and Eulalie Jones. Two crotchety, ninety-something-year-old roommates spending the remainder of their days bickering and pecking each other to death. They were a riot.

Those two would argue about the color of the sky if they had the chance. Every Monday, almost without fail, I could hear them from down the hall, more than twenty feet before I reached their door. Today was no exception.

"I'm tired of hearing about it every damn day!" That was Ms. Franny. "If I have to listen one more time to how you marched on Birmingham with Dr. King, I'm going to get out of this bed and march on your skull!"

"Well, pardon me, your whiteness!" Ms. Eulalie had a thick southern drawl. "Excuse me if I happened to be proud of doing something to change this world for the better."

"Aw, you never changed anything but your big ol' underwear. And even that you don't do anymore. So tighten up your diaper and be quiet."

"I don't have to be quiet! I don't have to be quiet just because some white lady say I do! I don't take orders from nobody."

"ANYBODY. Jesus H. Christ, will you learn to speak English for once before you die? Which I hope will be any moment now."

"Don't you go taking my Lord's name in vain, you she-devil! You leave my sweet Jesus outta your conversation. You sure enough leave him outta your heart. That is if you have a heart, which I seriously doubt that you do."

"Hello, ladies!" I sang loudly, peeking through the door-way.

Ms. Franny threw her bony arms in the air. "Oh, thank the devil. Get your butt in here, Blythe, so I don't have to listen to this broken record anymore." She patted a spot her bed and I plopped down on it.

"See?" Ms. Eulalie gestured emphatically at her room-mate. "See how she thank the devil? You'd think that some-one who has everything but one toe in the grave'd be a little more polite to God. Not that she's got much of a chance to get into heaven. Not at this late a date."

"If you're going to be in heaven," Ms. Franny said, "then I'll pass." She nestled back into her pillows looking satisfied.

Ms. Eulalie clucked and crossed her arms. "You're lucky I'm a merciful woman. Lucky I have Christian charity. Lucky I put your name on the prayer list down at the Baptist church every week. I get the message to Pastor Morris to say your name loud and clear every Sunday."

Ms. Franny wheeled around on her. "Will you stop putting me on that damnable prayer list? You only do it because you know it drives me nuts!"

Ms. Eulalie smiled. "A woman got to do what a woman got to do." She cackled with shameless amusement.

I shook my head at the pair of them. "You two are worse than a couple of five-year-olds, you know that?"

Ms. Franny sat up suddenly and squinted at me. "Wait a second." She drew shaky circles in the air right in front of my face. "What's going on with your eyes? Have you been crying? Look, Ukulele, our girl's been crying!"

"What?" Ms. Eulalie clutched her chest. "Oh, no! What you been crying for, baby?"

I shrugged them off. "Nothing." I forced a smile and waved their question away with my hand.

"Now you just tell us." Ms. Eulalie gave me the Eye and spoke firmly in her no-nonsense tone. She had developed that tone over decades of raising many children, and not all of them her own. "You know we heard everything in this life there is to hear about. You tell us what's wrong and we'll tell you how to fix it. Something go wrong at school? Somebody not being nice to you?"

Ms. Franny shook her head. "Better not be, or I'll have to call up my old friend Joey Gambino." She winked and placed her knobby index finger beside her nose. "I'm connected, you know."

I got up to straighten up the knickknacks around the room. "You've mentioned it before."

"About a thousand times," Ms. Eulalie added under her breath. Then louder, "Watch that figurine, girl. My Josephina gave me that for my seventy-fifth birthday. God rest her soul." Ms. Eulalie had outlived all four of her children.

I planted one hand on my hip and cocked my head at her. "And you've mentioned *that* about a thousand times," I teased. Ms. Eulalie was a robust woman. Her muscles might have slackened and left her skin looking slightly deflated, but there was no mistaking that Ms. Eulalie's body had once been stout and strong.

"Now, tell us what happened. Was it a boy, baby?" Ms. Eulalie gave me a knowing look.

"Actually, it was," I said. "His name's Luke Pavel and he's this jerk senior at Ash Grove who hates me for absolutely no reason besides the fact that I'm the principal's daughter and I used to go to Meriton." I'd already told them the whole moving and switching schools story.

"Pavel?" Ms. Franny said with a *humph*. "Is he *Polish*?"

Ms. Eulalie snapped, "You are the biggest racist I ever met in my whole living life."

"Calm down, Rosa Parks. I didn't say anything bad about Polacks, I just asked about his heritage."

"See? You just called the boy a 'Polack'!"

"That's not racism!" Ms. Franny cried. "That's bigotry."

"Dear, sweet Jesus, why'd you put me in this room?" Whenever Ms. Eulalie'd had enough of Ms. Franny, she'd start praying to the ceiling. "I been good to you my whole life, so why, Lord, why? What terrible thing did I do to deserve this? Whatever it was, Jesus, please forgive me. Or call me home and end my misery."

"Yes! Pick that last choice, Jesus!" Ms. Franny interjected.

"Don't you get involved! Don't you go trying to queer things 'tween me and Jesus."

Ms. Franny tried to rise up out of bed. "Oh, so it's 'queer' things, is it?" She had a grandson named Darren who was a highly successful dancer-slash-choreographer on Broadway. Ms. Franny was fiercely protective of Darren's sexual orientation. "How dare you use that word! *Now* who's the bigot?"

"I don't mean it in that sense!" Ms. Eulalie waved her hands like she was erasing the air. "You know that I don't mean it that way, woman. Now close your mouth and let baby girl talk!"

They both shut up and looked at me expectantly. I began the story and told them every detail, from last year's scavenger hunt to my conversation with Dad barely half an hour earlier, including how I thought I'd convinced him to cancel the Senior Scramble and possibly the yearbook. They sat silently, even after I finished. "What?" I asked them. "What's wrong? You guys have a look."

Ms. Eulalie clucked and shook her head. "You going about making friends the wrong way, sugar."

"I'm not trying to make friends," I said. "I'm trying to stand up for myself and for other victims of bullying." It had sounded rehearsed. Maybe because I'd said it to myself so many times.

"Oh, that's horseshit," Ms. Franny said.

"Watch your language, you hussy!"

Ms. Franny went on like she hadn't even heard Ms. Eulalie. "Don't try to blow smoke up our asses, cupcake. We may be old, but we're not stupid."

Ms. Eulalie straightened her pajama top and nodded slowly. "Mmm-hmm."

"What do you mean?" I think, deep down, I already knew.

Ms. Franny leaned over and snatched her knitting out of the wicker basket on her bedside table. She unwound the baby-blue yarn from the needles and set into knitting a row. The aluminum needles clacked together rhythmically. "What I mean is, you're not interested in standing up for any victims. All you're interested in is getting even."

"That's right." Ms. Eulalie rocked back and forth slightly. She drummed her fingertips together in her lap. "Ain't nothing good going to come of that."

I couldn't stand the thought of Ms. Eulalie and Ms. Franny thinking I was a spiteful person, even though I recognized the complete hypocrisy in that. I tried to deny it, though. My feelings had been hurt, I explained, and I was only looking for justice.

They saw right through me.

"You done got justice mixed up with revenge, baby girl," said Ms. Eulalie. "You need to stop and think on things for a spell."

"Now, Blythe, we're all in favor of being strong and not letting bullies win," said Ms. Franny, "but you're going about it all the wrong way. What's the best-possible situation that could come out of this? You think everyone's going to realize they were wrong, call you a hero, and throw you a ticker-tape parade?"

"Mmm-mmm." Ms. Eulalie closed her eyes and calmly shook her head. "Lord, no."

Ms. Franny's hands moved the yarn and needles like a

shuttle on a loom. "Here's what's going to happen, best-case scenario. So make sure this is what you want. The seniors won't like you because you ruined their turn to be on the fun end of the stick for a change. The juniors won't like you because you came out of nowhere and took away a tradition they've been waiting for all year. The sophomores won't like you because they know they'll never even have a chance to look forward to it. And the freshmen won't like you because freshmen do what everyone else does."

"But . . ." I began.

Ms. Eulalie pointed her finger up in the air to stop me. "Oh, she ain't done."

"She's not?" I said.

"No."

I searched Ms. Franny's expression for confirmation. She kept her eyes on her knitting. "No, I'm not. That was the best-case scenario. Now here's the worst. All of that stuff still happens but on top of it, your father loses his job, your brother has to live down your reputation when he gets to high school, and you continue to get bullied, more than before. But that isn't even the worst of the worst."

"It isn't?" I asked. "What's the worst of the worst?" I was thinking maybe she meant I would get beaten up or something equally horrific. But I was wrong.

"The worst of the worst," Ms. Eulalie answered, "is that everyone finally come to realize that the biggest bully of all is you."

Her words halted my breath. That couldn't be true. Could it?

Ms. Franny stopped knitting mid-stitch and peered over the stilled needles at me. "That's the worst," she said. She waited a moment, and then her hands went back into motion. The needles clicked and clacked.

"So what am I supposed to do?" I asked. "Dad always said that the only way to stop a bully is to stand up to him."

"Standing up to a bully," Ms. Franny said, "is not the same thing as becoming one."

"Amen," Ms. Eulalie agreed. "You have to try to find a peaceful, non-violent resolution. You know, back in Birmingham, Dr. King said—"

"Oh Christ, here we go again."

Ms. Eulalie slapped both hands down on her mattress. "I already said! Don't you take the Lord's name in vain!"

"Aw, somebody make her stop. Make her stop!" Ms. Franny threw her head back on the pillows. "I can't take it anymore!" She grabbed both knitting needles in one fist and pretended to stab herself repeatedly in the neck.

"Ladies," I implored, "please!" I heard shoes squeaking on the floor behind me and knew who it was before I even had to look: Darlene, the head floor nurse. She was overweight, middle-aged, and seemed to have gotten sick of nursing about twenty years ago. I never had a conversation with Darlene where she didn't complain about something. She was that type of person.

"What on EARTH is going on in here? Why do I have to come in here every SINGLE day?" She glared at me. "And why is it always worse when YOU'RE here?"

Ms. Franny bolted upright and brandished her knitting needles like a sword. "You lay off her!"

Darlene sneered and hitched her thumb at the door behind her. "Blythe, go in the common room and call bingo. They're ready to start. Go on."

Ms. Eulalie started humming a hymn, which is what she does when she's trying to bite her tongue. Ms. Franny doesn't even bother trying. "You are such a sad and hateful woman; you know that, Nurse Ratched?"

Darlene sneered. "Oh, ha ha ha." She'd been called the name of the evil, sadistic nurse from *One Flew Over the Cuckoo's Nest* many times, especially by Ms. Franny.

Darlene smiled snake-like. Slit-eyed and all. Her hands clenched the hem of her Snoopy scrub top. "Watch out, or I might forget your Oxycontin."

"Ha!" Ms. Franny laughed. "As if I don't already know that you're stealing it to sell to drug addicts on the street. Got to buy yourself some more fake fingernails and stripedy hair color, huh? Well, here's a little secret for you, darling. Fancy striped hair doesn't make you look any less rotund!"

As Ms. Franny spoke, Darlene's eyes seemed to swell out of her bulging, crimson cheeks. She pursed her lips into a tight, wrinkled bud. She clearly had zero experience with the lady look.

Ms. Eulalie hummed louder.

Darlene growled through gritted teeth, "BL-YTHE?" When she was really livid, Darlene added syllables to words.

I slid off Ms. Franny's bed. I didn't want to leave and go call bingo, but Darlene had the authority to fire me from volunteer work. I didn't want that. So I kissed the ladies and followed Darlene through the door. Two steps out, I heard

Ms. Franny start up again back in the room. "Talk about a bully," she said. "Well, thanks a heap, Ukulele. Fat lot of good your peaceful, non-violent humming did to help me out . . ."

Darlene's white orthopedic nursing shoes squeaked so loudly that I couldn't make out another word. I felt like a scolded child following her down the hall, but she wasn't the type of person who would walk beside you, either. She always had to be a step or two in front. I sped up and tried to walk next to her just to see if she'd turn it into a race, but she veered off toward her desk.

The common room could seat about a hundred people, but there were only maybe fifteen white-haired bingo players there. Actually, fifteen was a pretty good turnout. One time, I called six games of bingo for one lovable old woman. She had the time of her life. She just couldn't believe she'd won six bingo games in a row.

So fifteen was a decent number of players. I just wished they'd all sat up front near where I stood and pulled each ball out of the wire barrel. Instead, the people were scattered throughout the room, and I had to call each ball several times, yelling as loud as I could until everyone finally heard me. By the time I'd called four games of bingo, I had pretty much lost my voice. I had very little hope that I'd be able to tell Tara the saga of my day.

CHAPTER 7

"GOD, YOU SOUND LIKE YOU'VE BEEN SMOKING KITTY litter or something," Tara said.

"I had to call bingo," I rasped. "They decided to be extra deaf today."

"How dare those old bastards!" Tara teased. "So it was a craptastic day at Ass Grove, huh?"

"Pretty much."

"Then ice cream for dinner, it is. It'll be good for your throat too. Come on. I'm buying."

I tried to object, but Tara shushed me and dragged me over to Baskin-Robbins, where we each got a chocolate chip cookie dough sundae.

"It's just as well that you can't talk," Tara said, "because I have some stuff to tell you. Remember how we thought Jenny Pritzkey was faking having her period because she was actually pregnant?"

I shoved a huge spoonful of ice cream in my mouth and said, "Yearagh." My mother would've been mortified.

Tara pointed her long pink spoon at me. "Well, you are not going to believe this."

From here, she launched into a long, convoluted tale of

Jenny Pritzkey's spring break pregnancy scare. I won't go into the boring details. It was pretty dull even for me, and I know Jenny Pritzkey. I pretended to hang on every word of Tara's, though, because there's nothing she likes more than to spread good gossip, and there's nothing I like more than Tara. So she talked and I listened. In every close friendship, there is one talker and one listener. It didn't take a genius to figure out which was Tara and which was me.

To tell you the truth, I really hadn't been looking forward to rehashing the drama of my day for the third time, so I was grateful to have the sordid tale of Jenny Pritzkey's tardy period to fill out the conversation.

When I got home a couple of hours later, Mom was cleaning the cabinet under the kitchen sink and Zach was doing algebra problems at the table.

"You got homework already?" I asked. "On your first day?"

"Hi, sweetie," Mom called from under the sink.

Zach flicked his pencil up and down like a seesaw. "No big deal," he said. "We did this stuff last fall at Meriton."

Mom sat up. "You're kidding?" She sloshed her rag in the bucket of sudsy water beside her, wrung it out, and ducked back into the cabinet.

"Hilarious as that is . . . no," Zach said. "Works for me, though. I'm gonna cruise through the end of the year." He scribbled an answer. "More time for gaming."

"You already play video games far too much," Mom said inside the cabinet. Zach rolled his eyes and made a "blah blah blah" gesture, opening and closing his hand like a mouth.

Mom scooted out and pointed to a spray bottle on the

counter by the stove. "Pass me that bleach spray, will you, Blythe? There's some kind of stain under here I can't get out." She arched her back and winced.

"Seriously, Mom," Zach said. "Why don't you just hire somebody to clean?"

Mom wiped the sweat off her forehead with the back of her hand. She hadn't thought to take off the gold and diamond watch that Gran and Granddad had given her for her fortieth birthday. And her manicure was destroyed. "Maids cost money, Zach."

"Yeah, but don't you have like a gazillion dollars in a trust fund from Gran and Granddad?" Zach asked, finishing a problem in about five seconds.

I handed the bleach spray to Mom. She gave Zach a sly grin and said, "And would you like me to spend it all before you have a chance to inherit it?"

Zach stared at her for a few seconds and then said, "Get back to scrubbing, woman." He and Mom shared a laugh and she went back inside the cabinet to launch her bleach attack.

"It's not a gazillion, anyway," Mom said from under the sink. "And it's tied up in long-term investments. It's more of an emergency fund, and a dirty house is not an emergency."

I plopped down in a chair. "Where's Dad?"

"At a school board meeting" Mom said. "Ugh, this isn't working either. I'll just have to put something on top of the stain." She sat up again and blinked away the chlorine fumes. "He told me that you had kind of a rough first day. Are you holding up okay?"

Kind of rough?

"I'm fine," I told her. I didn't want to be a liar, so in my head, I said, *Fine: as in thin, fragile, and about to break.*

Mom knew me too well, though. "Want to talk about it?"

I shook my head. "Nothing to talk about."

"Do you have homework?"

"Not really." I had to translate a paragraph, which would take about three minutes since Ash Grove was also about two semesters behind Meriton in Intermediate French.

"Well then, would you mind folding the laundry in the dryer and putting it away? There's a showing first thing tomorrow." She crossed her fingers in the air.

Without thinking, I said, "I can't believe you're so eager to sell the house. Doesn't it bother you at all?" It had slipped out and produced an immediate effect on Mom. She hauled herself up to her feet. There was no lady look on her face. She didn't try to hide her displeasure a bit.

"Of course it bothers me, Blythe. This is my home too. My life is changing too. But you know what? These are the sacrifices we make for the people we love."

"Person," I corrected her.

"Pardon me?"

"The *person* you love. Not *people*. Person. Dad."

Her eyes saucered. "No, Blythe. I mean people. For Dad, yes, but also for you and Zach. Everything your father and I do, or choose, is to benefit you kids. You may not see it when you don't look past the end of your nose, but it's a fact."

Ouch.

"And even if it wasn't, your father has given so much to this family. We can give him this. His happiness counts too,

Blythe. It matters. And what's good for your father is good for the family. So before you start another diatribe about how unfair your life is, like you apparently did at school today, maybe you should think about things more carefully." She picked up the bucket and walked out of the room.

"Don't sweat it," Zach said as he finished his algebra and shoved the paper in his backpack. "She gave me the same speech yesterday."

"It's not just about happiness, anyway," I said. "It's about money. God, I do not understand what their hang-up is about using Mom's trust fund to help out the family."

"It's a guy thing," said Zach. "Men are hunter-gatherers. They want to provide for their tribe."

"Yeah, but we're the ones paying the price," I said.

"What are you complaining for? You've got another year and a half, tops. I'm stuck here for half a decade." He tossed his backpack by the kitchen door and headed outside. "Later. I'm going to Jack's."

"What about dinner?" I asked. It was nearly five thirty.

"It's fend for yourself. I'll get something at Jack's." The storm door slammed behind him like it always did. Such a familiar sound. Even that would be gone soon.

I opened the fridge. Fend for yourself was when you had to grab something to eat on your own because neither Mom nor Dad had the time or energy to cook. I was thrilled that I didn't have to sit at a table and make small talk with my parents tonight. I grabbed a leftover ham and cheese sandwich and took it to my room, where I stayed for the rest of the night. I forgot all about folding the laundry.

. . .

The next morning, Dad was gone by the time I came downstairs. He must've needed to get to school early. I grabbed a giant mug of steaming coffee and trudged back up to my room. I selected an adorable polka-dot jumper to wear and then remembered that Ash Grove wasn't as fashion forward as Meriton. I didn't want to draw attention to myself, so I opted for leggings and a cream chiffon tunic. I remembered to make my bed before I left.

Walking into school, I kept my chin high and my profile low. I resolved to be dignified but non-confrontational. I hoped that people would be finished laughing at me for the yearbook caption contest, and thankfully, they seemed to be. The obvious way they looked straight through me didn't exactly give me the warm fuzzies, but I'd take that over ridicule any day.

I made it to homeroom. Made it to first period. By second period, though, I began to notice whispering. I saw pairs of girls hunched over the invisible space between them, heads inclined toward each other, mouths moving. A group of guys stood stock still except for the one doing the talking. I was desperately curious, but who could I ask about it? Nobody. Maybe Cy and Jenna.

In the hallways between classes, I kept an eye out for Jenna's bright hair, but I didn't see it anywhere. I finally caught up with her and Cy at lunch. They were back at the same table in the corner, but they were sitting on the opposite side. I'd have to sit facing the room today. I got my yogurt and pretzels and made my way over.

"Can I sit here again?" I asked. They turned in unison

to face me. For a few seconds, neither one said a word. It almost felt like I'd barged in on them or interrupted their privacy. Jenna shrugged one shoulder and said, "Sure."

I inched my way around the table to give them time to change their minds if they wanted to. Neither one did, so I sat and tore open my pretzels. "Tear, not pull," I said to Cy, trying to break the ice. He gave me one solitary nod. He was wearing the same army jacket as yesterday. Jenna had on a Betty Boop tee. They seemed to be somehow guarded.

"Is something wrong?" As soon as the question left my lips, I immediately felt like I'd asked something too personal. Like we were old friends who cared enough to ask that kind of thing. Which we weren't. So I segued right into, "Everyone's whispering and talking about something. Do you guys know what it is?"

Cy crinkled his forehead and frowned. "Yeah." That was all.

I blinked a few times. "Well, can you tell me?" I'd tried not to sound sarcastic, but I wasn't very successful.

Jenna and Cy locked eyes. Silence passed between them. Jenna turned to me and said, "There's a rumor going around that Principal Mac is canceling the Senior Scramble."

He was actually considering it? I took a moment to make sure my expression had enough surprise in it. "What?" I said. "He is?"

I hadn't seen Dad since yesterday. So what had made his mind up?

"Apparently, yes," Jenna said. She added, "Rumor has it, you're behind it."

Cy asked me, "So are you?"

I waffled. I didn't want to confirm the rumors, but I didn't want to lie either. If there was one thing I never wanted to be, it was a liar. I also didn't want to jeopardize the only quasi-friendships I'd made at school, frail as they were. Jenna and Cy didn't seem like snitches, so I went ahead and told them about my conversation with Dad, emphasizing the "stopping bullies" theme. Again, it sounded like a flimsy excuse. Cy and Jenna didn't buy it for a second. Only when I admitted what Ms. Eulalie had suggested—that I might've been looking for a small smidge of revenge along with justice—did Cy and Jenna accept my answer.

"Kind of a dick move," he said.

I nodded and mumbled, "I had good intentions. I thought I did, anyway. Apparently, they were hiding a couple of not-so-good ones." I desperately wanted to offer Jenna and Cy a reason not to hate me. A reason for me not to hate myself. I straightened up and snatched the lid off my yogurt. "You know what? Dad would never do it. I bet he'd never do it. He won't. You guys matter too much to him. His students." I crumpled the foil lid into a tight pebble. "Don't worry."

"But you're his daughter," Jenna said.

I smiled sardonically and shook my head. "Not here, I'm not."

Cy snagged one of my pretzels and popped it in his mouth. I took it as a tentative gesture of forgiveness and pushed the bag toward him.

"Here's what I don't get, though," I said. "The entire conversation happened in his office, with the door closed. How could the rumor even start? Dad wouldn't blab. He'd know it'd make things worse for me. Plus, if he ended up deciding not to cancel the Senior Scramble, he wouldn't want anyone to know that he was even considering it in the first place."

"Wait a sec," Cy said. "You were in your dad's office?"

"Yeah."

"The door was closed?"

"Yes."

He chuckled. "Was Mrs. Bolger still there?"

Jenna suddenly caught on to what Cy was hinting at. "Oh my God! That must be it. I cannot *believe* that woman!"

I looked back and forth between them waiting for them to explain. "Who's Mrs. Bolger?"

"The head secretary. Mrs. Bolger," Cy said.

"Gladys?" I asked. "Is her name Gladys?"

Jenna nodded. "Yeah, Gladys Bolger."

"What about her?"

"Oh my God," Jenna said, collecting herself. She held both hands up to set the scene. "Okay, here's what happened. This one time Cy got called into Principal Mac's office for threatening this jerk who was saying crap about me. I ditched class to go with Cy, but I didn't want to get caught, so I waited out in the hall. So I'm out in the hall, right? But I keep peeking through the glass every now and then, to see if Cy's done. So at this one point when I'm peeking in, I see Mrs. Bolger, who's the only other person there, I see her tiptoe up to Principal Mac's door and listen for a sec. I thought, that's weird, right? So I keep watching. She goes straight back to her desk and pushes a button on her phone and leans down to it. I finally figure out what she's doing, and I know I have to stop it. You know, for Cy. So I barge in there and she jumps like a frigging monkey, smacking at the phone. But it's too late. I heard Principal Mac's voice loud and clear through her intercom before she finally hit that button. I didn't let on that I knew, of course. But I did. She was totally listening in on them."

I gaped at Jenna. "Oh my God, she eavesdrops on his private meetings?"

"Yup." Cy chucked another pretzel in his mouth.

Jenna leaned back and snuggled into Cy's chest. "Bet that's how everyone knows about the Senior Scramble." Cy wrapped his arms around her and fed her a pretzel.

"Unbelievable," I said. "She seems so nice."

Cy gave a sarcastic laugh. "Yeah, well, so do serial killers. It's a total front. Don't trust her. She gets off on stirring up shit for students."

"How pathetic," Jenna muttered. She picked the black polish off the tip of one of her fingernails.

I sat up straight as a rod and poked at the air. "You know what? She's the one who told my dad about the yearbook picture yesterday too!"

"See what I mean?" Cy said. "Stirs shit up."

"Unbelievable." I grabbed my spork as something zinged past my head. I looked up in the direction it came from and saw a Tater Tot winging toward me. I've never had quick reflexes, and even if I did, I'd never had someone throw food at me before. Ever. Especially not at Meriton. So I didn't even flinch, and the Tater Tot smacked me in the middle of my forehead.

Cy and Jenna wheeled around to see the bunch of goons three tables down who had broken into hysterics. I touched my forehead and had opened my mouth to say something, when one of the guys launched another Tater Tot at me. Only this one was covered in ketchup. I tried to dodge, but it hit me square in the chest, splattering my cream tunic with red goo and grease.

Cy growled, "Give me your yogurt," so fiercely that I didn't dare disobey. I handed it to him and he stood up. His thick-soled black boots thudded on the linoleum floor as he strode over to the guy who'd thrown the ketchup. Without hesitation, Cy tipped the container upside down over the guy's head and squeezed the entire cup of strawberry yogurt into his spiky, over-gelled hair. The guy leapt to his feet and shoved Cy backward with both hands.

Now, besides the fact that Cy rocked a fairly psycho-killer look, he also was taller than pretty much everyone in the junior class. So all he had to do was come at the yogurt-covered douche bag like a madman—yelling and waving his arms and pointing to me—and yogurt douche backed down. Cy didn't need to lay a finger on him. Yogurt douche took a couple of stumbling steps backward and then pivoted and stormed out of the cafeteria. One of the underpaid, under-educated teachers monitoring lunch followed him out like an obedient dog. None of the other monitors had even noticed the fight until it was already over.

"Now you watch," Jenna said softly. "Cy's the one who'll get in trouble." In her eyes was the tenderest affection I'd ever seen. I'd never noticed anything like it between couples at Meriton. Even the ones who'd been together for years. I sure hadn't ever felt it myself.

When Cy headed back to us, Jenna's demeanor and tone did a complete one-eighty. She went into sex-kitten mode. She arched her back and lifted one of her feet in black patent-leather Mary Janes onto the bench. She wiggled in her seat as he came closer. When he got there, she reached out for him and purred, "God, that was hot. I love it when you do brave hero shit." She slid her hands around Cy's hips and drew him closer, gazing up at him standing above her. He slipped one hand behind the nape of her neck, bent down, and pulled her face to his. They kissed hard and deep.

I sat, mesmerized.

When they were done, Cy tossed the empty yogurt container onto the table and it skittered toward me. "Here you go," he said. "Thanks for the loan."

I was still gripping the spork tightly in my fist. I hadn't really moved a millimeter since handing over the yogurt. Finally, I managed to say, "I should be thanking you." I picked up my lone, useless napkin and tried to wipe off the ketchup. "I've never . . . That's never . . ." The spot just smeared. It was more than a spot; it was a stain. It was a violation. It was a message. It was a symbol of the fact that, for the first time in my life, I was disliked. By pretty much everyone. Except for the two people in front of me. These unlikely allies.

"Thanks, Cy," I said weakly but totally sincere. "I owe you."

"Don't worry about it." His eyes bored into Jenna's, but

he spoke to me. "I only did it because I knew it would turn her on."

She cradled his face in both of her hands and said, "Oh, yeah, right. Sure. That's the reason. God forbid anyone should know you're secretly a good guy."

"God forbid," he said, and went in for more kissing.

I whispered a paper-thin "See ya!" not to disturb them. I stood up and hoisted my messenger bag onto one shoulder. I left the pretzels for Cy and headed for the hall bathroom to clean myself up.

I didn't get three steps out of the cafeteria doors when I nearly slammed into the one-and-only person who could put the cherry on top of my hot crap sundae. That's right, Luke Pavel. Why was I always running into this guy? And I mean literally running into him.

I was too frazzled to stop and chat. I could feel the moisture from the ketchup seeping into the cami I was wearing under the tunic. It was damp and cold and I really didn't want it to get any worse. Nor did I want to strip off the ketchup-soaked tunic out here in the hallway. This required bathroom privacy.

I tried to dart past Luke, but he hooked his finger in the strap of my bag. "Holy crap, what happened?"

I must have looked pretty pathetic, because there wasn't even a note of ridicule in his voice. That I could tell, anyway. For all I knew, Luke could be an expert faker and master manipulator. Yet for whatever reason, I suspected that wasn't the case.

"Oh, you know," I said. "Just a little present from the Ash

Grove welcoming committee." I sidestepped him, but Luke jumped in front of me again. God, this guy was like a bionic jackrabbit or something.

"Wait a sec. Wait a sec." He held one palm up to me. The other hand straightened his glasses. His eyes became steel-blue agates behind them. "You mean someone threw this at you?"

I sighed heavily and switched my bag to the other shoulder so he couldn't snag it again. I rolled my eyes at the ceiling and said, "Look, just let me go, okay? Don't pretend you give a shit."

I would like to take a moment to point out that, on the whole, I'm not a potty mouth. I try not to swear because I think there are almost always more precise and descriptive words to use instead. But occasionally, as in this exchange with Luke, the swearword is the more precise and descriptive word. Plus, I wanted to use the word as a weapon.

It produced the intended effect. Luke drew back, looking astonished. He opened his mouth, and while he was momentarily distracted by the effort of thinking up what I'm sure would have been a scathingly witty retort, I slipped by him, yanked open the bathroom door, and slipped inside.

Once the door closed behind me, I took a deep cleansing breath like my dad always did. Then another. Then I checked the stalls. They were empty. The cafeteria was on its own hallway off one wing of the school, so I figured that unless someone had a violent intestinal reaction to Mystery Meat Monday, these bathrooms probably didn't see much action.

I dropped my bag on the floor, peeled off my tunic, and washed it out in the sink. I noticed a wet spot on my cami from the moisture that had leached through, so I blotted it with a paper towel. That wasn't helping much, and the bell rang anyway, so I tossed the paper towel, wrung out my sodden, spoiled tunic, shoved it in the bottom of my bag, and left.

Thank God there was no sign of Luke outside the bathroom door, or anywhere. I melted into the torrent of students like slushy snow into a rushing spring gully and disappeared down the hallway.

By the end of the day, the watermark on my top had dried into a wobbly O right in the middle of my cleavage. It was a minor battle scar, I decided. I was just about to declare day two at the Ash Grove Penitentiary a victory when the afternoon announcements came on. Instead of hearing Gladys Bolger's voice like yesterday, I heard my father's.

Attention, Ash Grove students, this is Principal McKenna.

I know some of you have heard rumors circulating today about the Senior Scramble. Although I realize that the Senior Scramble is a long-standing tradition here at Ash Grove, recent as well as past events have caused me to re-evaluate the role and effect the Senior Scramble has on the lives of Ash Grove students. Because I cannot, in good conscience, sanction an event that can so easily result in criminal behavior, as well as emotional harassment and bullying of other students, I feel that it is in the best interest of the school to hereby prohibit the Senior Scramble from this point onward in Ash Grove history. I know many of you will be unhappy with this decision, but I must remain firm in my obligation to protect the welfare of the entire student body. Anyone caught participating in anything resembling the Senior Scramble faces suspension.

On an unrelated note, there has been a snag in the yearbook publication schedule. Final yearbooks will not be available until mid-July. At that time, they can be picked up at the front office, as the administration will remain open throughout summer vacation.

And finally, Luke Pavel, please stop by my office before you leave for the day.

Thank you very much, and have a pleasant afternoon.

My first impulse was one of self-preservation. I wanted to run. To leap out of my chair and make a break for it. If mere rumors caused me ketchup stains, I couldn't imagine what would happen to me now. I pictured myself tearing down the hallway and through the parking lot to the safety of my car, then locking my doors and frantically scrabbling to get the key in the ignition while being overtaken by a mob of ravenous zombies with fake tans.

It didn't take long for me to realize that there'd be many, many more people out in the hallway than were here in the classroom. So despite having everyone around me flip out and start yelling, and despite being pummeled with insults and angry stares, I drilled myself to my chair and stayed put. I made eye contact with no one.

Since nobody wanted to stick around school any longer than necessary, soon enough the classroom emptied out and I was alone. The next breath I took felt like the first one in hours.

Then I waited. I sat there and waited for the rush of satisfaction I was expecting. I'd gotten what I wanted, after all. The Senior Scramble, the yearbook, even Luke Pavel. No doubt, he was being read the riot act by my father at that very moment and was probably being threatened with disciplinary action if he didn't cease and desist publishing *Buried Ashes*.

So I should have been elated.

Except, I wasn't.

I felt only one thing.

Fear.

I tried to talk myself out of being scared. Tried to justify my actions. Tried to convince myself that I'd done this for the greater good. For everyone in all the other nose-picking or drunken or sexting pictures out there. The only problem was, obliterating the Senior Scramble and derailing the yearbook and screwing over Luke Pavel didn't really help those other people. It didn't really help anyone at all. It didn't, I finally realized, even help me.

Ms. Eulalie and Ms. Franny had been right. There was no good scenario that could've come out of my actions. And now it was too late. Too late for the Senior Scramble. Too late for the yearbook. But maybe not too late for Luke Pavel.

I jumped up, grabbed my things, and sprinted down the hall toward the main office.

Much to my disgust, but not my surprise, when I slammed open the outer office door, Gladys Bolger shot five feet out of her chair and started smacking her phone like it was covered in spiders. I glared at her, resolving to tell my dad about her deception after all this was over, and barged into Dad's office. He was alone, sitting at his desk with his head in his hands.

"Where's Luke Pavel?" I cried.

He raised his head. "He just left. I told him to pull the online newspaper."

"Did he agree? He didn't agree, did he?"

A cold quizzical look came over my father. "Agree? Agree to what? I threatened him with expulsion, Blythe. That's the penalty for bullying under my zero-tolerance policy. There was nothing for him to agree to. Either he terminated the newspaper or he didn't graduate high school. Why do you look so shocked? I did everything you wanted."

I stood there rooted to the carpet, my mind a mile above the room. My ears buzzed and my pulse hammered inside my skin. I seemed to be inhaling and exhaling at the same time and I couldn't quite figure out how to breathe.

"Dad," I said barely above a whisper, "I think I made a mistake."

CHAPTER 8

I RAN. I WAS CRYING AND RUNNING AND I DIDN'T know where I was going. I saw lockers flying by in a blurry smear. I could still hear Dad's voice in my ears, furious, yelling. Could see the confusion on his face. Disappointment in his eyes. Accusation.

I rounded a corner and kept going, thinking I'd hit an exit sometime. Instead, I hit a dead end. I was in the cafeteria hallway. Instead of a door to escape through, there was just a huge, nasty mustard-and-green Ash Grove Fighting Eagles flag. I spun around and ran the other way. I saw a person start to cross the end of the hallway. When I realized who it was, I froze.

I ducked inside the girls' bathroom just before Luke Pavel had a chance to see me.

I collapsed against the concrete-brick wall and slid down to the floor, crying even harder. It was the kind of sobbing cry you know you can't stop, so you just have to ride it out. After a few more minutes of shuddering and hiccuping, my brain finally let my body relax a bit. I forced myself to breathe in and out. I could only get air through my mouth, though. My nose was completely blocked. My eyes burned too. That's probably why I didn't notice right away that the bathroom ceiling was clouded with smoke.

At first, I thought the school was on fire. Then I saw feet under the door to the handicapped stall. Feet wearing thick, black, high-laced boots and patent-leather Mary Janes.

"Jenna?" I called. "Is that you? Cy?"

The stall door opened a crack and Jenna peered out. She saw it was me and started cracking up. Her face disappeared behind the stall again and she said way too loudly, "It's just Blythe!" I heard Cy snort and snicker and then snort again, and the two of them stumbled out of the stall. "Holy crap!" Jenna said, trying to lean back on the windowsill behind her. "I thought we were so busted!" She and Cy fell into sniggering hysterics again, clutching at each other for support as they tipped left and right.

"Are you guys getting high?" I pushed myself against the wall and stood up. "Oh my God, you're smoking pot in the school bathroom. How cliché is that? God, this is such a bad after-school special."

Cy shook his head at me for several long seconds before he finally said, "Nobody ever comes in these bathrooms."

Jenna came over and wrapped her arms around me. "What's wrong? Is it your dad?" I nodded, and her pink shaggy hair poked me in the cheek. Jenna pushed herself off me and held my shoulders. A smile bloomed on her face and her eyebrows danced up and down. "Wanna get high?" Cy wagged a small silver pipe in front of my face. It looked like something a garden gnome would smoke.

"Oh, ho . . . !" I made myself chuckle to be polite, but I

waved the offer away. "Oh, no thanks. Thank you. But no. Thanks."

Cy leaned his elbow on Jenna's arm, which was still riveted to my shoulder like an I beam. "I hate to break it to you, Blythe," he said as he waved the pipe widely through the air, stirring the haze into swirls, "but you already are." The two of them dissolved into a snorting, giggling mass again.

Of course, they were right. There was probably enough secondhand smoke in there to knock out a horse. I didn't want to add "getting stoned" to the long list of reasons for my dad to hate me right now, so I grabbed my stuff and said bye to Cy and Jenna. I pushed the door open, ready to meet some fresh air.

Instead, I met Luke Pavel. Waiting for me outside the bathroom. He must have seen me after all.

For a reason I couldn't comprehend, the first thought to cross my mind was what a mess I must look like. And smell like.

I pushed that aside, and the next thought was that Luke was pissed. Not furious or livid or enraged. He was pissed. That was the precise word for it. I knew he had every right to be.

"Have fun getting high?" he asked. "Now, what would dear Daddy say about that?"

"No!" I objected. "I'm not—"

"Please," he sneered with condescension, "I could smell it from down the hall. Go ahead and lie if you want, though. Your bloodshot eyes pretty much say everything." I opened my mouth to explain, but he took a step toward me. Instinctively, I retreated. He nodded toward the door. "I guess you were having yourself a little celebration in there. Congratulations are in order, after all. Yippee for you, Blythe. You won. Way to go. I hope you're happy, because no one else is. It took less than two days for you to screw over the entire school. You're like a hurricane. Hurricane Blythe, a category-four crap storm. Oh, it was social suicide, no doubt. But impressive nonetheless."

I stood there silently taking his chiding. I had a right to deny the pot, but nothing else. I tried to bear up with dignity, but by that point, my eyes were too used to crying. With almost no warning, they started up again. I tried to fight it, but all that did was make my chin and lips quiver uncontrollably while the fat tears tumbled down.

I got no sympathy from Luke. "Oh, here we go!" he said. "Things don't go your way, so you start the waterworks. Such timing. Is that how you manipulate Daddy?" He laughed sarcastically. "You are some piece of work, you know that? And to think I actually felt bad for you today when you got pelted with ketchup. And yesterday, I thought I saw a glimmer"—he pinched the air in front of me—"just a tiny hint that you might be a smart, brave, decent human being." He dropped his hand and drew upright. "But I was so wrong."

He spun around to leave, but this time I was the jackrabbit. I rushed in front of him and planted my palm on his sternum. "You think you know me?" I cried. "You think that just because you recognize me from a photo, you know me? That since you know my father, you know me? Well, you don't. You don't know anything about me, Luke. Because if you did, you'd know how hurt I was when you posted that picture last year. You'd know how long it took for me to get over it. You'd know how confused and betrayed I felt when my father took my home and my friends and my life away from me. How terrified I was of coming to school yesterday. How right I'd been to be scared. How degrading it was just to walk down the hall. How stupid and naive I was for thinking that maybe if I spoke to you, you'd realize that it was partly your actions that were making things horrible and difficult for me, and then maybe you'd stop. Maybe you'd turn out to be a smart, brave, decent human being yourself. But I was wrong too, Luke. It looks like we were both wrong."

He locked eyes with me for a few seconds. Then he knocked my hand off his chest and walked away without a word.

I stood and watched him go. He didn't look back. He didn't even toss me a glance when he turned the corner at the end of the hall. Now I understood why Mom never wanted me to be walked-out upon. It hurts. Even when you despise the person who walked out on you. You feel like garbage tossed aside that even *they* didn't want.

At least I didn't back down, I thought. *At least I said my piece.*

Except, I was wrong. I'd forgotten a few key points. Like how sorry I was for ruining *Buried Ashes*. Or how I had raced to my father's office to try to keep that from happening. Or how my father had freaked out on me and pretty much hated me now. Or how grateful I was to Luke for showing concern earlier that day—at that very spot—when I was covered in ketchup. How sorry I was for being so rude. How wrong I'd been about everything.

I forgot to say any of that.

I heard Jenna squeal and Cy laugh inside the bathroom. I didn't want to be here when they came out. Didn't feel like seeing all that happy-happy or explaining why I wasn't that way. So I grabbed my bag and left.

Luckily, I got home before Dad did. Mom was buzzing around in a silk blouse and pearls, using a hand vac to suck up the potato chip crumbs that Zach evidently had dropped in a zigzag trail between the pantry and the couch. He sat munching a handful of them with the phone tucked under his ear, yakking about some video game. "Dude. No. The best first-person shooter is definitely *Battlefield 3*." Bits of potato chip shot out of his mouth as he talked. The front of his shirt was littered with debris.

"Zachary!" Mom barked. "You're getting them all over the place! That's it! No more food in the family room until we get a sales contract. Hi, Blythe!" She waved to me with one hand, running the hand vac up and down the front of Zach's shirt with the other. He reared back into the cushions and looked at her like she was deranged.

I knew that if I lingered downstairs, Mom would eventually notice my crying face, if not the stain on my top and the reeking stench of pot smoke. So I said a quick hello and dashed upstairs to take a shower.

When I was dry and dressed in my favorite gray pajama pants and a clean black hoodie, I fished the tunic from the bottom of my bag, grabbed the rest of my dirty clothes, and sneaked downstairs to the laundry room. I sprayed the ketchup stain and rubbed it as well as I could. I tossed it in the washing machine with the rest of the load, hit Start, and hoped for the best.

When I walked into the kitchen, Mom's expression of frustration was instantly replaced by one of bewilderment. "Why are you in your pajamas already? I need you to take Zach to his friend's house!" She said it as if I should've known that somehow, like what an idiot I was to put on pj's when I still had to go out. She yanked open the refrigerator and started pulling out the drawers and stacking them on the counter beside the sink. "We have a showing in an hour. I have to finish cleaning."

"Mom," I said as gently as I could. "I don't think they're going to pass on the house just because the cheese drawer isn't spotless."

She started slapping half-empty packages of deli meat on the counter. "Yes, they might. They might see the cheese drawer and think, Well, if they can't take care of something as minor as the cheese drawer, what else have they neglected? You know what Marjorie said, Blythe. Now please stop arguing with me and give Zach a ride. That was one of the conditions of having your car, remember? You drive Zach when I need you to. You don't stand there lecturing me."

Why is it that whenever parents are frustrated or angry about something, they start bringing up every wrong thing you ever did or every right thing you didn't do, even if those things have absolutely nothing to do with why they're upset?

I didn't possess my mother's hang-up about wearing pj

pants in public, so Zach and I headed out to my car. When we were buckled in, I asked, "Where are we going?"

Zach stretched his leg out and dug in his front pocket. He pulled out a scrap of paper and flipped it onto my lap. "Kid named Brian."

The paper had directions scribbled on it. I followed them in my mind and realized that they led to Ash Grove. "Hold on, is this a kid from your new school?"

"Yeah." He let out a long, resonant belch. "Can we get going?"

I rolled down my window. Started the engine. Backed out of the driveway. "But we only started school yesterday," I said.

"So?"

"So how can you two be friends already?"

Zach shrugged. "He's got *Elder Scrolls: Skyrim*. What's the big deal?" He grabbed my CD case and started flipping through it. "Sucks. Sucks. Sucks. Sucks balls."

The big deal, which I wasn't about to tell my little brother, was that in two days he'd managed to transition painlessly to his new school and make friends good enough to hang out with at their house. Whereas all I'd done was antagonize my entire school, including its principal, and obliterate any hope of making a single friend there.

Luke had been right, though. It was an impressive accomplishment for only two days. Hurricane Blythe.

I dropped Zach off and realized I was only a few blocks away from our new house. I figured I'd do a little drive-by and check on it. When I got there, I thought I'd stop in the driveway for a minute. Once in the driveway, I thought maybe I'd get out and peek through a window. After all, it was a reality, this house. It wasn't something I'd been imagining or denying; it was real. It was happening. We were moving here and this would be my home. As foreign as that seemed, I had to get my head around it.

Outside, a damp, cold wind swirled up the street and cut right through my wet hair to my scalp. I pulled up my hood and tucked my hands inside my sleeves. I slunk up the front walk and peered through the sidelight window beside the front door. It was beveled leaded glass though, and the view was disjointed and angled like a kaleidoscope. I could barely make out the staircase.

I stepped into the front garden and shimmied behind a couple of low bushes so I could see through the front picture window. I had to stand on tiptoe, but I had a clear view inside. Maybe it was the slant of the afternoon light slicing the rooms into uneven wedges, but the house looked even emptier than it had the week before. Forlorn. A dormant shell holding nothing but unfulfilled purpose.

I started to see that there was something humble and honest about an empty house. Stripped bare of all the decoration and flair. With its flaws—chips in the woodwork, marks on the paint, stains on the carpets—all in full view. No pretty paintings hiding holes in the wall or curtains covering cracked windows. No disguise. No pretense of perfection. Fully exposed.

Looking at an empty house, its old owner would see the vacancy. The absence of everything that had made it a home.

But a new owner would see only potential. How the empty spaces could be filled. How the house's purpose of being a home could be satisfied once again.

I realized that it's exactly the same with people. If you meet someone and all you can see are the decorations, the trappings she's gathered around herself, you know you aren't seeing the real person. You aren't seeing the flaws she's disguised, only her version of her perfect self. You make assumptions about her based on what she has chosen to show you. Often, you presume that there isn't any more to her than that.

But if she makes no effort to conceal her flaws, you know you are seeing the genuine person. If she's honest and open—not weak or vulnerable, just uncluttered—you wonder what else she might be. You sense her potential. The person would find a certain security in that mystery. In fact, if she wanted it, she would find a chance to start over, just the way an empty house starts over with its new owners.

Could that happen for me?

Was it too late to undo the past two days? Was there still a chance for me to erase the judgment everyone had passed? Judgment I'd led them to all by myself? I wasn't sure. All I knew was that I envied that house. I wanted people to look at me and see potential too. To wonder. To sense mystery. I wanted those things even more than I'd wanted to ruin things for everyone at Ash Grove.

In fact, that's what I had wanted all along, I realized. I had wanted them to see the real me. Not the girl in the picture. Not the principal's daughter. Just Blythe.

Yet I never gave them the chance. I had walked into that school pretending to be perfect. Pretending not to hate them. Hiding my scars. Trying to manipulate everyone. The only true, honest moment I'd had at Ash Grove was when I'd yelled at Luke in the hallway. Touched him and told him who I was. Of course his reaction was something less than positive.

I'd made a start, though.

I knew the next step I had to take.

CHAPTER 9

I SPENT HALF THE NIGHT WORKING OUT THE DETAILS of my plan, then got to school early and waited by Luke's locker on the senior wing. When he finally rounded the corner and noticed me, I thought I saw his eyes widen behind his glasses for half a moment before narrowing to tight, blue pebbles. I watched his shoulders heave with a forced sigh as he got nearer. When he was in front of me, I amicably stepped out of the way. He spun the combination on his lock as if I weren't even there.

"Can I talk to you for a minute?" I asked.

"I think you've said enough already." He yanked his locker open. I'd stepped to the wrong side, and now the door blocked me from his view. I skirted around to the other side of him.

"Please?" I asked. It felt foreign to say that. I'd never really had to plead or beg for anything in my life before, besides pleading with my father not to move us here. And when I begged Dad not to take *Buried Ashes* away from Luke yesterday. Actually, I was begging more and more, it seemed.

Luke shut his locker and stepped back from me. The expression of contempt on his face made my stomach lurch. "No," he said.

He made a motion to leave, and I gently placed my hand on his arm. He froze, his muscles tightening under my fingertips. "Luke," I said, willing myself to be open and honest. "I'm sorry. About *Buried Ashes*. About everything. I was being so selfish." I let my arm fall to my side. It felt odd dangling there.

Luke's face grew taut behind his glasses. The muscles in his shoulders flexed. "*Buried Ashes* was important to me," he said. His voice was husky and deep. "It helped to get me accepted to college for journalism. *Buried Ashes* was a record of my work. It also did what a newspaper should do: expose truths and change the way people think." He pressed his lips into a hard line. "Taking it down yesterday was . . . very difficult."

"I know," I said, "and I'm really sorry. I begged my dad to let you keep it. I tried everything I could do to get him to change his mind, but he wouldn't. He said he couldn't go back on his word. It would undercut his authority. That's why I was so upset when you saw me." I suddenly felt compelled to clear up something else. "My eyes were red because I was crying. Not from smoking pot. That was . . . other people in the bathroom." I wouldn't snitch on Jenna and Cy. They were the closest thing I had to friends.

Luke was surprised, I could tell. I hoped it was about me begging my dad, not about the pot smoking. Either way, it kept me going. "I was wrong about a lot of things. *Buried Ashes*. The Senior Scramble. All of it. I was so focused on getting back at everyone. I was angry. I was hurt. I admit it." *Show your imperfections, Blythe,* I kept telling myself. *No disguises.*

Luke stuck out his chest and crossed his arms like he

was trying to hold tight to his grudge against me. His eyes gave him away, though. They were the slightest bit softer. Understanding.

I dropped my gaze and made sure my voice was non-confrontational when I asked him the next question. "Why did you post that picture of me last year?"

Luke was quiet. I looked up at him. Our eyes locked for several loaded seconds. I felt a blush rise on my cheeks for no reason.

"I was trying to get a rise out of Principal Mac by lampooning his family," he said. "I never intended to target you directly." The edges of his voice had smoothed. His eyes crinkled affably. "Besides, everybody picks their nose. It really didn't seem like such a big deal. *Then*, anyway." Even though people milled all around us in the hallway, it felt strangely like Luke and I were alone. He said, "I apologize. If I'd known it would hurt you like it did, I never would have posted it. That's tabloid territory. That's not what *Buried Ashes* is about." A knot of anger began to coil up inside me, and I wasn't sure why. Then Luke said, "That's not what I'm about, either," and the knot unwound. I had wanted the integrity to be his, not just the newspaper's. I wanted to know that posting a hurtful picture wasn't merely something that *Buried Ashes* wouldn't do; it was also something Luke wouldn't do. That he wasn't that type of person.

"Thank you," I said softly. Before I lost my nerve or broke the delicate, newborn bond I had with Luke, I took my chance. "If you're into it, I have an idea. About doing the Senior Scramble."

Luke's eyebrows shot up and he gave me his first genuine smile. "Didn't your dad say that anyone caught doing the Senior Scramble would be suspended?"

My body vibrated with excitement, terror, and rebellion. "That's why we're going to have to be careful," I said.

Luke's eyes flashed like white sunlight on blue ocean. He leaned closer to me, looking mischievous. "We?"

"I can't do it alone," I said. "I'm not a senior, but you are. Plus, you know everyone. I don't. I'm new."

Luke laughed. It was fresh and bright. It made me think of bubbles popping. "NO KIDDING," he said, mimicking the way I'd said it on Monday.

"But if anything happens and we get caught," I said, "I'm taking full blame. It's my idea and if I could do it without your help, I would."

With his arms still crossed, Luke tipped sideways onto the lockers. I watched his eyes dance around the different parts of my face, down my body, back to my eyes. My cheeks went hot again. "Tell me your plan," he said.

I steadied myself and tried to focus on my idea rather than where Luke's eyes had just gone. "My plan," I said, "is to take the Senior Scramble underground. With your journalistic integrity and experience with *Buried Ashes*, you become the communication hub. We set up a private forum with anonymous members. The juniors sign up with fake names. We'd be the only ones who knew everyone's real identity. People would drop off the scavenger hunt items at a secret drop-off point. Or maybe just upload pictures of the item. But you'd verify each one and send the information for the contestant's next item. Then you could update stats on the forum so everyone knows who's in the lead and post reports on the status of the hunt. It'd almost be like journalism. You'd be sort of a war reporter. It's not a replacement for *Buried Ashes*, but at least it's something."

Luke pursed his lips together for a few seconds. "Why can't everyone just register under a fake name without using their real identity at all?"

I stepped an inch closer to him. "Because there wouldn't be a way to keep someone like, oh, let's say . . . my father or Vice Principal FINKler, excuse me, I'm terribly sorry, I mean Hinkler, from creating a profile." I caught a flicker of amusement crossing Luke's face when I insulted the VP. I liked it.

"They could easily sabotage the hunt or set a trap for the other contestants," I explained. I knew it was possible to sabotage the hunt because I had thought about doing that myself, last week. "We even could have each junior hand you a pencil or a scrap of paper or something the day after they sign up to prove that he or she really was that person who'd applied."

"Not necessary," Luke said. "I have a program to track IP addresses. It's accurate down to the latitude and longitude of the router. I can check the locations against the student directory." He still looked unconvinced, though. "Won't the winner's identity be blown when they get the prize?"

"The seniors would hold a fake drawing for the exact same prize," I said. "You guys could call it a gift to the junior class in lieu of the scavenger hunt. The winner of the hunt becomes the winner of the fake drawing, obviously."

"And your dad doesn't have to go back on his solid-gold word. He gets to stay respectable as principal."

I wasn't entirely sure if Luke was being sarcastic or not, but I answered him with the truth. "Exactly."

He shifted his weight and nodded thoughtfully. "I'm not sure the entire junior class would be willing to risk suspension."

"We'll be the only people who know the players' real identities. If we don't tell, no one else can know."

"No offense, Blythe," Luke said, "but my trust in you isn't exactly rock solid."

Crap. I hadn't considered that. I'm trustworthy, and I automatically assumed Luke would see it. How naive of me. "Okay," I said. "How about this? I don't have to know any-one's real name. You'd be the only person who knows. If you don't tell, then nobody gets caught." Luke said nothing but appeared more satisfied. I noticed that his rosy lips were parted slightly, and I could see his bone-white teeth behind them. He must have seen me staring because he snapped his mouth shut.

I continued. "But there's one condition: if we get discov-ered, I take the full blame. I become you. I'll say that I'm the only person who knows the identities. I won't reveal them, obviously, because I can't. I'll deny that you were involved at all. And don't even think about getting all chivalrous or being some tough-guy hero here because this is non-negotiable. I won't jeopardize your graduation."

Luke tapped a rhythm on the steel locker door. "Prin-cipal Mac would have to suspend his own daughter. How would that look for him?"

"I don't care about getting suspended, and I don't care how it would make him look," I said, surprising even myself. "My sole objective is to get the hunt going again."

Luke reached up and cradled his jaw with one hand. His index finger rubbed against the light stubble on his cheek. He studied my face. "I just don't see what you'd get out of it. What's in it for you? Credit for bringing back the hunt?"

Don't hide, I told myself. *Don't mask the real reason with some flowery, fake adornment. Let him see.* "Yes," I said. "I want to start over here. But I can't start over until I undo the damage I've done. I have to take care of that first." I stood there, open and honest. I let Luke Pavel scrutinize me. I wanted to know if I'd managed to change his assumptions about me. I wanted to know if he thought I held potential.

The bell rang.

Luke slapped once on the steel locker. "I'll think about it," he said, and strode off into one of the classrooms.

I lingered there, knowing I was already late for homeroom. There'd be a tardy on my report card. An imperfection. A flaw.

I was shocked at how little I cared.

I finally got moving. As I turned into the hallway of the junior wing, I passed Cy and Jenna heading out. Jenna was wearing her puffy hooded coat over her outfit of a tartan pleated miniskirt with striped leggings. Cy was wearing his black army coat with black pants, but that was basically what he wore all the time. "Where are you guys going?" I asked.

"Ditching," Cy said. His shoulders were slack and his

hands were deep in his pockets. He didn't have his normal impish countenance.

Jenna looked at Cy but spoke to me. "Told you he'd get in trouble for lunch yesterday. For the yogurt? He got two weeks of detention. He watches his little sister after school. Now his mom will have to rearrange her shift at work, and her boss is a dick." Cy shot a look at her, telling her to shut up.

"What?" I cried. "Cy, you were defending me! Did you tell my dad that?"

"We saw the vice principal and the lunch monitor, not your dad," Jenna answered. "Just now."

"Did you at least tell them that the guy had been throwing food at me first?"

Jenna shook her head, no. The sideways glance she gave Cy told me that she didn't quite agree with keeping silent.

"We're not snitches," Cy said. He circled Jenna's shoulders with his arm and tugged her along to walk with him.

To hell with that, I said to myself. I decided to take a little detour to the main office. When I got there, I gave Gladys a slimy smile and knocked on my dad's door. It was halfway open, and the smell of fresh coffee drifted through it.

"Come in," he said. "Oh, Blythe. Hi." He glanced at the clock on the wall. "How come you're not in class?"

I ignored his question. "You know how Cy Mason got detention for dumping yogurt on some kid's head?"

He wove his fingers together and leaned forward on his desk. "Yes. Vice Principal Hinkler mentioned it just now. Why?"

"The reason Cy did it was because he was defending me.

That kid was throwing food at me and had nailed me in the chest with a Tater Tot covered with ketchup. All over my clothes."

"Someone was throwing food at you?"

"Yes. Some jerk with a neckless head like a Weeble. His whole table thought it was just hysterical."

Dad's eyebrows squeezed together. "I'm sorry about that, honey. You should have said something yesterday."

"Well, I'm saying something now. So can you override the vice principal's authority and cancel Cy's detention? He babysits his sister after school."

Dad picked up his mug of coffee and leaned back in his chair, which squeaked. "No, I'm sorry, I won't do that."

I couldn't tell whether I was feeling disbelief, disappointment, or embarrassment. "*Won't?* Why not?"

He sipped his coffee and didn't answer me for a moment. "Because that's not how it works. Cyrus Mason committed an act that requires discipline. It doesn't matter why he did it. I'm sorry about his sister, but he should have thought of her before acting. Look, even if I had a problem with how Vice Principal Hinkler handled the situation, I wouldn't override her authority. Student discipline is her jurisdiction. I trust her to make the right choices."

I crossed my arms and glared at him. "And the jerk who threw food at me? He's getting detention too, right?"

Another sip. Another silence. "I can ask the lunch monitor about it, but she never mentioned anything about it to VP Hinkler, as far as I'm aware, so I doubt she saw anything."

"Isn't my word good enough?"

He set his mug down on the Formica desktop in a spot that already had several coffee rings on it. Dad was nothing if not methodical and predictable.

Or so I thought.

"To be honest, Blythe, I think I've played all my favoritism cards with you on the Senior Scramble and the yearbook."

"But the kid was—"

"I'm sorry, but that's my decision."

He shut me down, and that was that. He was perfectly fine with punishing Cy for something but not punishing some egghead moron for the same thing. Unbelievable. I'd always thought that my father was the epitome of reason and high standards. That he was more interested in justice and fairness than in his appearance and reputation. Apparently, I hadn't been looking closely enough.

Oh, and guess what else? He didn't even give me a late pass to homeroom.

If I had any doubt that it was the right thing to take the Senior Scramble underground, the rest of that day wiped it out. The snickers and pointing from my first day at Ash Grove were nothing compared to the treatment I got for ruining the scavenger hunt. Nobody called me "booger girl." Instead, they called me "bitch." They told me to get the hell back to Meriton. I sat alone in the cafeteria since Cy and Jenna ditched. I doubted even they would've sat with me. Grapes were on the menu, and all through lunch they whizzed by my head and pelted me in the back. In the hallways, people slammed into my shoulder as they passed. Knocked my books out of my hands. They were sly enough to do it when no teachers were looking, too. What could I do? Go crying to daddy again? No way. I just took it. But I had no idea what I'd do if Luke said no. I wasn't just embarrassed or humiliated; I was genuinely scared. Luke had to say yes.

I didn't get an answer from him until after school. He called to me as I was hiking across the vast, pitted, asphalt wasteland otherwise known as the student parking lot. Most of the sludge-stained patches of snow had melted, but the sun still had the iron quality of winter.

"Blythe!" Luke called. "Hold up!"

When I heard him call my name, I immediately spun around. The way he half-jogged toward me showed that he was more athletic than he'd seemed at first. I caught myself doing the supermodel runway walk in his direction. I'm sure Mom would have advised me to be coy and wait for him, but that would've been phony.

When we finally reached each other, the crisp wind gusted and we both ran our hands through our blowing hair simultaneously.

"Okay, so I asked around," he said, "and everyone thought it was a good idea, even if it came from you. You're going to do the hunt yourself, right?"

"Of course. Don't worry; there'll be plenty of blood on my hands too. Lady Macbeth will have nothing on me."

A quizzical look and a half smile were on his face for a fleeting moment. He swiped a strand of hair out from behind his wire-framed glasses and straightened them. "How do you know nobody's going to turn you in?"

"I don't," I said. "I have to take that risk."

"Well, if they turned you in, the hunt would be off again, so it doesn't make sense that anyone would."

"I don't know," I said. "I'm pretty sure some of the juniors would do anything to get me kicked out. Or just kicked. It was rough today."

"I bet it was," he said. "I'm not surprised, though. Ash Grove isn't Meriton, Blythe. Once word gets around that the Senior Scramble's back on because of you, it'll die down."

"Does that mean you're in?" I asked. Luke winked and it shot right through me. His blond curls bobbed in the wind. My long hair whipped around my face. I let it go. There was no use in trying to keep it in place.

"I'm in if you're in," he said. "Two things, though. The list of items and clues for the hunt took forever to put together. The seniors who compiled it say they can tweak it to work online, but there's no time to make a new one. They're worried that if word gets out that the underground hunt is using the original list, they'll be implicated. So if that happens, they'll just say the list got stolen."

"If they get in trouble, I'll blow my cover and say I found it somewhere at school," I told him.

I thought for a second he was going to object, but he just said, "Cool. And second, I can't monitor the site twenty-four seven, so a couple of my closest buddies are going to take shifts. I'll make it so that they can't see any of the real identities."

"Okay," I said. "I trust them if you do."

"I'll set up the forum tonight. I figured we could incorporate that Sherlock Holmes 'The game's afoot!' quote."

Oh my God, Luke Pavel was actually a geek. In a kind of adorable way. He was also wrong. "That wasn't Sherlock Holmes," I said.

"Yes, it was."

"Not originally."

"Of course it was." His tone clearly indicated that he thought I was an idiot.

"Oh yeah?" My tone told him to prepare for an intellectual smackdown. "Want to bet?"

He cocked his head slightly and narrowed his eyes at me. "Something tells me I shouldn't. But my honor and masculinity say otherwise. What do you have in mind?"

Don't do it, I told myself. *Don't say something even remotely personal or quasi-flirtatious, Blythe. Say something inane like a pack of gum or a dollar. Say a dollar, Blythe! A dollar!*

"An apology," I said. "An apology for being rude on Monday and calling me 'kid' and 'McMussolini's daughter.'" There was teasing in my voice and he could tell, so I pushed it a bit further. "And for hiding behind the First Amendment like a coward."

His face was bright, his mouth half-open like a comma on its side. He crossed his arms and shifted his weight to one hip. "Fine. And what do I get if I'm right?"

I took a step closer to him and coyly mirrored his crossed-arm posture. "You're not."

He slid both hands into his back pockets. "Prove it."

I pulled out my iPhone and opened the web browser.

"Wow," he said. "Nice phone. By Ash Grove standards, I mean. By Meriton standards, I'm sure it's garbage."

I ignored him and brought up a website of Shakespeare quotes. I typed in *Once more unto the breach*. When the passage came up, I handed the phone to Luke.

He glanced at the first line. "Shakespeare? This isn't it. I know this speech."

"Then you should recognize the last four lines. Scroll to the end and read," I said, and then added, "Out loud, please."

He straightened his glasses and pursed his lips at me but did as I said. His voice was low and resonant, like a bass drum.

"I see you stand like greyhounds in the slips,
Straining upon the start. The game's afoot:
Follow your spirit, and upon this charge
Cry 'God for Harry, England, and Saint George!'"

"Well, crap," he said. He scrolled up and down to read again. "I guess Meriton really does give you a better education."

He tapped the screen a few times to close the browser and handed the phone back to me with a sly smile. His bright eyes bored into mine and I forgot to breathe. I knew why. Even as I admitted it to myself, I tried to mentally beat the idea into submission. I already had way too much to handle without getting a crush on Luke Pavel. He was a senior. He had a god complex, probably. Maybe. Maybe not. I didn't have time for this! He wouldn't be interested in me anyway. Not after seeing so many of my flaws. So why was he still grinning at me like that?

Luke checked an invisible watch on his wrist. "Well, I'd better bolt. See ya." He started to go.

"Hey!" I laugh-squealed and grabbed his arm. Immediately, I realized it was a mistake to touch him because instead of pulling away from my grasp, he moved into it. And that sent sparks up my arm and into my body.

"Did you need something else?" he teased. He was too close. Too familiar. I wasn't ready to be that open and honest. I didn't even know Luke Pavel.

I let go and pulled back. "I believe you have a debt to settle?"

"Oh, that. Yes." He stayed silent.

"Well? Aren't you going to apologize?" I tried not to sound as rattled as I felt.

"Absolutely." Luke smirked and backed away from me. "But I never said I'd do it today." He shrugged, turned, and loped off.

What?

Had I just been played? Was Luke Pavel actually an infantile jerk after all? It sure looked that way. What an idiot I was for giving him the smallest amount of consideration as crush material. I was glad I'd let go of his arm. I just wished I'd been the one who walked away.

I texted Tara and arranged to meet her at the Daily Grind, the coffee shop in Meriton. I couldn't wait to tell her about Luke and what a tool he seemed to be. Apparently, he was not an adorable geek; he was an ass. And so was I, but for different reasons. She'd understand. Best friends don't need that kind of explanation. Still, I wanted to tell her everything.

I spent the whole drive back to Meriton composing the

perfect monologue about my day that only Tara could fully appreciate. So you can imagine my shock when I got there and she wasn't alone. Melissa was there too. Sitting across from Tara. Sitting in my spot.

I have to be honest: I didn't feel terribly charitable at that moment. I should've been gracious to Melissa. I should've dismissed my jealousy as unwarranted. Yet, I did neither of those things. I closed up, walked over, and sat down.

"Hey girl!" Tara sang. She slid a tall cup across the table to me. "I got you a peppermint and white chocolate chai latte. Taste. It's orgasmic." I took a sip as Tara kept talking. "Isn't it good? Melissa turned me on to them. I tried hers yesterday, and I was totally craving one all day today."

I swallowed hard. Tara got coffee with Melissa yesterday too?

My disappointment must have shown on my face because Tara covered quickly. "We ran into each other in front of the library. I was coming out, she was going in."

Melissa caught on. "I had to get rid of the latte anyway. I couldn't bring it inside the library."

"Total coincidence," Tara added, with a fake "no big deal" gesture that was a bit of overkill, in my opinion. Why did it suddenly seem like I was the charity case for those two? "So what's up with you?" she asked, obviously trying to change the subject but sincerely interested, I could tell.

The next thing I did surprised me at the time, but looking back, it makes sense. I plastered a huge, garish lady look disguise over the gigantic imperfection of a day I'd had. I smiled a perky smile and said, "Nothing." Then I cheerfully agreed that the peppermint white chocolate chai latte was exceptionally yummy and let them believe everything was fine and dandy with me.

I justified it by telling myself that I was trying not to be selfish. But really, I was trying to hide. I know that now.

I sat and listened to Tara gab about everything at Meriton. Fill me in on all the news. Catch me up on all the gossip. The irony is, I'm sure she thought she was trying to keep me connected to Meriton, but all she really did was underscore the fact that I was set apart from them.

I didn't let on, though. I knew Tara's intentions were good. So I listened attentively until my phone on the table pinged, telling me I'd gotten an e-mail. When I glanced down and saw who it was from, well, let's just say that my attention got diverted from Tara. As inconspicuously as possible, I slid the phone onto my lap and opened the e-mail.

from: lpavel@hotmail.com
to: blythespirit@gmail.com
subject: Settling up

To Blythe:
"The quality of mercy is not strain'd,
It droppeth as the gentle rain from heaven
Upon the place beneath. It is twice blest;
It blesseth him that gives and him that takes:
'Tis mightiest in the mightiest: it becomes
The throned monarch better than his crown;
His sceptre shows the force of temporal power,

The attribute to awe and majesty,
Wherein doth sit the dread and fear of kings;
But mercy is above this sceptred sway;
It is enthronèd in the hearts of kings,
It is an attribute to God himself;
. . . We do pray for mercy
And that same prayer doth teach us all to render
The deeds of mercy."

—Luke (and William S.)
P.S. Hope you don't mind that I gacked your e-mail addy
while you weren't looking.

His apology. He hadn't wanted to blow it off. He'd wanted
to get it right. With Shakespeare! Adorable geek status officially
reinstated.

I read the e-mail again. And again. And again, until I
noticed that Tara had stopped talking. Oops.

"Hellooo?" she sang. She could tell I was reading something on my phone. So much for being inconspicuous. "Anything you want to share with the rest of the class?"

I thought about it. It should be. But was it? Normally, I
wouldn't hesitate to tell Tara all about a semi-non-jerk possible crush. I switched off my phone and dropped it in my
bag. "Nah," I said. I took another sip of my chai latte and
Tara went back to her gossip.

I tried to follow her conversation, but my mind kept
sneaking back to Shakespeare and ocean-blue eyes and blond
curls blowing in the wind. I had to stop thinking about him.

My life was already complicated enough without adding a guy into the mix.

Back at Meriton, I'd been very careful not to get so involved with someone that it would interfere with my future plans. Bryn Mawr didn't accept average students who spent their entire high school career video-chatting or getting felt up in the bowling alley parking lot. I went out with guys all the time, but I didn't get serious with anyone. I never saw the point. It's not like I was going to marry someone I met in high school. Especially if the guy didn't want to go to Haverford. So it seemed like a waste of time.

Now that I was going to graduate with *Ash Grove* on my transcript, I had to step up my game. Work harder. Focus more. I had to be at the top of my class. I had to have some seriously worthwhile extracurricular activities. As it was, the Senior Scramble was going to eat up a huge chunk of time. There simply wasn't room in my life for a crush.

Even a tall one with blue eyes and strong arms and a laugh like bubbles popping.

CHAPTER 10

BY THE END OF THE WEEK, WORD HAD SPREAD THAT the Senior Scramble was going underground because of me, and I was finally out of everyone's crosshairs. The name-calling stopped, the food-throwing stopped, and people stopped looking at me like they wanted to sink their fangs into my skull. It felt better than any day at Meriton ever had.

Luke had set up the members-only website anonymously, and its address had not-so-mysteriously circulated throughout the entire school in about seventeen minutes. He'd named the site the Revolting Phoenix. *Phoenix* because it came out of *Buried Ashes* (out of the ashes, get it?) and *Revolting* because it was a revolt against the administration. But the graphic he created for the homepage banner was this hideous, messed-up bird on fire so that it seemed the "revolting" meant disgusting. Pretty clever, actually.

After school on Friday, I went online in my bedroom and opened a private web browser so my browsing history would be clean in case my parents or Zach came snooping. I pulled up the Revolting Phoenix website. I clicked on the Join button and typed my name into the membership application, but a pop-up appeared saying that a profile had already been made under that name. What? I tried again and got the same result. Almost immediately, my phone pinged. I clicked over to my e-mail in-box. It was from Luke. It read: *I took the liberty of signing you up already. Hope you don't mind. Enjoy!* Underneath were what I assumed were my profile user name and password:

kate4eva

iluvpetruchio

Kate forever? I love Petruchio? Oh my God, Luke was calling me a shrew in need of taming. Ugh! So evil! Yet hilarious. I could tell he was just aggravating me for kicks. Still quasi-jerky, but I could let it go. I logged on and almost immediately a window popped up with an IM from someone called *profmarvel*. When I started to read it, though, my stomach started squirming. In a good way.

> profmarvel: it's luke. found your way in, i see. like your name?
>
> kate4eva: i'm sure you're enjoying it more than i am. how did you know i was on the site?
>
> profmarvel: ip address tracking program. you're the only one whose hub city is meriton
>
> kate4eva: how big brother of you
>
> profmarvel: thanks, i thought so too
>
> kate4eva: what does your name mean?
>
> profmarvel: professor marvel in wizard of oz film—the guy behind the curtain pretending to be oz
>
> kate4eva: "pay no attention to that man behind the curtain!"
>
> profmarvel: you got it
>
> kate4eva: ah, i see. v. clever

profmarvel: gracias

kate4eva: the book was better than the movie

profmarvel: they always are

kate4eva: surprised you didn't use shakespeare

profmarvel: i love the bard, but this worked

kate4eva: my dad (& family by default) = huge shakespeare nuts

profmarvel: my mom used to be an actor & made me read s'peare plays out loud with her

kate4eva: omg me too! dad did same

profmarvel: freaky

kate4eva: very

kate4eva: so what time does the hunt start?

profmarvel: 1st item's clue drops @ midnite

kate4eva: how many juniors have signed up so far?

profmarvel: 97

kate4eva: holy crap

profmarvel: no kidding

kate4eva: we are going to be so busted

kate4eva: not "we." i mean "i"

profmarvel: nah. the admin will find out about it, but they can't find out who's behind it

kate4eva: not unless you blab

profmarvel: as if. journalists protect their sources

kate4eva: how many are in the jr class?

profmarvel: around 250. not everyone will do it. too risky

kate4eva: wimps

profmarvel: i never pegged you as a rebel

kate4eva: me neither

kate4eva: thought i'd feel more guilty

profmarvel: lol

kate4eva: gotta go. parentals calling me for dinner

profmarvel: be back @ midnite

kate4eva: just like cinderella

profmarvel: see ya. don't forget to delete your browsing history

kate4eva: already in private browser

profmarvel: smart move, kid. bye

kate4eva: GRRR! BYE!

profmarvel: heh heh

I exited the site and closed the browser. I checked my history anyway, just to make sure the web address wasn't there. Then I trotted downstairs.

It was odd sitting at the dinner table with my dad, knowing that I had entered into an act of subterfuge against him. I tried to pick apart the threads of emotions that had balled themselves up inside me. There was fear, sure, but there was a deliciousness about it. I think it came from the bond of secrecy I shared with Luke and the other juniors now. Yet I also felt an edgy anticipation, like when I was a kid on the country club swim team and I stood on the blocks getting ready to dive into the water. Was I feeling competitive? I didn't consider myself competitive. Mom believed that a competitive spirit was highly undignified in a young woman. All that bravado and trash talk of opponents were at cross-purposes to the humility and graciousness she believed a young lady should exemplify.

As I sat there at the dinner table, I realized that I hadn't been involved in any kind of competition since the swim team. At Meriton, I'd been fairly aggressive about maintaining my grade-point average and my class standing, but that wasn't a true competition like the Senior Scramble. The only person I had worked against was myself.

Now I found myself completely unprepared to handle a hot desire to win that smoldered inside me. It grew hotter and hotter with each minute closer to midnight that passed. Should I smother and suppress it? Should I fan it? Do I let it consume me? Should I just keep it on a slow burn?

I also had to figure out how to deal with the guilt. I'd never blatantly disobeyed either of my parents before. I'd never even lied to them. I had little doubt that I'd have to lie over the next few weeks. I didn't like it, but it had to be done. I figured I should practice alone a few times first, though. I'd rehearse like an actor in a play.

Unfortunately, I never got the chance to practice. Right there above my plate of pre-made cheesy chicken casserole, I was forced to improvise.

"So tomorrow," Mom said, "there are two showings, one at ten thirty and the other at one o'clock." She delicately coaxed one saucy noodle onto her fork with her knife. "I don't want any messes happening in between, so everyone needs to be out of the house until after the second showing." She eased the food into her mouth and gingerly chewed.

Excellent, I thought. *I'll probably need all day to search for the first scavenger hunt item anyway.*

Then she said, "So we're going to spend the day at Gran and Granddad's house. They've offered to take us to the club for lunch."

Gran and Granddad had retired to an exclusive gated community about an hour away. Lunch at their ultra-swanky country club took at least three hours. Plus, there would be visiting time before and after. We wouldn't be home before five o'clock, I was sure. By then, everyone else in the Senior Scramble would probably have the first item turned in and be on to the second. Or maybe even the third! That strange competitive ember inside me flared up into a flame.

"I can't go," I blurted without having thought of what to say next. Big mistake. First rule of lying: Figure out your lie before you open your mouth.

Mom shot me a scolding look. "Why not?"

I shoved a hunk of chicken in my mouth to buy some time. Mom wouldn't expect an answer until after I swallowed. No talking with our mouths full!

I chewed and chewed and kept chewing as my brain spun. Should I say I was meeting Tara? No, not important enough. Mom would make me cancel. Homework or an essay? Nope. She'd say I had plenty of time tonight and Sunday. My excuse had to be something she couldn't override and had to happen tomorrow.

I had it.

I swallowed and said, "There's a special afternoon tea over at Shady Acres tomorrow at one o'clock. I volunteered to help." I added, "They're really short-staffed because it's Saturday." *Pretty good*, I thought. *Mom's a firm believer in honoring commitments.* She'd never abide by my skipping out on Shady Acres.

It worked.

"Well, if they're counting on you, then you should go. Just don't come home until after the buyers leave from the second showing, okay?" Mom said.

"No problem." Maybe I didn't need lying practice after all.

Second rule of lying: Play on your opponent's sympathies and weaknesses.

"Speaking of the club," Dad said, "did you cancel our membership yet, Anne?"

Cancel the club? Was he kidding? Mom's entire social life revolved around the Meriton Country Club. She played golf; she played tennis; she played bridge. We spent every summer at the club pool. She had lunch in the restaurant weekly with all her club friends. They were iconic examples of Ladies Who Lunch.

"Not yet," she said to her plate. "I want to wait until we have a sales contract on the house."

Zach opened his mouth to talk, and I could see that it was full of pulpy food. He had selective memory when it came to table manners, much to Mom's dismay. "How come you can't stay in the club?" he asked.

Mom answered, but there was a rigidity to her demeanor that I could tell she was trying to repress. "To be a member of the Meriton Country Club, you must live in Meriton."

"So join the Ash Grove Country Club," Zach said before slurping his milk loudly.

I knew for a fact that there was no Ash Grove Country Club, but even if I hadn't known, the shudder that rattled through Mom would have spelled it out loud and clear.

Ash Grove had a public pool, a mini-putt golf course, and a Denny's. Not exactly country club standards, if you know what I mean.

"Unfortunately, that's impossible," she said. Her voice sounded like it had snagged on something in her throat. Her face, however, presented a flawless lady look. "We all must make sacrifices."

Sure, I thought. *Everyone except Dad, that is.*

How could Mom bear to give up her club membership? How could Dad bear to force her to? Who was this guy? Who had he become? Had he always been like this, but I never noticed? Because until then, I'd seen him as a model father who put his family first. Not anymore, though. I couldn't believe that his whole superintendent fantasy was going to upend us all. Even Mom. Yet he didn't care.

I didn't need any more justification than that to do the Senior Scramble. My guilt evaporated. My resolve hardened. As much as I was doing the Senior Scramble to resurrect my reputation, from that moment on, I was doing it even more to defy my father. I couldn't wait. I couldn't wait for midnight and for the hunt to start.

I learned something at that dinner table that would be confirmed many times later in life: the propulsive nature of anger overrides the immobilizing nature of fear, every time.

After dinner, I was on dish duty, which, since there were showings tomorrow, really meant scrubbing the dishes, sink, counter, cupboards, floor, appliances, molding, light fixtures, knobs, cookbook shelf, top of the fridge, and windows. Followed by organization of the pantry, pots and pans, plastic containers, silverware, and cooking utensils. I truly couldn't imagine how a cleaning person could finish an entire house in an afternoon. It took me nearly two hours just to do the kitchen. I was tempted to cut corners, believe me. Even to cut so many that the buyers would run away in disgust and horror. But I knew that Mom saw her house as a reflection of herself. The kitchen especially represented her.

By the time I finished, I was exhausted and stank of sweat, grease, and Knock-Out All-Purpose Spray Cleaner. Which, for future reference, isn't for all purposes. It leaves streaks on the windows and won't bleach the black mold growing in the caulk behind the faucet. Truly, no sixteen-year-old girl should know this.

Mom came to inspect my work, and once she approved it, I bolted straight upstairs for a shower. She hollered after me to be sure to wipe down the tiles when I was done. On second thought, wipe down the whole bathroom, she said. I called myself an indentured servant under my breath, but I did as I was told. Good, reliable, obedient Blythe.

Maybe not so much anymore.

By the time midnight came around, my body was rested, but my nerves were lit up. They were frantic little live wires coursing and sparking through every crook and bend in my anatomy. I sat at my desk, staring at my laptop and watching more and more members log on to the Revolting Phoenix. The count topped out at 123. So many. I checked the clock on my screen: 11:58. Two minutes until I was fully committed to rebellion. Was I sure? Should I bail?

No.

At midnight, the first clue popped up on the screen and my new, ferocious, competitive spirit kicked in. It obliterated any doubts I might've had. I was absolutely, totally, unequivocally sure.

The Senior Scramble was mine.

CHAPTER 11

Welcome to the Senior Scramble: Underground Version!

Due to recent events of which you're surely aware, the Senior Scramble is going commando this year. No, that doesn't mean that everyone will play without underwear; it means that we have to work fast. Get in and get out quickly. Strike and then vanish.

Obviously, we must take certain new precautions to protect everyone. So instead of turning in a scavenged item to a senior at a drop-off point, this year contestants will upload a photo of the found item. Yes, this makes it possible to cheat in a variety of ways, but we'll be on the lookout for fakes and Photoshops.

Any player who submits one will be disqualified.

Besides, if you cheat, you're a butthole and everyone will hate you.

So play nice.

Once your photo is verified, you'll receive the next clue. There will be ten clues in all. Be sure that nothing identifying is in the background or foreground of your snapshot and clear any properties from the picture that might point to you.

For security reasons, you'll only be able to access this site from the IP address you registered under, so don't count on uploading pictures from your phones.

Also, when you log off the forum, remember to delete your browsing history or use a private browser from the start.

We know you've taken great risks to play this year, so let's make this Senior Scramble the best one ever. Keep your eyes open and your mouths shut. Try not to be seen. Protect each other. And above all, have a fantastic time.

Here is your clue to item #1:

1812–1903 was when I walked around.
Now I lie forever here beneath the freezing ground.
Find that spot and of my stone a picture you must take.
One more hint: the place I am is right beside a lake.

GOOD LUCK, PLAYERS!
THE GAME'S AFOOT!

He used the phrase. What an adorable geek.

Okay, so clearly the clue was referring to a grave. I needed a picture of a certain grave. The problem was, I had no idea where the Ash Grove cemetery was. Or cemeteries. There could be a few. There probably was only one near a lake, though. Hopefully it would be a small cemetery so there wouldn't be too many graves to check before I found the one with those exact dates.

I pulled up a satellite map of Ash Grove. I scanned every inch of the entire township, but I didn't see a lake anywhere. There were a few ponds in housing developments, but there weren't cemeteries anywhere nearby.

I opened another tab and Googled cemeteries in Ash Grove, PA. Maybe if there were only one or two in town, I could just search the whole cemetery for the grave.

There were six cemeteries. Six! Two public and four church ones. There was no way I could search every grave in six cemeteries.

I had a brain wave: maybe *lake* was actually a word in the name or address of the cemetery. I scrutinized each name and address, but the word *lake* didn't appear anywhere. Oh, no! Maybe Lake was the name of the person buried next to this guy. How could I possibly find this? What was I going to do?

I knew what I was going to do. As soon as my family left tomorrow morning, I was going to drive by those cemeteries and see what I could find out. Maybe if I was lucky, I'd notice a junior or two somewhere. Reconnaissance was definitely in order.

I scribbled down the dates from the clue. The rest I could remember; I wanted as little physical evidence as possible around. I logged off, double-checked my history, and shut down my laptop. I shoved the paper into the bottom of my purse and then crawled into bed. My body still thrummed with the adrenaline that had rushed through it when the clue first appeared. It wasn't until sometime after one o'clock that I finally fell asleep.

I woke to the sound of my mother clucking and sighing in my doorway. I peeled open one eye and knew right away that she was already at DEFCON 1. She didn't think I was awake, so she made no effort to disguise her displeasure. Her eyes darted around my room and finally settled on my open eye.

"Why are you just waking up now?" she asked. "It's after nine! I need you to get up and straighten up this room right away. Please." That was one of those *pleases* that didn't really mean "please." It meant "do it now."

I didn't argue, even though my room looked fine. My clothes from yesterday were on the floor, there was some stuff on my desk from last night, my curtains were half-closed, and I was presently in the unmade bed (the horror!), but those things would take two seconds to fix.

It didn't register with Mom, though. Ever since our house went on the market, she'd developed a black-and-white attitude: a room was either picture perfect or it wasn't. It didn't matter whether there was a pile of laundry on the floor or just a pair of socks, her reaction was the same.

"I'm up," I said, pushing myself up on one elbow to prove it. I squinted at the bright slivers of sunlight cutting through the thready clouds and skewering my eyeballs.

"I want everyone out of the house by ten o'clock. This room had better be in order." Then almost as an afterthought, she said, "Where are you going before you need to be at Shady Acres?"

The question caught me off guard. I hadn't made something up to cover the fact that I planned to spend all morning stalking cemeteries. My sleep-fuzzed brain wasn't functioning at full capacity yet, so I just started babbling random excuses. "I'm meeting Tara. Um, at the library. To research. A paper. She, uh, has to . . . research one too." So lame! "We have to have some book sources. I mean, I do. For mine. I don't really know about hers." Stop talking!

I faked a yawn and watched my mother for signs of suspicion. She was focused on the state of my bookshelves, though, so she didn't seem to notice my string of poorly executed lies. "Just make sure this room is decent," she said, and walked out.

I fell back on my pillow even though I wasn't tired. My spontaneous lying had flipped every switch in my body to the On position. My heart thudded in my throat, and my eyes were open so wide that it felt like the lids had retracted completely inside. I took a long breath and let it seep slowly from my lungs.

When I'd finally settled down, I got out of bed and immediately made it. If Mom came back to check on me, which she most likely would do any minute now, at least that much would be done. She'd be satisfied with even a little progress because it meant that the job had been started.

I threw on some jeans and a gray hoodie that both looked like they could belong to any generic teenager who might be wandering around in graveyards on a Saturday morning. I finished perfecting my room, grabbed some breakfast, and was out of the house along with everyone else by ten o'clock. Once I had driven out of sight of my family, I pulled over to the side of the road. I grabbed my iPhone and went to the webpage with the names and addresses of the six cemeteries in Ash Grove. I mapped them, and the closest one was at First Lutheran Church, so I set its address into the GPS in my phone and hit the gas.

Twenty minutes later, I pulled into the church parking lot. I did a quick scan of the cemetery. It was empty. Above-ground anyway, ha ha ha. I got out and pulled my hood over my head so I'd be less recognizable if anyone else showed up. Plus, there was a damp wind slicking down the back of my neck. The sky couldn't seem to decide whether it was cloudy or sunny. There were swaths of cirrus clouds here and splotches of cumulus clouds there with patches of blue sky behind. Some insistent rays of sun burst toward the earth, and the next moment, it would be dark as dusk. Changeable weather typical of March and mischief.

I entered the cemetery gate and noticed that all the head-stones appeared fairly modern. Sharp angles, crisp engrav-ing, twentieth-century dates. I wandered deeper into the field, thinking that maybe the older stones were toward the back. That wouldn't make sense, though, because the Luther-ans would've started burying people close to the church and worked outward. Sure enough, the farther back I went, the more recent the dates became. Hold up, when was this church built?

I trotted back to the gate and climbed the front steps to the stone church. Just to the right of the arched wooden dou-ble doors was a plaque that read, *Dedicated June 5, 1953*.

Argh! Why didn't I think of checking that first?

I dashed back to my car and searched on my iPhone for each individual cemetery and the church it was affili-ated with, if there was one. Two more of the four churches were dedicated after 1903. The two public ones and the cemetery at the Catholic church were each older than that.

I typed the address of the nearest one into the GPS and drove off again.

It was one of the public cemeteries: Oak Hill Cemetery. When I got there, I saw three or four teenagers out among the graves. I couldn't tell whether they were other juniors, but when they turned in my direction, I instinctively ducked down below the dashboard so they couldn't see me.

Why? Why would I hide? Why didn't I want anyone to know I was doing the Senior Scramble?

Part of me was worried that they'd think I'd be cheating by having the inside scoop with Luke. That was so unlikely, though, since Luke was well known and trusted. Another part of me wanted to keep the competitive edge of stealth. If I got ahead, I wouldn't want anyone to know it. But there was something else. Something more sinister.

It was shame. I felt ashamed. My father would be so disappointed in me, and as mad at him as I was, I still cared what he thought of me. I guess I wasn't such a rebel after all. Maybe I had to work up to it in small amounts. I wasn't turning back, though. Once I made a commitment, I followed through with it. That tidbit looked great on college applications as well.

A few minutes later, I peeked up over the dash and the kids were gone. So was the maroon sedan that had been parked at the far end of the parking lot. I crossed my fingers that all of them had left. I pulled my hood tighter around my head, slipped on a pair of sunglasses, and crept out of my car. Right away, I felt tiny droplets of rain start to dab my face and dot my sunglasses. Perfect.

I hustled up the path through the graves toward the older stones. I crested a small hill, but still there was no lake anywhere in sight. No section or path named Lake. Even nothing with a proper name of a lake, like Superior or Tahoe. I hugged my arms tightly to my chest and stooped over against the spitting rain.

Way at the back of the cemetery, I found a section with death dates from the beginning of the 1900s, but I didn't see any with the dates 1812–1903, nor any stones mentioning anything remotely to do with a lake. Beyond the fence were thick woods, and I realized how far I'd have to hike back to my car.

The rain fell heavier. Low thunder rumbled in the distance. I knew I was standing in a pretty stupid spot to be in a thunderstorm, so I marched swiftly back up the path. Just as I reached the top of the hill, the sky lit up and thunder exploded over my head. I jumped, and my arms and legs shot straight out like a cartoon cat who'd just stuck his tail into an electrical socket. When I landed, I didn't even take a moment to recoil. I sprinted down the hill, across the parking lot, and flew into my car exactly as I would if I were being chased by a velociraptor.

I cranked the engine and turned the heat on full blast. My clothes were soaked, and I was damp and cold right through to my bones. I held my icy fingers to the vents, but the engine wasn't warm enough yet, so I cupped them around my mouth and blew on them. My phone rang. My hands shook so much, I could barely answer. I checked the ID. It was Tara.

"Hey T."

"Hey chica, what's up?"

"N-n-not much-ch." My teeth were chattering like a jack-hammer.

"Wanna come hang? My place?"

Of course I couldn't; the Senior Scramble clock was ticking. I didn't want to hurt Tara's feelings, though, so I tried to sound interested, at least. "I'd love to, but I can't. Stupid . . . school project." Wow. Not only did I spontaneously lie to my best friend, but I also immediately tried to convince myself that it didn't count as a lie since it was a project and involved school. Both of those things balled up into another hot lump of shame in my belly.

"Need any help?"

Yes, I thought. Tara would be a huge help. But then I'd have to explain to her why I was doing this and who Luke was and why I kept thinking about his eyes and why I was trying to fit in at Ash Grove after Tara and I and everyone else at Meriton had been bad-mouthing that white-trash school for years. Plus, I had to keep the Senior Scramble a total secret. Even from her. There was no way I could risk having word about it leak out and be traced back to me. "I wish. But no, it's cool. Thanks, though." In a rush to ease my mounting guilt, I added, "If I finish quick, I'll give you a shout and come over or something."

"Sounds coolio. Talk to ya soon."

"'Kay. Bye."

I hung up and dropped my phone on the seat like it was a dead rat. Who was I all of a sudden? Why was I acting like this? I told myself that I was acting like this because I was trying to survive in a hostile environment. I was a refugee. I was an insurgent. I was a junior at Ash Grove High School, and I had a grave to find.

CHAPTER 12

THE RAIN CAME DOWN LIKE IT HAD A POINT TO PROVE. There were none of those wavering moments of maybe-letting-up. It was angry, loud, and unrelenting. It was resolute rain. It was taking no prisoners.

I'd been sitting in the Oak Hill Cemetery parking lot for twenty minutes without being able to see the hood of my car through my windshield. Imagine going through a car wash, only the car wash is at the bottom of a flooding ravine. That's what it was like. There was no use even trying to drive. While I waited, I pored over the satellite maps of the last two cemeteries to see if I had missed something. The Catholic cemetery was ginormous, so I decided to leave that one for last. Maybe the weather would dry up by the afternoon.

I entered the address in my GPS for the last cemetery, Ash Grove Memorial, the other public one, at 122 South Jefferson Avenue.

Earlier, I'd read that Ash Grove Memorial was the original town cemetery. Looking at the satellite map, I could see that it sat close to the center of town and took up an entire block. I zoomed in and could see how closely the graves were packed in. There wasn't an empty spot anywhere, from

Jefferson Avenue on the south to Ridge Road on the north or from Huron Street on the west to Adams on the east.

Wait a second.

My brain tripped over something. What was it? There was a thought drawing toward me like a fuzzy black-and-white movie slowly coming into focus. Then it was right there, in full clarity.

Huron Street. As in Lake Huron.

The place I am is right beside a lake. The grave could be somewhere along that fence line. Right beside Huron Street. Right beside a lake.

Up yours, rain! I slammed the car into gear and started to drive, hoping to God that my GPS would tell me if I was about to run off the road or speed through an intersection. My windshield wipers thumped away at full tilt. With each swipe, I got a millisecond of sight. Just enough to get me the next twenty feet or so. Foot by foot, I edged my way the entire four miles to Ash Grove Memorial.

Despite the stupidity of driving any more than necessary, I circled the cemetery to get an idea of the layout. There was street parking all around and a gate in each one of the four sides of the black wrought-iron fence. I could have parked on Huron, but I wanted to keep out of sight. I parked on the north side of the cemetery, on Ridge Road, just before the corner where it intersected with Huron. I was pretty sure that when the rain let up, I'd have a clear view down the entire line of graves that bordered Huron. I'd make sure no one else was there, and then I'd sneak in.

After cursing myself for not keeping an umbrella in my

car and idling at the curb for another fifteen minutes, I started to worry about the gas situation. If I turned the car off, I'd have no heat. If I let it run, I'd have no gas, the car would die, and I'd still have no heat.

I was delaying the inevitable; I had to go out in the rain again. On the plus side, if this was in fact the cemetery with the answer to the clue, then the storm would probably keep the other contestants away. I cranked the heat to warm myself as much as possible before I left and cinched my hood tight around my head. I stretched out my right leg and slipped my phone into my front pocket. I pulled the hem of my hoodie down over it in an attempt to protect it from getting wet and kicked myself again for not having an umbrella. I rubbed my hands in front of the heat one more time, turned off the ignition, and bolted out into the storm.

In less than ten seconds, I was saturated. There wasn't any point in trying to stay dry any longer, so I stopped shielding my head and hunching over. Without the windshield to splatter the sheets of rain, outside I had a better view of the churning sky. Shades of dark and pale gray mottled and smudged into each other like an impressionist painting. Especially if the artist was suicidal. The smell was anything but depressing. It was that warm, earthy scent of expectancy that only spring rain carries. The scent of something coming. A comingling of promise and warning.

For a moment, I had this tantalizing impulse to stretch my arms wide and race through the rain, shouting to the clouds like a madwoman. I reminded myself that I was on a covert mission, though, and kept my head down. I crossed through the wrought-iron gate and headed straight for the line of headstones along Huron Street.

One by one, I checked the dates. At the same time, I tried to concoct an excuse for why I was there, in case I ran into anyone who knew me or if someone asked why I'd decided to visit a grave during a monsoon. I wanted to have my story straight. Okay, I'll say it: I wanted to have my lie well rehearsed.

I stepped from grave to grave, lining up excuses and shooting them down. Was today my dear departed's birthday? Nah, I'd never find a gravestone with March 17 on it. Was I doing research on genealogy? That was hardly something so urgent it couldn't wait until the rain stopped. Was I just out walking and got caught in the storm? What, and sought shelter in a graveyard rather than any of the stores within fifty feet of here? Yeah, right. Plus, anyone could have seen me get out of my car. This whole lying business was a lot more difficult than I'd anticipated.

My attention drifted. How great would it be to have an online forum where you'd say, "I need a lie for *X* situation," and people all over the globe would post suggestions?

"Blythe?" The voice was female.

I froze. I didn't look at her, because the immediate status was that she wasn't sure it was me, and I didn't want to be all, "Hey! Look at my face!" So I did the only thing I could think of. I collapsed at the foot of the headstone in front of me and pretended to bawl inconsolably. "Why?" I moaned. "Why did you have to go? I miss you so much my dear, sweet, uh . . ." I peeked at the name on the stone. Oh, crap. " . . . Ebenezer! Why did I have to lose you?" I glanced at the dates and realized this guy died in 1897. Oops. I hurled my arm over the front of the stone to cover the date and pretended to cry into it.

"Oh my God, you so need medication," a male voice said. I peered under my arm and saw a thick-soled black boot park its toe on my hip and then shove me over into the soggy, brown grass. I looked up at Cy and Jenna grinning at me. A guarded relief washed through me. Maybe I didn't entirely trust Cy and Jenna, but at least it wasn't yogurt-douche guy or the skank with the bedazzled fingernails who first called me the booger girl.

"What the hell are you doing?" Cy asked.

I scrunched up my face like I was confused about it myself and raised and blinked a few times. "Nothing," I said, and shook my head vigorously to emphasize the point.

They both burst into laughter. Jenna cried, "Blythe, you are the worst liar on the entire planet!"

I pouted. "Well, excuse me. I haven't had a lot of practice."

"Lemme guess," Cy teased, "that was your very first one."

I pushed myself up on my hands and knees and stood up as I said, "As a matter of fact, I happen to have told some very convincing lies just yesterday." I wiped off my hands and stuck my chin out at Cy. "To my *parents*, no less." At the same time, they both went, *Ahh!* and nodded with approval. I smirked.

"No offense," Cy said, "but your father's not exactly a polygraph machine. We've been lying to him for years and he has no idea."

"The irony is," Jenna added, "whenever we're telling the truth, he thinks we're lying." Her tri-color hair stuck to her face and neck beneath the rim of a wet, woolen cap. The eyeliner on both of their eyes ran down like black tears. She glanced at Cy. "Except for yesterday."

"What happened yesterday?" I asked, digging the fingers of each hand inside the sodden sleeve of the opposite arm like a Chinese finger trap.

Cy scratched his head. "Yeah, so yesterday after school, as soon as I get to detention, he calls me down to the office and tells me that I can go home. My detention's canceled."

"No way, it is? Awesome!" I cried.

"It seems *someone* tipped off your dad about the other kid who threw the Tater Tots at you," Jenna said with exaggerated innocence in her voice. She meant me. Luckily, she seemed to be thanking me—and not calling me a snitch—which was a huge relief. "When your dad checked with the lunch lady, she confirmed it. Since Cy wasn't the instigator, he was off the hook. Right, babe?" She beamed at Cy. He leaned in and kissed her full on the mouth for an eternity of awkwardness for my part.

I was getting used to Cy and Jenna so I said, "Helloooo? Could we perhaps table the foreplay for some future moment when I'm not standing next to you in a raging thunderstorm?" As if on cue, a crack of thunder tumbled across the sky. Cy and Jenna broke apart and laughed, still looking into each other's eyes. They were so in sync. They didn't even need to speak.

I wanted that.

Lightning flashed nearby and brought me back to reality. Thunder followed almost instantly, and I had to get moving. I didn't want to admit to Cy and Jenna that I was doing the hunt, though. I thought for some reason that it would lower their opinion of me. I was struggling to find something to say when Cy pointed to his left and said, "The guy's down there. Next to that one stone with the cross on top."

I felt my eyes open too wide. "What guy?" I asked, my eyebrows going up and down like a couple of spastic caterpillars. "What are you talking about?" Jenna tried not to laugh, but it spurted out of her anyway. Cy just shook his head and gave me a half smile.

"The dead dude," he said. "For the clue? You know exactly what I'm talking about. I don't know why you're even pretending . . . God, you are the *worst* liar!" He laughed out loud and I saw genuine delight on his face. I could tell right away that it wasn't something he let slip very often. He was more guarded than that. So I have to say that I was kind of proud to make him react that way.

Jenna tugged Cy by the arm toward the grave. "Here, we'll show you."

"Unless . . ." Cy stopped her. He held out his open hand to me and feigned sympathy. "You need more time to mourn your beloved Ebenezer."

I burst into fake tears and covered my face. "How could you remind me of that? Oh, Ebenezer." I gently laid my hand on his headstone. "Oh, my love. How I miss thee."

"*Thee?*" Cy mocked. "Okay, I'm sorry, but you are way too much of a dork to be seen with us anymore. We're going

home. I don't know if you've noticed, but it's started to rain."
He turned to go, but of course he was only kidding. Jenna
pulled him along and they showed me the right gravestone,
so close to the foot of an oak tree that the tree must have
been planted after the burial or else the roots would have
prevented digging. The headstone itself was small, but the
grave was lined with white fist-sized rocks set into the earth.
I knelt down and read as rivulets of water streamed down
the stone and collected in the bottom of each carved letter
and number.

William Caleb Symons
1812–1903
"And this our life, exempt from public haunt,
Finds tongues in trees, books in the running brooks,
Sermons in stones, and good in everything."

I wrestled my iPhone from my wet jeans pocket as
the damp denim fought to hold on to it. The pink rubber
sleeve had kept the phone dry enough. I kneeled down and
snapped a picture, and then I checked to see if it was okay.
The words were in perfect focus. The headstone seemed
larger than it had appeared at first. It was banked with white
rocks, cradled in roots, and awash in tributaries of rainwater.
Stones, trees, and running brooks. Exactly as it should be. I
couldn't help but think that William Caleb Symons would've
been pleased.

I saved the photo and wriggled the phone back into my
pocket. I stood up and tried to brush some of the mud off

my knees, but it just smeared down my shins. Another secret load of laundry I'd have to do before Mom saw.

The rain was finally starting to ease up. I had to bolt before anyone else from school got there. "Thanks, guys," I said to Jenna and Cy. "I owe you . . . uh . . . well, actually, I guess I owe you a couple."

Cy waved me off. "Consider it payment for having my back with your dad."

"But you had my back with that Weeble-headed yogurt douche bag." I looked down and muttered, "That's what I call him." Not exactly the picture of charity, but oh, well. Cy and Jenna were the type of people you might as well be honest with because they could spot a fake a mile away.

"Because that's what he is," Jenna said. She gazed at Cy. "You were so heroic that day. It was so hot." She went in for more kissing with plenty of tongue action as the last of the rain slicked down their faces and over their lips.

"Seriously?" I said. "Again?"

They dragged themselves apart as Jenna playfully rolled her eyes and Cy leered at me, saying, "Come on, you love it. You know you do." He flicked his tongue in and out at me like he was tasting my air.

"EW! NO!" I grimaced and squeezed my eyes shut.

Jenna purred, "I know I love it."

When I opened my eyes, they were throat-deep in each other again. "You guys! Are you kidding? For real? God, I feel like I need a condom just to stand near you." Without breaking their kiss, Cy pulled a gold foil-wrapped condom out of his back pocket and flung it at me. I shrieked like a two-year-old and sprang out of the way, but I slipped on a patch of mud and did a completely humiliating backward-running-man for a few steps before falling flat on my butt. I heard the mud squelch beneath me and felt it seeping into my jeans. Naturally, the sight of my sweet comedy stylings made Cy and Jenna completely lose it. At least I'd put my iPhone in my front pocket, not the back; otherwise it'd be shattered. Which might be iRonic, but I'd be iRate. That was a little Apple humor. Be sure to add something to my tip jar later.

I gracelessly heaved myself to my feet as Cy and Jenna struggled to recover from crumpling in hysterics.

"Oh, yes. Laugh away," I said, pulling on the seat of my ruined $150 jeans to dislodge some of the mud clumps. "Go ahead. Enjoy it, please. I exist only for your amusement, after all. Oh, crap, doesn't that girl go to Ash Grove?"

Cy and Jenna's heads swiveled in unison. "Ella Chambers," Cy muttered.

"Fake, evil bitch," Jenna added.

I stepped nearer to Cy and Jenna. "I don't want her to see me. I don't want anyone to know I'm doing the Senior Scramble."

Without demanding a reason or even hesitating, Jenna took my hand and the three of us ran. I couldn't believe how much noise came out of my squelching sneakers. *Shlurp-shlurp-shlurp-shlurp.* If Ella Chambers couldn't see me, she probably could hear me at least. We ducked into an open mausoleum close by, out of sight of Ella but with a perfectly hidden view of William Caleb Symons's gravestone.

After all they'd done for me, I felt I owed Cy and Jenna

an explanation. I told them that even though it was my suggestion to resurrect the scavenger hunt, I wasn't ready to assume the role of career delinquent yet. "Plus," I said, "a lot of people still hate me enough to turn me in, just so I'd get in trouble. I wouldn't care about that, but the hunt would be found out and spoiled for everyone, and that's what I really don't want. I'm trying to earn people's respect, not make them even angrier."

"Why?" Cy asked, aghast. "Who cares what they think?"

I swiped a wet lock of hair off my cheek. "Look, you two have been outsiders for . . . how long? I'm guessing pretty much forever. It's part of who you are. And you have each other. But you've got to understand something: I've never been an outsider. Over in Meriton, I had a ton of friends. Pretty much everyone liked me. But here? Pretty much nobody does, and I can't take it. I'm not used to being disliked. It sounds shallow, but it's true." When I spoke those words to Cy and Jenna, it was also the first time I admitted them to myself. It tied right into the shame I felt earlier. I was ashamed to be so superficial as to want to be well liked. But there it was. "I'm sure that if you two were there, you would've hated me."

"You wouldn't have been who you are now, though," Jenna said.

"Exactly," Cy agreed. He slid an arm around Jenna's waist and touched his forehead to hers. "You are so smart," he whispered to her.

"Yeah, but does that make me a better person or worse?" I asked.

Cy turned to me. "Neither. Both. Who cares? Look, we get it. You don't have to justify or rationalize why you want to do the Senior Scramble. It doesn't make any difference because you're not going to win."

"I'm not?" I asked meekly.

"Nope," Cy said, looking sly. "'Cause Jenna and I are going to beat your ass." He grinned at me and chuckled. "We helped you today in a moment of weakness, but no more!" He pointed in the air dramatically. "From here on out, you're on your own. So you might as well get used to being a looooo-ser!" He turned his fingers into an L and moved it toward me.

I smacked his hand away playfully. "Hold up, you two are doing the hunt? What happened to 'We're not exactly joiners'?" My macho imitation of Cy's voice threw Jenna into giggles.

"Are you kidding?" Cy said. "The cops go so easy on Ash Grove juniors doing the Senior Scramble."

"Most of them did it themselves in high school," Jenna added.

Cy rubbed his palms together. "I've been looking forward to the mayhem for months."

Jenna leaned closer. "Plus, there's a rumor going around that the prize this year is two front-row seats at the Strokes concert, with backstage passes and a room for the night in the same hotel the band is staying at."

"That prize is so mine," Cy said, grinning.

"Holy crap," I said. "Where do they get the money for all that?"

"Everybody chips in," Jenna said. "Students, staff, parents, whoever."

"People in Ash Grove are pretty tight," said Cy. "Most of them went to school here."

"That's wild," I said. "But what if the rumor's wrong?"

Cy hiked up the collar of his army jacket and wrapped it snug around his neck. "Maybe it is. But I can't pass up the chance that it might be right."

"So you're doing the hunt," I concluded.

"We're doing the hunt," Cy confirmed.

"Last night, right after we figured out the clue, we came here and found the grave," Jenna said. "It was dark, but Cy knows this place, so we figured it out pretty quick."

"What do you mean, you know this place?" I asked Cy, without thinking.

He went silent.

"I'm sorry," I blurted. "I didn't mean . . ."

"My brother's here," Cy said to me. He turned to face the rain. "He died two years ago. Car accident."

Jenna leaned closer. "It was his older brother, Shane. After Cy's dad took off, Shane sort of became Cy's surrogate dad. Now Shane's gone and it's just Cy, his mom, and his little sister."

Cy's shoulders stiffened.

"Wow, Cy," I said. "I'm so sorry."

He nodded.

Suddenly, he clapped. "So yeah," he said, changing the subject, "we've been spying here all day to see who else was doing the hunt."

"Who did you see?" I tried not to sound anxious but wanted to know if I was far behind. It was nearly one o'clock. Plenty of people could've gotten to the cemetery earlier that morning.

"Let's see. You and"—Cy used his tongue to swivel the enormous stud below his lip while he remembered—"Megan McGillicuddy, David Davidson, Biff O'Toole . . . Who else? Oh, Fabian Bonaventure, Carlito Montoya el Diablo Ramirez, Arizona St. Cloud, Dick Dangler—"

"So many?" I blurted. "Who are they? I don't know any of those people!"

Jenna snickered behind her fingerless lace gloves. "Blythe, he's messing with you! Nobody's been here but you and Ella Smella."

"Those were all fake names?" I still doubted Cy.

"Come on," he cried. "Carlito Montoya el Diablo Ramirez? *Dick Dangler?*"

"Well, yeah, when you say them like that, they sound fake," I said. "Okay, so I'm a naturally trusting person. So sue me."

"The word isn't *trusting,*" Cy said, "it's *gullible.* But don't bother looking *gullible* up in the dictionary. It's not there. Did you know that?"

I sneered at him. "Oh, ha ha. As if I didn't play that joke on my brother like a thousand times when he was little."

"How old's your brother now?" Cy asked.

"Twelve," I answered vaguely as I tiptoed to the mausoleum door and sneaked a glance outside. I was worried about the time. I had to get home so that the minute the buyers left the house, I could run inside, wash my clothes, and have them dry before Mom, Dad, and Zach got back. I checked for any sign of Ella Smella. I couldn't see her or anyone else anywhere. "I'd better make a break for it before tons of other people start to show up," I said.

Jenna spied around the other side of the mausoleum doorway, toward Jefferson Avenue. "I hope they do. It was so boring until you got here. Wait, hold on. A bunch of jocks are getting out of a pickup truck. Holy crap, how do you fit five football players in the cab of one pickup truck? Idiots. That's what you call natural selection."

I spun toward Jenna and clasped my filthy hands together in prayer. "Please promise me that you guys won't tell anyone else where the grave is. Please? Ooh, or better yet, tell them it's in the Catholic church cemetery! That place is huge. They'll be there for days."

Cy shook his head and tsked at me. "My, my, that's not a very sportsmanlike attitude for the principal's daughter to have."

He was joking, but it still stopped me cold because what he said was true. What I said next was also true. And cold. "I don't care. I want to win." To top it off, I added, "The less like my dad I am, the better. So roll that up in your pot pipe and smoke it."

Cy scoffed dramatically and chuckled like I was a precious moron. "It's called a bowl, not a pipe. The thing you roll is . . ." He hesitated. "Ah, forget it. You know what, Blythe? It's not information you're ever going to need." He poked his head outside and checked all around. "Coast is clear," he said.

I thanked them both again and sprinted for the car. And by sprinted, I really mean waddled in my mud-caked jeans like I was wearing a loaded diaper, while my sopping-wet sneakers went *shlurp-shlurp-shlurp-shlurp.* So sexy.

I yanked open the car door and searched around for something to sit on to protect my seat upholstery. I didn't care about the dingy velour fabric; I just didn't want another mess to have to clean up. I had too many messes on my hands already.

I spotted the corner of my history textbook on the floor in the back, peeking out from under the seat. It must have slid under there at some point. I hadn't noticed it was missing. Normally, I didn't lose track of things like textbooks or other items that don't belong to me.

There was zero time to delve into that right now, though. I grabbed the book, opened it near the middle, and splayed it facedown on the driver's seat. I sat down and got the wedgie of a lifetime, but the book kept the seat clean, and that was all that mattered. I didn't need perfection; I just needed a temporary solution.

A strange sensation of hot pride flared up inside me. I wasn't accustomed to finding quick fixes. Usually I did things the proper way or not at all. Now, all of a sudden, my eyes were open to the benefit and thrill of just squeaking by.

I drove off as the stubborn sun burst through and sparkled the raindrops left everywhere. When I finally turned down my street, I could see that Marjorie's and the buyers' cars were still in the driveway. I pulled over to the curb and parked where I could see my house but nobody would notice me. The rain started misting again, so I switched on my wipers. I wanted to get a good look at the people who might be living in my house. I was suddenly very curious about them. *They'd better not be jerks,* I thought. I didn't want jerks walking around my house, cooking in my kitchen, climbing my stairs, sleeping in my room.

My room.

Someone was going to take my room. Steal it away from me like a bully snatches a toy. My room wouldn't be mine anymore. It would belong to someone else. All the dreams I'd imagined and the plans I'd made and the secrets I'd whispered into my pillow at night would be gone too.

I'd never see my pale pink walls that I helped paint. Never see my fuzzy beige carpet that I loved to dig my toes into after I'd slept late on weekends. Never hang my spring wardrobe in perfect order on the closet rod. Never open or close my linen curtains. Never watch out the window for a boy I liked to walk up the street. Never read inside my closet so Zach wouldn't bug me. Never see the inner edge of its door where I scribbled *I ♥ Kevin Bailey* in third grade. Never hide secret notes from Tara under the loose corner of the carpet. Never see the crack in the ceiling light from when I tossed up the baton I got for my tenth birthday. Never lock my door and cry.

Never feel my room keeping me safe.

All of that would be gone.

I wondered if Dad had thought about that. If he'd counted all those things when he tallied up the list of sacrifices he would ask his family to make for him. No, not even for him—for his job. Not the whole of him, just one part. Except that lately he seemed more and more "Principal McKenna" and less and less "Dad." He spoke to Zach and me like we were students. He treated Mom like a staff member. I couldn't even remember the last time he wore sweatpants.

The front door to my house opened and the thieving demon-buyers stepped outside, followed by Marjorie. The buyers were a man and woman who looked like overpaid, underbred yuppies. Mom called them "nouveau riche." Newly rich people. People with more money than class who flaunted their wealth every chance they got. They hadn't been rich long enough to learn that wealth was a private matter.

For example, these two were dressed in designer labels on a Saturday afternoon. Wearing wool and cashmere in the rain. They didn't even have enough experience with those fabrics to know what wetness does to them. I hoped his wool sweater smelled like dirty gym socks and her too-tight cashmere top itched like chicken pox. Then again, there was a good chance their clothes were synthetic knockoffs. Those two probably couldn't tell the difference.

They sauntered down the front walk, talking and gesturing to the roof or the chimney. The man accidentally stepped in a puddle on the concrete and immediately yanked his foot up. He hopped around on the other one while he checked the condition of his fine leather dress shoe. Unfortunately, he accidentally bumped the woman while she was contemplating her manicure and knocked her off balance. She stepped off the walk, and the entire five-inch spike heel of her knee-high suede boot sank deep into the spongy, rain-soaked earth. She let out a little cry, twisted her boot out of the mud, and started hopping around on one foot, just like he was. They'd just managed to clasp each other's shoulder when her clean boot landed in his puddle and splashed them both again. It was comedy. I had to laugh. Especially since it's so hard to get water marks out of suede.

When they finally got into their hybrid SUV crossover and followed Marjorie down the street, I pulled into the driveway and ran inside. I peeled off my filthy clothes and threw them in the washer. I set the machine to Extra-Heavy Wash and switched it on. At the last second I remembered that my phone was in my jeans. I fished it out of the load of clothes, slammed down the washer lid, and sped upstairs. I scrubbed my hands and face in the bathroom. Still completely naked, I dashed to my desk, cleared the properties from the headstone picture, and uploaded it onto the Revolting Phoenix website. One minute later, I had my second clue.

CHAPTER 13

Congratulations! You have successfully uploaded a valid picture of item #1.

Here is your clue to item #2:

Long ago in Gettysburg, a famous speech was heard
In it was a number, not in digits, but in words.
Find that many soda cans, and then when you are done,
Stack them up and take a pic. (Recycle every one!)

How cute that the seniors wanted us to recycle! For some reason, it seemed like Luke's idea. I bet it had been. Okay, soda cans. I needed how many? I recited Abraham Lincoln's Gettysburg Address, "Four score and seven years ago . . ." All right, I remember my American History teacher in Meriton last year said a score was twenty. So four score is eighty, plus seven is eighty-seven. Eighty-seven soda cans. Where the heck was I going to find eighty-seven empty cans?

Recycling day wasn't until next Thursday, so trash-picking wasn't an option; I couldn't wait that long. It dawned on me that I could just buy eighty-seven cans of soda. I pulled up my desktop calculator and divided eighty-seven by six.

That would be 14.5 six-packs, so I'd have to buy fifteen to get the half pack. Those were about three bucks each, so I needed . . . $45?

Um, no.

That was a mani-pedi plus tip at my salon.

Forget it.

I had to think of a source. What kind of place would use a ton of soda but only in cans? Restaurants all used fountains. Vending machine sodas were mostly in plastic bottles. Even if one had cans, it wasn't like people stood there, chugged the soda, and then tossed the can in the nearest trash. An airplane would work. Flight attendants opened soda cans all day long. Unfortunately I was nowhere near an airport, and even if I was, I highly doubted I'd be allowed anywhere near the trash.

No, I needed someplace more local. Someplace with a lot of people who liked to drink out of cans. Or drank weird stuff that only came in cans. Or the place used cans like the airline because they didn't have a fountain, but they needed small servings of a wide variety of beverages to accommodate a lot of picky drinkers.

Wait a second . . . picky drinkers . . . Aha! I had it! I couldn't believe how obvious it was.

Shady Acres. There were over three hundred picky, opinionated diners and drinkers in that place. I remembered volunteering in the dining room my first year there. I had gone into the kitchen for something and noticed shelf upon shelf of beverages, most of them in cans. I later found out that certain residents would only drink certain brands of certain sodas or juices or sparkling water, but not every day. So the staff ordered a few pallets of each to keep on hand.

I couldn't believe I hadn't thought of it sooner! I checked the time. There were still a couple of hours before my family would get home. Long enough to run over to Shady Acres and see what I could find. It would almost make my lie about going there for an afternoon tea a truth. Shady Acres . . . afternoon . . . beverages . . .

Almost a truth.

I threw on some dry clothes. I didn't bother with hair or makeup, which wasn't like me. Normally, I wouldn't leave the house without at least a five-minute face and a perky ponytail.

But I was in a race. A race against the clock, a race against the other players, and a race against my family. There was no time for vanity. Vanity was for losers! Plus, Tara always said I was naturally cute enough.

When I got to Shady Acres, instead of parking in the visitors' parking lot like I usually did, I pulled around back to the loading dock. To the right of that, I spotted two enormous Dumpsters, one black and one blue with a recycling symbol. The only problem was, they were locked behind a six-foot-high slatted wood fence. There was a gate where the garbage truck could gain access, but it was padlocked. I got out of the car and peered through the slats. The sides of the fence met the wall of the building on either side of a steel door labeled Trash Repository Room. I couldn't get to the recycling from the outside, but maybe I could from the inside.

I left my car in the back and walked around to the front door. I waved to the front desk attendant, who knew me by sight. I vaguely remembered that the trash room was off the kitchen, so instead of turning left toward the resident rooms, I veered right toward the dining hall. Inside, staff members were milling around setting up for the dinner service (which started at three thirty!). People would pass in and out of the swinging kitchen doors so many times that nothing seemed odd when I went through the doors too.

That was as far as I got.

The place was a zoo. People in white uniforms ran everywhere yelling at each other or chopping or stirring or mixing or frying. Food and utensils were scattered and piled on every inch of countertop. Discarded peels and stems littered the floor. Steam and smoke billowed up from the stoves.

I guess dinner for three hundred took a lot of work.

The heat was stifling. The overwhelming smell of so many foods cooking at once was nauseating. Far across on the other side of the kitchen, I spotted the door to the trash room in a little vestibule off to the side. I was almost glad that there was no possible way I could reach it unnoticed, because I had to get out of there before I passed out.

Back in the dining room, I leaned over one of the tables to catch my breath. The cheap polyester tablecloth seemed to slicken beneath my sweaty palms. How was I going to do this? I couldn't wait until after dinner. It ended at five thirty and my parents would be home long before that.

I needed an accomplice. I needed a diversion. I knew where to find both.

I couldn't help but stop to listen outside their door for a second.

"I happen to *like* the smell of my Jean Naté After Bath Splash," Ms. Eulalie cried.

"It smells like a whorehouse in here!" Ms. Franny bleated.

"Well, you would know."

"What's that supposed to mean?"

"Just what you think it means, Jezebel."

I knocked on the door and pretended I hadn't heard a thing. "Anyone home?"

"Blythe!" Ms. Franny exclaimed. She picked up a magazine and fanned her face. "Go open that window, will you? Get some fresh air."

"Oh, no, you don't!" Ms. Eulalie said, holding her hand up to me. "Don't you do any such thing. It's already colder than an icebox in here."

Ms. Franny smacked the magazine down on her side table. "Nonsense. It's plenty warm."

"On your side! You got the heater! I got the leaky, drafty window! And you're so stingy with that heat, too. Like you're gonna use it all up or something. Got to *save* it so we don't run out."

Ms. Franny stuck her tongue out at Ms. Eulalie, then turned and stared at me for a moment. A shadow of confusion fell over her face. "Wait a minute. What day is it? Why are you here? Is it Monday? I thought it was Saturday. When did it get to be Monday? I'm losing my marbles."

Ms. Eulalie pointed to the floor. "There goes one."

"No, no," I said. "It is Saturday." I perched on the edge of

Ms. Franny's bed and leaned in close. "I'm here on a special mission. I could use your help, though. Both of you. If you're up for it."

"What kind of help?" Ms. Eulalie asked.

"What kind of mission?" Ms. Franny followed. "Will there be guns involved? I've got good aim. I'm a dead shot."

"No, there will be no guns," I said.

"Damn," Ms. Franny mumbled. Ms. Eulalie glared at her for swearing but let it slide.

I proceeded to give them the whole story. I told them they'd been totally right. After Dad canceled the Senior Scramble and everything, I'd felt like a bully. I told them about Luke's online newspaper and how I apologized to him and proposed the idea of taking the Senior Scramble underground. The ladies had nobody to tell, but I swore them to secrecy anyway. I explained how everything in the hunt worked and what yesterday's clue was like and told them my plan for getting the cans.

"So what do you think?" I asked them. "Are you in?"

The ladies looked at each other for a few moments, then at me. Ms. Franny opened her mouth, held it there, and then finally said, "So who's *Luke*?"

"That's what I want to know too." Ms. Eulalie's eyebrows danced up and down. She grinned at me.

"You guys!" I cried. "No!" I thought I'd done a good job of covering up my semi-crush. Apparently not. "He's just some senior. I don't . . . He just . . . It's nothing. I mean there's no 'it' even. There's nothing. He's n-not anybody. I mean of course he's somebody, but I mean he's not . . . you know. *Somebody*."

Once they were sure I was done babbling, Ms. Eulalie went, *"Psssh!,"* and Ms. Franny went, "Ha! Yeah, right."

"Lord love you," Ms. Eulalie said, "but you tell lies like Ms. Franny sings: hard to listen to and even harder to believe."

I expected Ms. Franny to come back with some witty retort. Instead, she said, "On this point, I have to agree with the old fart bag. Blythe, you stink at lying."

"So I've heard," I muttered to the floor.

Ms. Franny clapped her knobby hands together. "Well, I for one am in on Operation Soda Pop. How about you, Ukulele?"

"Lord save me, yes. I'd never say no to you, baby girl. Not after you been so good to me all these years."

"The only problem is," Ms. Franny said, "Nurse Ratched's going to be coming around in a little while to wheel us down for dinner. After that, it's lights-out."

"We get so tired after dinner, you know."

I nodded in agreement even though I didn't want to agree to what I knew Ms. Franny was about to say.

"Can we postpone till tomorrow?"

"Nurse Darlene is off on Sundays, remember." Ms. Eulalie winked at me.

Good point. "I hadn't thought of that," I said. It definitely would be easier without Darlene around. She'd know something was up and bust us, no question. I hated to lose all that time on the hunt, but I couldn't afford to blow this. I had no other soda can options. "What's the Sunday floor nurse like?" I asked.

Ms. Franny blew a raspberry. "A moron."

I stood up to leave. "Okay, what time tomorrow?"

"Say, one o'clock?" Ms. Franny said. "That's the peak hour for Sunday visitors. The place will be crawling with people, and nobody'll bat an eye if we're out of our room."

"I agree," Ms. Eulalie said.

"Sounds good," I said. I was already collecting a list in my brain of lies to tell my parents. "I'll see you then. And thanks, ladies." I kissed each of them on the cheek and left.

I pulled into my driveway just as my parents' car did. They were home early. At least I didn't have to lie to them about where I'd just been. My stomach lurched at the sight of my mud-coated history book on the floor beside me. I kicked it quickly back under the passenger seat.

"How was Gran and Granddad's?" I asked once we were out of our cars.

"SO boring," Zach said. "You're so lucky you stayed home. I had to sit through three whole photo albums of old dead people. Be glad you missed it."

Mom got out and smoothed the wrinkles in her camel pants. "How was the afternoon tea?" She said "afternoon tea" like it was a jewel on her tongue. A precious little gem that was lost to her now.

I felt sorry for my mom, so I did my best not to answer her with a lie. Not a direct one, at least. "Shady Acres was great. The dining room and kitchen were very busy. I had a good time with Ms. Franny and Ms. Eulalie. I'm pretty wiped out, though."

Mom beamed at me. "Well, I'm sure they appreciated your company. Why don't you go upstairs and have a little nap?"

Wow. Third rule of lying: Dance around the lie with distracting truths. They're far more convincing.

Dad got out, gave me a vague smile, and placed his hand on the top of my head for a second. I didn't have any truths that were appropriate to say out loud to him at that moment, so I kept my mouth shut. I followed him and Mom inside and then took a detour to the laundry room to toss my clothes in the dryer. Mom would probably think I simply felt like doing some laundry. After that, I went up to my room to check the stats on the Senior Scramble. All I could do was hope that other players were having as much trouble as I was.

When the Revolting Phoenix came up, I clicked on the statistics button. It displayed everyone's user name and what clue each person was on. Most of them hadn't turned in the photo for the first clue yet, which was a relief. A few had turned in the one for the second clue and were on to the third already. Crap.

My plan for tomorrow had better work or I was going to fall way behind. I logged off the site and suddenly realized that I was starving. I hadn't eaten since breakfast. I had forgotten completely. I try to eat smart. I drink plenty of water. I know what keeps my energy up and keeps my skin hydrated. Yet once I left the house this morning, I didn't have a drop to drink or a bite to eat and I didn't even notice. Weird. Well, I was hungry now.

I went down to the kitchen and grabbed the first things that looked appetizing: a bag of potato chips and a root beer. Not my normal diet. When I popped a chip in my mouth, though, it tasted like the most spectacular thing I'd ever eaten.

I finished the bag and guzzled the soda, then slouched back upstairs and fell asleep.

Mom woke me up for dinner, but my stomach was still heavy from the greasy potato chips. I ate a little salad, but I only picked at my pork chop. I didn't want any of the mashed potatoes. Instead, I made hash marks in them with the tines of my fork.

The phone rang. Mom excused herself and scooted back from the table. I heard her muffled voice in the kitchen talk for a few minutes. Then she came back and sat down. Her face had tensed up. Her jaw flexed in and out. She blinked a few times and then blossomed into a full-blown lady look. "The showings today went very well," she said. "We have two offers on the house."

Dad set his knife and fork down on his plate. "Are they any good?" he asked. I wanted to claw that eager expression off his face.

Mom sat down in her chair. "They both came in at the asking price. Marjorie will be stopping by after dinner to go over the details." She methodically laid her napkin across her lap, picked up her fork, and started eating.

That was it. It was done. Our home was gone.

CHAPTER 14

I DIDN'T CRAWL OUT OF BED UNTIL SOMETIME AFTER eleven Sunday morning. Marjorie had been at the house until almost midnight. She had shown up after dinner and presented the two offers on the house. One was from a family with five boys. The other was from the yuppie idiots I had seen that afternoon. The offers were exactly equal in price, timeline, contingencies, everything.

We thought that all we had to do was pick one, but Marjorie said no, now that there were competing bids, she could call the buyers' agents and ask for their clients' "best and highest" offer. I suppose it was the free-market system, but it felt unnervingly like a shakedown.

Marjorie called the other agents right there on her cell, and both agents said they'd get back to her within an hour. By eleven o'clock, we had the "best and highests." The family could only come up another five thousand dollars, but the yuppies tacked on ten grand. Marjorie said the buyers had given us forty-eight hours to decide before the offers expired. Until we accepted one and signed the contract, either one of the buyers could yank their offer at any time. The whole negotiation seemed quick and dirty.

Once Marjorie left, I did my best to sway my parents toward picking the family. What I really was doing was arguing against the yuppies. I had to be careful not to let it slip that I'd seen them. Zach liked the idea of extra cash, of course, so he argued their side. Mom and Dad didn't say much. That's how I could tell that they were overwhelmed and confused. Finally, they decided to sleep on it, so we all went to bed.

Now the morning sun was flooding my beautiful room that soon would belong to someone else. Even though I was curled up under my polka-dot comforter, I could hear Mom and Dad downstairs in the kitchen. I couldn't make out any words, but I was familiar with the tone. They were arguing.

They had to be butting heads about which offer to take. At least that meant that one of them wanted to give our home to the family with kids, which was encouraging. The other person wanted the money more. I could guess who was who. Mom came from money; it meant little to her. It meant a lot to Dad, though. He was trying to prove his worth to Granddad. How lame and insecure.

As far as I was concerned, there was no way those yuppies were getting their hands on my house. I slid my feet into my fuzzy white slippers and charged down into the fray. *Once more unto the breach, dear friends, once more.*

I passed Zach in the family room. He was sitting on the couch, throwing Cocoa Puffs into his empty orange juice glass. Mom must have relaxed the no-food rule now that we had buyers on the line. Every time Zach made a shot, he'd announce, "Two points!" The shots he missed were scattered across the glass top of the coffee table.

Dad and Mom stood in the kitchen, leaning on opposite counters, arms crossed, faces set. Mom's softened when she saw me, though. "Good morning, sweetie," she said. Dad kissed the air and winked at me. He didn't say anything.

"Morning," I said. "What's up?" I tried a non-confrontational approach. "Did you guys decide?"

Dad and Mom locked eyes. "Not yet," Dad said.

I poured myself a mug of coffee and nonchalantly said, "It would just be so nice to know there were going to be kids running around here and growing up. It's a family house, you know?"

"I agree," Dad said.

What? Hold up. Dad wanted to take the lower offer?

Mom shook her head. "Five boys? This place would be destroyed in a week. I won't hand over my home to people who aren't even responsible enough to use birth control."

"Anne!" Dad chastised. "You don't know that. Stop fabricating things."

"I bet they were trying for a girl," I offered.

"I don't care why they had five children," Mom said, not looking at anyone. "I can't let them ruin . . ." She pressed her lips together. Squeezed her eyes shut. Couldn't stop the tears from running down her cheeks.

Dad crossed the room and wrapped his arms around her. He stroked the back of her head and said, "Whoever buys this house will be buying it because they love it. They'll take care of it. You don't need to worry. And you'll have the new house to make your own. We'll build new memories. We'll still have the old ones too."

I watched Mom's rib cage heave in and out with silent, jagged sobs. Then it stilled. Mom straightened up and wiped her eyes. Sniffled once and walked out of the room. This argument wasn't over.

I found it odd that Mom would dig her feet in about this decision, yet when Dad asked to move to Meriton, she rolled right over. Why hadn't she stood up then? Why hadn't she burst into tears then? Why hadn't she disagreed with him when it really mattered?

Maybe she had. Maybe she'd done all those things. And maybe when she walked out of the kitchen just now, she was saying, I've given you enough.

"Take the damn money!" Zach hollered.

"Don't swear," Dad said meekly. It was nothing more than an automatic response. His gaze had focused in the air somewhere between the tile floor and the table leg. Yet, he looked like Dad again. Not Principal McKenna. Only for a moment, though. Then he snapped to attention and asked, "What's on your schedule for today, honey?"

I took a big slurp of coffee to buy a second and steady myself. I swallowed and said, "Just running some errands. Nothing big."

"Good." He nodded and slipped away into his thoughts again.

"I'll be back late this afternoon," I said.

"Okay."

"Don't make any decisions without me."

"Nope."

I could've told him I was running off to marry a gay

kangaroo and I would've gotten the same robotic response. I counted myself lucky that he didn't pry. And even luckier that Mom was still in her room when I left the house just before one o'clock.

I drove over to Shady Acres and parked in the back again. The visitor lot was packed anyway. Ms. Franny was right about this being prime visiting time.

Apparently, Shady Acres was a whole different place on Sundays. I knew that Sunday was the day that most guilty family members showed up to spend a few strained minutes with their ailing relative and then go home feeling better about themselves. I just didn't realize there were so many. And that they all seemed to come at one o'clock. I guess it made sense. The visiting family wouldn't feel obliged to take their relative to lunch. Plus, they could still get home in time to watch the football game or wash the car or do whatever else they'd rather do than sit here pretending that their relative wasn't withering in front of them. Or saying they'll see their relative next week, when they know he might not be here then. Or even hoping he might not be here.

Their visits were a joke.

I'm sorry. I shouldn't be so cynical and judgmental. But the sight of all those people who could visit anytime—but didn't—made me angry.

I shoved my anger deep inside and concentrated on the task at hand. I stopped by Ms. Franny and Ms. Eulalie's room, but it was empty. I found the ladies in the common room in their wheelchairs. They'd cornered one of the few male residents, Coleman Watson, who had outlived his wife by almost forty years. Let me tell you, the women in this place were like horny piranhas around the widowers. There was flirting, touching, possessiveness, giggling, lying, eyelash-batting, jealousy, and backstabbing. Just like high school.

Ms. Eulalie saw me first. She patted Ms. Franny's shoulder and pointed to me. "Here she is, look. She's here right now."

Ms. Franny turned and gave me a conspiratorial wink. "Well, Coleman," she said loudly (he was pretty deaf), "Eulalie and I have some business to attend to. I hope we can continue this conversation later." I swear to God, she stroked her braid and smiled at him like a schoolgirl. Then she stuck out what little boobs she had left and shimmied her shoulders. Gross!

"Let's go, Franny pack," Ms. Eulalie muttered, "'fore you shake your womb out onto the floor."

Ms. Eulalie could wheel herself, but Ms. Franny wasn't strong enough, so I pushed her. She and I led the way so we could clear a path through the crowded hallway for Ms. Eulalie behind us. We rolled into the dining hall and closed the double doors. We weren't alone, though. A few families still sat at the tables where they'd finished lunch. Servers cleared the other tables, clinking glasses together, piling plates and silverware, and swooping tablecloths into a big canvas laundry bag on wheels. It smelled like French onion soup.

They had stopped serving lunch at twelve thirty, so when I peeked in to check the kitchen, it was fairly empty. A couple of the kitchen staff stood at the giant dishwasher against the left wall, hosing off pots and plates. They were listening to their MP3 players, though. Between those and the noisy rush of the dishwasher, the workers probably wouldn't even notice me unless they turned around.

The real problem was the servers bringing in the dirty dishes. I needed to keep them out of the kitchen for a few minutes. We had it all planned, though. Ms. Eulalie would distract them while Ms. Franny and I sneaked through to the trash repository room. She'd keep a lookout at the door while I went inside and stuffed eighty-seven cans into the black garbage bag I had tucked in my coat pocket. At first, I had wanted to go out to the Dumpster and toss the bag over the fence into the parking lot. But yesterday when I told the ladies my plan, they insisted that I stack the cans in their room so they could see it. I wasn't sure why. I guess when you live inside four little walls, anything unusual becomes a treat.

I glanced around the dining room again. The last few diners got up from their table. Once they were gone, it was just the servers and us. "Okay, ladies," I whispered. "It's showtime."

Ms. Eulalie wheeled over to the far corner of the room, turned around, and set the brake on her wheelchair. Then she clutched her left shoulder and started to wail. "OOOOH, LAAAWD! PRECIOUS, PRECIOUS LAWD!" Every eye in the room turned to her. "I THINK I'M HAVING ME A HEART ATTACK! LAWD JESUS SAVE ME! SOMEBODY HELP!" A few servers jogged over to her. "HELP ME, PLEASE!" She stuck out her left leg and slid halfway down her seat. "LAWD

A-MERCY! I'M FADING, JESUS!" The rest of the servers rushed to help her.

This was our chance.

I grabbed the handles of Ms. Franny's wheelchair and pushed her through the swinging door to the kitchen. We raced across the floor so fast that my hair blew back and Ms. Franny's nightgown flapped around her shins. She waved her hands in the air, squealing, "WHEEEE!" None of the dishwashing staff seemed to hear a thing, just as I'd predicted. We careened into the alcove and I wrenched open the heavy door. I backed Ms. Franny just far enough into the doorway that her wheelchair propped it open. That way, I could hear her warn me if anyone was coming. I grabbed the trash bag from my pocket and ran over to the giant recycling bins that sat ready to be emptied into the blue Dumpster outside.

As quickly as I could, I counted by twos and tossed the cans into the bag. I had twenty. Then forty. Then sixty. "Everything okay?" I whispered to Ms. Franny.

"Fine and dandy," she whispered back.

Seventy cans. Now eighty. Then a few extra to make ninety in case I counted wrong. I knotted the bag and dragged it over to the door.

Oh, crap. I hadn't thought about how to carry it back to the room. Originally, I was going to throw it over the fence. How was I going to haul this bag and push Ms. Franny at the same time? The bag wasn't heavy; it was just huge and bulky. "I can't carry the bag and push!" I hissed to Ms. Franny. Time was ticking. My heart pounded.

"Give it here!" she said. "I'll hold it on my lap. People will think I'm just a crazy old bag lady who likes to carry her garbage around."

There was no time to argue. I hoisted the bag onto her lap and she hugged it with her bony arms. I gripped her wheelchair handles and we zoomed through the kitchen again. I think one of the guys with the hose saw us, but we were through the door to the dining room before he could say a word.

Ms. Eulalie was still wailing and grabbing her chest while the people around her stood or squatted or held her hand. A nurse was stooped over her, listening to her heart with a stethoscope.

When Ms. Eulalie caught sight of us zipping past, she sat straight up and said, "Oh, you know what? I feel much better all of a sudden. Yes, I do. I do believe I feel just fine now. Thank you for your kindness anyway. I think I'll be leaving. Bye, now." She released the brake, grabbed her wheels, and gave them a firm shove. The nurse followed along for a few steps, still trying to check Ms. Eulalie's heartbeat. Her wheelchair finally broke free and she sped toward us.

I held the door open for her with my foot, and we all rolled out.

It was clockwork!

As we wheeled down the hall, several visitors looked at Ms. Franny funny because of the garbage bag. She just kept yelling things like, "I got body parts in here" or "Hands off my pocketbook!" or "Who wants my big bag of poop?"

Once we were safely back in their room, the ladies and I whooped and clapped and gave each other high fives. I held up the black garbage bag like it was a pirate's booty and shook it to rattle the cans. When we finally got ahold of ourselves and settled down, I said, "You guys were so great!"

"I gotta hand it to you, Ukulele, you should get an Oscar for that performance," said Ms. Franny.

Ms. Eulalie still panted a bit from the ride back to the room. "Mark down the date!" she said between shallow breaths. "Frances Calhoun gave somebody a compliment."

"Enjoy it while you can, because there won't be any more. Not in your lifetime, anyway. A compliment from me is like Halley's Comet."

"You got that right," said Ms. Eulalie. "It flies by fast and then you forget all about it for the next seventy-five years."

I helped the women back into their beds and folded up the wheelchairs so there'd be more floor space to stack the cans. I kept getting almost to the top and then accidentally knocking them over because the ladies kept asking me questions about Luke, and I couldn't concentrate. Talking about him made me nervous.

They wanted to know every detail about him, so I went over what he looked like, what he wanted to study in college, conversations I'd had with him. When I told them about his e-mail apology, Ms. Eulalie said, "An E-MAIL?" like it was the rudest thing ever. So I explained that he'd needed to look up the Shakespeare quote first. Then they started teasing me about liking him and demanded that I read the e-mail to them. Of course when I did, they really let loose with the ooh-ing and aha-ing and mmm-hmm-ing.

By the fourth time I tried to stack the cans, my hands

were shaking like crazy. I was just about to put on the final few cans when Ms. Franny shrieked, "WATCH OUT, BLYTHE!" and I jumped and knocked the whole thing over again.

"MS. FRANNY!" I yelled as I spun around to her. She was cracking up and clapping for herself. When I saw her wrinkled face so open and happy and drawn back into such a fulfilled smile, I couldn't help giggling too.

"Oh, you an evil, evil woman, Franny pack," Ms. Eulalie said. Yet, her belly bounced up and down as she chuckled silently.

Finally, I successfully stacked the cans and snapped a picture with my phone. I gave each of the ladies a few balls of Ms. Franny's yarn and they threw them at the stack like a carnival game. Between the cans falling and the ladies cheering, the noise was pretty loud. The Sunday floor nurse stuck her head in the door to see what was going on, but Ms. Franny threw a yellow yarn ball and hit the nurse right in the forehead. "Bull's-eye!" Ms. Franny cried. "I told you I had good aim!" The scowling woman vanished.

I stuffed the soda cans back into the black trash bag and thanked Ms. Eulalie and Ms. Franny again. As soon as I was through the door and out of their line of sight, I heard Ms. Eulalie say to Ms. Franny, "You know she could'a just asked for those cans. They'd'a given them to her."

"Sure," Ms. Franny answered, "but where's the fun in that?" Then they laughed some more.

I hadn't even thought about asking for the cans! My brain had gone directly to thievery. When did I start thinking like a bad girl? Had I stopped being a good girl? I couldn't tell.

The only thing I was sure of was that being bad was fun. A lot of fun. I finally understood the appeal for people like Cy and Jenna.

The question was: Did bad girls get into Bryn Mawr?

I started to see my happily-ever-after plans in a new light. A light that showed how dull they were. How riskless. How tame.

I didn't want to be tame. Or tamed. Domesticated, like a dog or a horse or a sheep. I didn't want to unlearn whatever instinct it was that made me "take" instead of "ask for." I didn't want someone else telling me what I could and couldn't have. Or should have. Or should want.

Had I read so many happy endings that I thought I should want one? That every girl wanted one? That good girls wanted one?

Did I really want that happy ending I'd envisioned? Or had someone told me to want it?

What did I really want?

Why didn't I know?

The bag on my back felt heavier. I hitched it higher on my shoulder and trudged through the front door of Shady Acres. I rounded the corner and headed to the back parking lot. The wind blew so hard against me that I had to lean into it. The weather was just one more unpredictable thing about that March.

After I ran the cans out to the recycling plant, I went home. I had a slight gnawing in my stomach that Mom or Dad would ask me where I'd been. I decided to tell them that I'd left my phone at Shady Acres yesterday so I ran over to get it and stopped to visit with the ladies. That had enough truth to it that I could talk about it convincingly.

I walked into the kitchen. Mom was slicing carrots and putting them in a slow cooker. When she saw me, she said, "Good, you're back. Stew for dinner." That was it. No questions about where I'd gone or how things went. She looked right through me. I'm not saying I was disappointed that I didn't need to lie to her, but it bummed me out that she didn't even care where I'd been.

I snagged a piece of carrot and went up to my room. Two seconds after I logged on to the Revolting Phoenix, an IM window popped up from Luke. A jolt of excitement shot through my abdomen. He hadn't even hesitated to IM me. It must have been his shift to mind the website for item verifications.

profmarvel: having fun?
kate4eva: sure—pouring rain, digging through garbage, petty theft, lying to my parents . . . good times
profmarvel: just wait until the next clue
kate4eva: why?
profmarvel: you'll see once you solve clue 2
kate4eva: done. was about to upload it
profmarvel: go do it. i'll verify.

I clicked over to the main window of the site and uploaded my picture of the cans. I waited for Luke to verify it, and then the next clue came up.

Congratulations! You have successfully uploaded a valid picture of item #2.

Here is your clue to item #3:

Playboy, Penthouse, Hustler are all types of this. But wait . . .
You have to get a certain kind, and not the type that's
straight.
Proof of purchase necessary! In your picture, show
the item and its paid receipt, and onward you will go.

I clicked on the IM window again.

kate4eva: OMG A GAY PORN MAG?????
profmarvel: have to upload pic to see if you're right
kate4eva: you guys are so EVIL!!!!
profmarvel: mwahahahaha
kate4eva: i hope you're enjoying this
profmarvel: i am
kate4eva: the receipt was a nice touch . . .
kate4eva: so we have to buy it, which is illegal < age 18
profmarvel: my idea
kate4eva: I'm not surprised. you're despicable
profmarvel: think so?
kate4eva: know so
profmarvel: that's a shame—i was just beginning to like you

I inhaled sharply. Was he teasing? Was he being ironic?
Did he actually like me? As in *like* me? My fingers hovered,

trembling, above the keyboard. I couldn't hesitate too long or he'd know something was up. I had to type something. Now.

> kate4eva: that's a conflict of interest anyway . . .
> kate4eva: aren't journalists supposed to be impartial?
> profmarvel: depends
> kate4eva: on?
> profmarvel: how strongly they feel

Both my lungs shrank to the size of walnuts. Not a molecule of air went in or out. What did Luke mean by that? Was he being cryptic and flirting with me? Or was he genuinely talking about journalism? I reread the message. He had to be talking about journalism. Right?

> Kate4eva: have you ever lost impartiality?

There was a pause. Definitely a significant pause. Maybe he was trying to puzzle out his feelings. Maybe those feelings were about me. Or maybe he just had to scratch his foot or take a bite of his sandwich or finish the game of solitaire he was probably playing on the side because talking to me was so boring. Then his answer popped up.

> Profmarvel: no. not yet anyway

WHATDIDTHATMEAN? Did it mean he never had and never would? Or that he hadn't YET but was in danger of doing so soon? Either he was the king of innuendo and double entendre or he was really just talking about journalism and I was the queen of reading too much into things. My brain was whirring and my stomach was as tight as a stone. Before I could send a response, he typed,

profmarvel: someone's here. gotta run

His user name logged out of IM.

No! I reached out for the screen like I could grab him through it and stop him. He was gone. I was left searching for deeper meanings in his words. Could he possibly be implying that he was in danger of becoming impartial when it came to the Senior Scramble because he was feeling strongly about . . . me? Was that crazy? It had to be. Luke Pavel didn't like me. In that way.

I could almost convince myself that he'd been talking about journalism if not for the fact that journalists truly are supposed to be impartial. Remain objective. There was never a "depends" scenario. Luke would know that.

I decided a run-in was definitely called for. I'd "accidentally" bump into him in the hall at school tomorrow and see if his face told me anything his words weren't saying. Until then, all I could do was wonder.

CHAPTER 15

THE NEXT MORNING, I GOT TO SCHOOL A FEW MINUTES early. I found a parking spot fairly close to the door for a change. I took that as a good omen and strode into school with anticipation tickling the inside of my chest like a thousand fairy fingers. I dumped my coat in my locker and then backtracked to the senior hallway. Along the way I fluffed the perfectly styled curls I had set in my hair and rubbed my lips together to even out my lip gloss. I ran my tongue over my teeth to make sure nothing was stuck on them. I straightened my top and my posture and smiled. No need for the lady look here.

I figured the best place to find Luke would be by his locker, so I hung out in the doorway of one of the classrooms down the senior hallway, where I had a clear view of it. After a few minutes of waiting, I saw him turn down the hallway and head in my direction.

He was wearing jeans and a red T-shirt with a silk-screened picture of the Ramones on it. It was cool and edgy, like something Cy would wear. It fit Luke perfectly, too. He wasn't nearly as skinny as I'd thought he was at first. He had lean but seriously noticeable muscles that filled out that

T-shirt like it was tailored just to show them off. I couldn't help watching him for a few seconds. His wavy blond hair was tousled from the wind outside. Or it just naturally had a flawless, windblown look.

He bent down to drop some books in the bottom of his locker. It was the perfect chance to walk up to him without him noticing that I'd been lurking in one of the classrooms. I stepped out of the doorway, a smile still firmly set on my face, and started to supermodel runway walk toward him. I got no more than three feet when a tall blonde in skinny jeans and a tight, orange V-neck stepped out from the crowd. She walked up behind Luke and tickled his sides with her talon-like fingernails. When he jumped up and whirled around, the girl pushed him against the bank of lockers. She pressed her body against him, grabbed the back of his head, and slipped her tongue down his throat, mashing her mouth against his.

I halted mid-stride, not knowing what to do. I couldn't turn away. I couldn't bear to watch. I couldn't believe that all this time, Luke Pavel had a girlfriend.

Luke had a girlfriend.

What an idiot I was.

I had to move. I forced my legs to propel my body forward. I needed maybe five steps to get past them. I started to count as I walked, but when I got to three, Luke saw me out of the corner of his eye. He pushed himself out of the girl's embrace and reached toward me.

I launched a level-five lady look. Eyes wide, smile wide, heart collapsed. It must have looked completely fake because

Luke's expression was sickened. I managed to flip him a quick wave and chirp, "Hi!" as I charged past. I hoped he hadn't seen what I was really feeling. This was definitely a time for decoration. A girl has the right to keep her dignity. Or try to.

I sped around the corner and bolted for my locker. The lump that had congealed in the base of my throat rose up behind my eyes and tried to push itself out through my tear ducts. I swallowed hard to force it back down. Pinched away the bit of wetness that had gathered in the corners and rims of my eyelids.

How could I ever have thought Luke Pavel might like me? Of course he wouldn't find some over-dressed snob attractive. I truly was a snob because it had never crossed my mind that a geek like Luke would have a girlfriend. Of course he would. Did I think I was the only person who noticed he was good-looking and intelligent and funny and mysterious? Did I really think that just because I was from Meriton and my father was the principal I could have my pick of guys? That any guy here would be lucky to go out with me? That I was better than everyone at Ash Grove?

I laughed at myself for thinking that maybe he'd been flirting with me yesterday online. Or with his e-mail. Or with the way he had spoken to me close and low when we talked about the Revolting Phoenix. Or the way he had looked at me in the parking lot last week, as if I were interesting. As if he were interested.

As if.

I was pretty good at reading guys' signals, so how could I

have been so off base with Luke? Unless he really was flirting with me, all the while knowing he had a girlfriend. Would he do that? Maybe his all-important integrity only stretched as far as journalism. Maybe he really was a player. How would I know? I met him a week ago.

I was sure that he'd been flirting with me at least a bit. And now I also knew he'd had a girlfriend the whole time. So the only conclusion I could draw was that Luke Pavel was a dirtbag. A manipulative egotist. Throwing Shakespeare quotes and literary references at me . . . come on, anybody could have looked that stuff up on the Internet in five minutes. Did I seriously think we'd shared some kind of connection? Like kindred spirits or something? What an idiot I was. Luke Pavel had never really cared about me. All I'd ever been to him was some girl in a photo. Some kid of the principal's. Something he could use. Something he could hurt if he wanted to.

Oh my God, maybe that was it. Maybe hurting me had been his motive all along. Maybe that was his reason for charming me with e-mails: it was all just part of a plan to get back at me for ruining his online newspaper and his senior year. Or to punish me for being a stuck-up daddy's girl from Meriton. Or both. Was Luke that Machiavellian? He was smart enough; that was for sure. Was he that cruel? Was he that malicious and vengeful? Was I that naive and blind? Or gullible, like Cy had said?

My heart throbbed and crashed against the inside of my chest. It felt three times too big. Swollen and sore. I was so confused and hurt and angry that I made four wrong turns on the way to my locker and barely made it into homeroom by the first bell. I took a seat in the back left corner. The loser spot. The spot where, at Meriton, the wasteoids would crowd together looking hungover and neglected. The place where people with something to hide sat. The place where no one would bother trying to connect with you.

I discovered that it wasn't the loser spot at all. It was the private spot. It was the only island in the room. I swiveled in my chair so that my back was to the critical eyes that had shot silent curses at me last week. There weren't any dirty looks today—due to the scavenger hunt, I was sure. It was the one positive thing about my life in Ash Grove. Mom had always told me to focus on the positives, so I clung to it like a starving refugee with a hunk of bread. I was the one who brought the scavenger hunt back. It was me. Of course, it was also me who made it disappear in the first place.

Focus on the positives, I told myself, because I still had the entire day ahead of me. And the rest of my days at Ash Grove. They stretched out in front of me like an endless path littered with rocks and thorns. I didn't want to be there. I didn't belong there. On that point, the Ash Grove student body and I agreed.

I pushed that thought from my mind and replaced it with Tara. She liked me. She loved me. She thought I was perfect.

I grabbed my phone out of my bag and crouched over it so the teacher wouldn't see. Phones were supposed to be off during school hours. The first-period bell hadn't rung yet, so I considered it before school hours. Not only was I getting better at lying, I was getting better at lying to myself.

I texted: *hey grl, whats up? I miss you. wish I was there.* I hit Send and waited.

And waited.

Then: *hey b! miss you too. so stupid w/o u here. let's meet up today.*

I had Shady Acres that afternoon but was totally free afterward. I wanted Tara all to myself, so I typed: *YES. I def. need some bff time. just you and me. coffee shop? 4:30?*

She sent: *perfect. See you then. SMILE.*

See? Even with just a few abbreviated texts, she knew I was feeling down. Tara truly was my best friend. I resolved to tell her everything about Ash Grove and my dad and Luke and whatever else I felt like saying about the past week. She'd make me feel better, just like always. That's what we did for each other.

My inflamed heart started to cool and shrink back to normal size. I slipped my phone back into my bag just as the first-period bell blared. I listed my positive things. I had four thirty with Tara, I had Shady Acres, and I had the Senior Scramble. Those three things would have to be enough to get me through the day.

Miraculously, they did.

By the last bell, I'd survived what had been a fairly uneventful day. I went to my classes, ate lunch with Cy and Jenna, and avoided Luke-Luke-who-makes-me-want-to-puke, as I now called him. There'd been a couple of times in the halls when he tried to catch my eye, but I disappeared into the crowd like an auburn-haired ninja. I narrowly missed running into him in the parking lot after school. Luckily, I had that great spot, so I jumped in my car and took off just as he got outside. I know he watched me drive past. Okay, I watched him too. But only to send him eye daggers to let him know I was on to him and his deceptive, charming ways. For that reason only. I swear.

As I drove over to Shady Acres, I devised my plan to get item number three in the Senior Scramble. I had to convince the ladies to help me out again. That would be easy. The hard part would be dealing with Darlene. I'd be putting my burgeoning lying skills to the test.

"A *what* kind of magazine?" Ms. Eulalie asked after I'd filled them in on the details.

"An . . . adult magazine," I said. "The kind you have to be eighteen to buy." I'd opted to leave out the gay part, for now. Baby steps.

Ms. Eulalie scrunched up her ashen face and tipped her head. She still didn't understand.

"A dirty magazine, you old prude!" Ms. Franny cried. "A nudie mag!"

Ms. Eulalie got it then. She gasped like it was her last breath and clutched the base of her throat. "Oh, sweet Jesus, no!" she cried. "That's sinful!"

"Oh, get over your holy self," Ms. Franny said. "Don't you want to get out of this dungeon for a while?"

Ms. Eulalie paused to consider it. "Nurse Darlene did mention something about a sponge bath," she muttered to the air. "That woman is about as gentle as a gator with a toothache." She closed her eyes and hummed a few bars of a hymn. "Lord forgive me," she said. "I'm in."

Ms. Franny slapped her hands together. "Crackerjack!" She started unbuttoning her nightgown. "Open that closet there, Blythe. Get out our human being clothes. I can't wait to get out of this prison uniform."

"Amen," Ms. Eulalie agreed.

I helped each of them into their street clothes, being careful to preserve their modesty by looking away whenever I could. Then we put their nightgowns on over their clothes so we could sneak out without suspicion. I tucked their shoes in my messenger bag and latched the clasp. Once the ladies were ready, I eased them into their wheelchairs. Their nightgowns were a bit bulky, but for the most part, you couldn't tell they were fully dressed underneath.

We wheeled down the hall to Darlene's head floor nurse desk. Her pudgy mouth frowned. "Where do you think you're going?" Her voice was nasal and accusatory.

"I thought I'd take them out for a spin around the garden," I said. As I spoke, I imagined myself doing just that and discovered that I sounded quite convincing. Fourth rule of lying: Picture the lie in your head as if it were the truth. "They want to see how it's coming up."

"I just love to see the first crocuses of spring," Ms. Eulalie added. *Go, Ms. Eulalie!*

Darlene narrowed her suspicious eyes. "Hold it," she said. "Stay here." Uh-oh. Her desk chair creaked as she pushed herself out of it. She waddled over to a door, pulled it open, and dragged down two wool blankets. She waddled back to us and thrust the blankets at me. "Put these on them," she said, like the ladies weren't even there. "They're not getting pneumonia on my shift." She circled her desk and lowered herself into her chair again. It squeaked loudly with complaint. She picked up a pen and started filling out some paperwork.

"Good idea," I said. "Thanks."

Darlene didn't even look up, so we wheeled past her and headed for the front door. I told the front desk attendant the same thing I'd told Darlene, and she showed the same lack of concern. She made me sign them out, though, which was nothing more than standard policy. I could have signed *Sleeping Beauty* and she wouldn't have noticed. We got outside and turned toward the garden. Instead of stopping there, however, we kept going until we reached my car parked on the other side.

I helped the ladies out of their nighties and into the backseat. I laid the blankets over them because I didn't want them to get pneumonia either, and it was a bit chilly. I folded the wheelchairs and stuffed them in the trunk. I felt like a secret agent. I jumped in the driver's seat and we sped off around the corner to the nearest seedy-looking convenience store. "Sped off" might be exaggerating a bit, to be honest. I don't think I got above thirty-five miles per hour. Even so, we got there in less than a minute. It literally was around the corner.

For Ms. Franny and Ms. Eulalie, it might as well have been on the moon. They couldn't stop grinning and chatting about this or that store or car or person or whatever they happened to notice. They couldn't get over the smell of the air: the fresh spring breeze mixed with car exhaust and deep-fried food from a nearby takeout restaurant. The ladies kept sucking it in like they were drinking it. I never thought how good it must be to get out of that stale medicinal smell of impending death back at the nursing home.

I helped them both into their wheelchairs, but before we went in, I crouched down and said, "There's just one more thing. The adult magazine we have to buy is . . . oriented . . . around men."

Ms. Franny went, *"Psssh!"* and said, "Honey, all of them are for men."

"Yes, I know," I said. "But what I mean is . . . it's for men . . . and it *features* men."

"Oh, my Lord," Ms. Eulalie whispered hoarsely.

Ms. Franny, however, got even perkier and said, "Terrific! I can send it to my grandson, Darren, when you're done with it. I'm sure he'd appreciate it."

I couldn't imagine that anyone would appreciate getting porn from their grandmother, but I agreed anyway. We wheeled into the store and parked ourselves in front of the counter. The pornographic magazines were kept behind the cashier. The pimply redhead at the register didn't even make eye contact with us. Instead, he stood at the counter flipping through a comic book and chomping a wad of gum.

I stepped forward. "Excuse me. We're looking for a magazine . . ."

"Aisle three," he interrupted without looking up.

Two men entered the store and went over to the coffee station. I leaned over the counter, closer to the cashier. "No, the kind of magazine we want is . . . behind you."

The pimply kid looked up. He stopped chewing his gum. He eyed us up and down and looked like he might vomit. "Ohhhhkay," he said. He reached up toward the rack behind him. "Which one?" He had his hand near the porno mags for women, which would've been a logical choice, but I waved him over. His eyes widened as he slid his hand to the typical straight men's porn magazines. I shook my head and waved even harder. A look of utter shock and horror came over his face as he reached for one of the mags for gay men. I nodded.

He lifted down a magazine and held it out to me. Ms. Franny snatched it out of my reach. She examined it, turning it back and forth. "Nah," she said. "I don't like this guy. He looks like he got hit in the face with a sack of ugly. Get me that one up there that was next to it."

Ms. Eulalie piped up, "Oh, sure, get the one with the *white* man on the cover. There's three of them up there with beautiful black men looking right out at you, but you go for the skinny white guy. Typical."

"I happen to like white men," Ms. Franny said.

"Well, I happen to like vanilla ice cream, but that don't mean I don't like a taste of chocolate once in a while."

The cashier stood there with his mouth open like a dead fish. His eyes were wide as pie plates. His already pale face had turned almost translucent.

"All right, fine," Ms. Franny said. "Get me one of those black guys up there." The pimply redhead got a magazine and held it up, as if he wasn't sure who to give it to. Ms. Franny took it and squinted at the cover. It showed a medium build, dark-skinned man in his twenties, oiled up, on all fours, and snarling at the camera. Ms. Franny tipped her head from side to side. "Not bad. What do you think, Ukulele?"

"Oh, don't ask me! I'm not involved!" Ms. Eulalie turned her head and tried not to look, but she couldn't help glancing at the magazine. She did a double take and peered more closely. She scrunched up her nose and shook her head. "Oh, no, not that one. His momma didn't feed him good enough. Looky there, you can see his rib bones poking right out! Poor child."

Ms. Franny slapped the magazine onto the counter. "No sale." She pointed her crooked index finger at the shelf. "Try that one with that muscle-y black fellow wearing the dog collar and leash, with the white guy behind him holding a whip. See, Ukulele? Vanilla and chocolate to make us both happy."

"Don't throw me in that batch of sin you're stirring up," Ms. Eulalie said. Then she added, "But he do look a sight better than the other one. At least this one's momma loved him, you can tell. Probably turning over in her grave at this picture, though. I know she passed 'cause she sure enough would'a dropped dead when she found out what he was doing for a living. Even if he do look like a young Sidney Poitier. Oh, my Lord. Mmm-hmm." Ms. Eulalie folded her hands over and over again and started humming a hymn to the fluorescent lights above us.

"Right, this one'll do fine," Ms. Franny said, sliding the magazine back on the counter. I pulled out my wallet and handed a ten-dollar bill to the cashier.

Before he took the money, he said, "Um, I need to see some ID."

"Oh!" I said, realizing that if I was paying, then that meant I was buying. "No. I mean, it's not mine." I swung the ten over to Ms. Franny, who snatched it and handed it to the cashier without missing a beat.

His gaze slid over to her. "I still need to see some ID," he said in the same monotone drone as before.

"ID? Boy, are you blind? Do I look like a minor? I've turned eighteen about five times by now!"

"What about her?" He nodded in my direction again. "She's paying, so I'm guessing the magazine is . . . for her."

Ms. Franny gestured dismissively at me. "She's got nothing to do with nothing. She just drives me around and holds my wallet so I don't lose it because I'm old and crazy. Last time I checked, this was still a free country where someone could buy themselves a magazine if they wanted, which is what I'm doing. So ring it up, young man." She thrust the ten-dollar bill at him. Ms. Eulalie hummed louder. The two men with coffee lined up behind us.

The teenage cashier eyed Ms. Franny suspiciously. Examined her wheelchair and blanket. "So you're telling me that this magazine is for you?"

"Yes," she said.

"This magazine."

"Yes."

"For you."

"Yes! Are you deaf or something, boy?"

"It's just . . . you're an old lady."

"Old lady? I'll have you know that for the past fifty years, I've been a fully fledged transvestite. Even *you* couldn't tell. Now, I'm horny and I want my dirty magazine, so ring the damn thing up!"

Ms. Eulalie's humming resounded throughout the store. The men behind us shifted their weight and hid their snickering mouths behind their steaming coffee cups. The cashier's face turned from white to red faster than a chameleon. I didn't know whether to laugh or run away. Luckily, he rang up the magazine and handed us the change and receipt faster than anyone I've ever seen. We were out of the store in a flash. I got the ladies into the car and we took off, laughing hysterically.

We pulled into the parking lot at Shady Acres and I parked over by the garden again. I smuggled the ladies inside and redressed them in their nighties. By the time Darlene poked her nose into the room to check on us, I'd returned the clothes to their drawers and everything appeared as though we'd never left.

"You were in the garden an awfully long time," she sneered at me as I re-folded the blankets. "They'd better not get sick."

"Don't you go talking about us like we're not even in the room," Ms. Eulalie said. She had even less tolerance for Darlene's disrespectfulness than Ms. Franny had. Darlene scowled as she grabbed the blankets out of my hand and left the room.

"If I was thirty years younger," said Ms. Eulalie, "I'd take her out behind the woodshed. I never met a single soul needing an introduction to the business end of a hickory switch more than that woman."

"I'd buy a ticket to see that!" Ms. Franny said, and cackled at the mental image.

I took the magazine and receipt out of my bag and snapped a photo of them with my phone. "Ms. Franny, do you want to write down Darren's address, and I'll mail this to him?" I asked.

"Nah, give it here. I decided we should give this to Coleman Watson and see if it lights his cigar. All those years and he never remarried? Sounds to me like he might be fishing in the other pond. What do you think, Ukulele?"

"As long as it's outta this room, I don't care," Ms. Eulalie said. "Else I'm going to have to start calling you Frank."

I tucked the magazine underneath Ms. Franny's knitting, at the bottom of the basket. I winked at her. "Let me know what he thinks."

"It'll most likely kill him," said Ms. Eulalie.

"Yeah, it might," Ms. Franny agreed. "But either way, it'll make for an interesting dinnertime tonight!"

"Well, I'd better get going," I said. "I'm going to meet Tara in a little while for coffee."

"Oh, Tara, yes," Ms. Eulalie said. I'd mentioned Tara a few million times to the ladies. "Tell me, how does she feel about you going to a different school?"

If I had more time, I would've told her that Tara and I were falling out of step a bit. That I was jealous of Melissa. That I was worried that I'd be replaced. But it was already two minutes after four. I'd have just enough time to dash home, upload the picture, get the next clue, and still make it to the Daily Grind on time to meet Tara. I didn't like to keep the Senior Scramble pictures on my phone any longer than necessary, and I wanted to know what was up next. So instead of telling Ms. Eulalie everything, I just shrugged and tossed off, "She thinks it stinks, but we're cool."

"The two of you have been friends for a long time," Ms. Franny said, as though she'd read my thoughts. "It's hard when things suddenly change."

"That's how you know if a friend is the best kind," Ms. Eulalie added. "If time and miles get between you, yet when you come back together, it's like you was never apart."

I nodded knowingly, although I really didn't know anything. "Yep. I'm sure we'll always be friends." I was trying to convince myself of it.

I didn't want to go any farther down this conversation road.

"Well, thanks again," I said. "You guys are the best. Ms. Franny, you made a totally believable transvestite. Wait, that came out wrong."

Ms. Eulalie started guffawing so hard she clutched the air like she could grab a breath with her hands. When she finally settled down, Ms. Franny shot her the stink eye but said, "Never you mind, Blythe. I know what you meant. I was happy to help, even if we did have to drag that ol' bag-o'-Jesus along with us."

"My Jesus follows me everywhere I go," sang Ms. Eulalie.

"Just like stalkers," Ms. Franny added.

"Oh sweet Lord, here we go again."

I kissed them both and said thank you and goodbye before the quibbling got worse. Outside, I hopped in my Civic and zipped up the street. Instead of going straight through two lights and turning right at a third, I decided to take a shortcut to pick up some time. I veered into the mini-mall and turned down the alley behind the stores, skipping all three traffic lights. I made it home and yanked opened the kitchen door just as Zach was barreling out of it. "Where are you going?" I called after him.

"Jack's," he said. "It's about to go nuclear in there." In one smooth motion, he lifted his bike by the handlebars, straddled the seat, and pedaled off. I didn't even get to ask him what he meant by nuclear. When I got inside, I didn't need to.

Mom and Dad were in the family room bellowing at each other about the offers on the house again. I didn't have time to get into that "pan o' hot eels," as Ms. Eulalie would say, so I sneaked through the kitchen to the hallway and bolted upstairs. I locked the door to my room and signed on to the Revolting Phoenix, noting the irony that Luke Pavel had turned out to be revolting after all. I uploaded the picture of the magazine and receipt, all the while praying that Luke wasn't minding the site and wouldn't IM me with more charming lies. Luckily, the only thing that came up on my screen was the next clue.

Congratulations! You have successfully uploaded a valid picture of item #3.

Here is your clue to item #4:

Pennsylvania license plates are everywhere around.
But only certain license plates are ones that should be
found.
Find a plate for every letter spanning A to Z.
Snap a picture, then you send all 26 to me.

Dear God, this was going to take a while. It wasn't like I
could just stand by I-95 and snap pictures of license plates as
cars whipped by. I was going to have to keep my eyes open
and my phone with me all the time. Especially at home. I
didn't want Dad scrolling through on some snooping mission
and finding them. Maybe he didn't know about the Senior
Scramble yet, but it might not be long before he got wind of
it. He couldn't know I was involved.

I logged off and deleted the magazine picture from my
phone. It sounded like the chaos downstairs had calmed
down, so I tiptoed to the kitchen as quickly as I could. I
hoped to slip out without them seeing me so I didn't have
any more delays on the way to meet Tara.

Mom was in the kitchen. "Where are you going?" she
asked gruffly. There was no sign of Dad anywhere.

"I'm meeting Tara in town for coffee." Strange. I felt
like I was lying even though I wasn't. For a split second,
I panicked and thought I'd slipped up, but I hadn't. Fifth
rule of lying: Never forget which is the lie and which is the
truth.

"Be back for dinner," was all Mom said. She started rifling
around in the fridge and pulled out a bottle of chardonnay.
"Six o'clock."

"No problem," I said. I heard Dad's footsteps in the hall. I dashed out the door before he had a chance to corner me.

When I got to town, I parked on the street near the coffee shop. I was already a few minutes late, but I couldn't help stopping to take pictures of all the license plates with letters that I passed. I got *A*, *E*, and *T* ones. I knew some letters were going to be easy to find and some would be brutal. Who the heck would have a license plate with an *X* or *Z*? I had to hope for vanity plates and luck.

I opened the door to the Daily Grind and spotted Tara at a small table beside the window. She saw me and waved, and I filled up with happiness. I'd forgotten to miss that. I remembered it now, though.

"Where've you been, girl? It's quarter to five," she said. She stood up and stepped toward me, smiling. "You've never been late in your life. One week at Ass Grove and your whole world falls to hell, huh?"

I wrapped my arms around her and let her hug the past seven days out of me. "Pretty much," I said.

"Sit. Talk," she said.

"Let me grab a coffee and I will." When I got to the counter, I opted for a hot cocoa with lots of whipped cream and chocolate shavings instead. It was definitely a day for chocolate.

"Sorry about bailing on you this weekend," I said, sitting down. "It's been crazy." I told her all about canceling the Senior Scramble, but I didn't tell her that we were taking it underground. I kept that secret locked up in the vault. I did mention Luke to Tara, but not in any particularly noticeable way. As far as I was concerned, he was negligible. That's what I kept telling myself.

"So by the third day, everyone pretty much hated me," I said.

Tara waved it off. "So what? Who cares what those freaks think about you? You don't belong there anyway."

"But Tara, I'm stuck there, whether I belong or not. You don't understand what it's like to have no friends. It wasn't even 'no friends' either, it was 'all enemies.' I'm not exaggerating when I say they hated me. And let me tell you, being despised and thought of as a loser? It sucks. It's awful."

"You're not a loser. Not at Meriton, anyway."

"Tara, I'm not anything at Meriton." Why couldn't she get that?

"Well, you should be," she muttered, circling the rim of her coffee cup with her perfectly French-manicured finger.

On the one hand, it was sweet that she clung to the idea that I was a Meriton student. On the other hand, it was absolutely no help to me.

Tara couldn't comprehend why I would possibly want to gain the respect of anyone at Ash Grove. That's because she wasn't on the front lines. She didn't see that I was in a survival situation. Had she always been that shortsighted? Or had I never noticed because I was that shortsighted too?

I'd always considered myself a fairly sympathetic person, but maybe I was only sympathetic to certain things I chose to see. Had I ever walked up to any of the so-called wasteoids at Meriton and asked what their story was? Had I ever spoken up when someone in my group started name-calling? Oh, sure, it was so easy for me to brag about being charitable and doing volunteer work, but had I ever done a true kindness to anyone fighting on their own personal front lines at Meriton? Had I even acknowledged those people at all?

I know Tara hadn't. She couldn't, even though one of them was sitting right in front of her. It was no use trying to explain more. I loved Tara, but she was just an oasis; she couldn't be a healing place for me when it came to this.

I steered the conversation toward Meriton and listened to her gossip for a while. When a car pulled into a parking spot right outside the window, I noticed its license plate began with a Z. I wrapped up our chat and told Tara I had to run. We hugged and I left, feeling more alone than ever.

CHAPTER 16

I WALKED THROUGH THE NEXT FEW DAYS IN FULL-ON zombie mode. You know when you go from home to school and home again and it's not until you're lying in bed that night that you finally realize you have no idea how you got there? That was my general state of being for the rest of that week.

There were a few landmarks. My parents decided to sell to the yuppies. Dad finally relented when they came back with an offer to close quickly on the sale. We'd be moving on April Fools' Day. What a joke.

In Senior Scramble news, I found twenty-four of the twenty-six letters on license plates. I still needed Q and X. Cy and Jenna had found them all by Wednesday. They were rocking the scavenger hunt. They told me their screen name was sid&nancy, and according to the stats and Luke's updates on the website, they were in first place.

That was about the full extent of my interaction (or lack of) with Luke Pavel. He kept trying to talk to me, but I dodged him every chance I got. I bumped into him outside the cafeteria again one day, but I plastered on ye olde lady look and pretended I was extremely busy and important. I didn't want him to know he'd rattled me. I didn't want to let on that I knew what a manipulative player he was. Probably was, anyway. I mean, all signs pointed to it. I even saw his slutty girlfriend accost him again Friday after school in the parking lot. It was so undignified. Luke must've thought so too because he ducked his head and wouldn't let her kiss him in front of everyone.

As far as Tara went, I texted and e-mailed her as usual, even though things weren't exactly "usual" between us. We made plans to go shopping with Veronica, Cerise, and Melissa at the mall on Sunday at four, though. I was looking forward to playing make-believe normalcy with them.

Even so, that Sunday afternoon I was running late yet again. I'd been chasing down a car whose license plate said XTRA SXY. I finally got the picture in the parking lot of that same convenience store that sells the porno mags. Coincidence? I think not.

I decided to take the shortcut through the alley behind the mini-mall on my way to meet the girls. I wheeled behind the buildings, and as I neared the back of the grocery store, an enormous black garbage bag shot out of a Dumpster and crashed to the ground in front of my car. I hit the brakes and slammed into my seat belt. Before I had a chance to wonder what kind of animal could possibly be throwing bags out of the Dumpster, a person's head popped up.

Luke Pavel's head.

I swear to God, this guy had some kind of evil cosmic tether to me. Only, this was in my neighborhood, not Ash Grove. He was the trespasser now. A flood of anger rushed through me and provoked this sinister desire to get back at him for toying with me when he had a girlfriend. I grabbed my phone, zoomed in, and snapped a perfect picture of him Dumpster-diving.

Eat that, Luke-Luke-who-makes-me-puke. Now who's got an embarrassing picture? I saved my fine example of photographic skill, tossed my phone on the passenger seat, and glanced up to see Luke staring at me and waving. Waving me over.

What choice did I have? Even in the throes of rage and vengeance, I was trained to remain civil and polite. Dignity, Blythe. Dignity. Besides, I was insanely curious.

I got out and strolled as far as my front bumper. I shaded the glare of the slanted afternoon sun with one hand. I stuck the other hand on my hip and struck an assertive pose. I said nothing.

"Blythe! Perfect timing. Can you give me a hand?"

I had always found it difficult to say no to someone who'd asked for my help. I recognized that this made me a perfect mark for scam artists and machinators, but I couldn't stop myself. Nevertheless, I didn't walk over to Luke right away. "A hand with what?" I called, without moving an inch.

"There's a whole case of eggs in here, but if I throw them, they'll break. Can I hand them to you?"

"You want to hand me filthy, rotten eggs out of the garbage?" I dramatically eyeballed my adorable green linen capris and matching wedge heels. "I don't think so."

Luke sighed equally as dramatically. "They're not filthy or rotten. They've just reached their sell-by date. They're good for at least another week."

"So?"

"Can you just take them? I'm standing in something soggy."

I reluctantly sauntered over to him as slowly as possible. He lifted down a case of about sixteen dozen eggs, which I took—touching as little as possible—and set on the ground. The case was still completely enveloped in plastic wrap as though it was right from the egg distributor. I didn't understand why it was in the garbage. "These eggs aren't even unwrapped."

"No kidding," Luke said. "There are three more cases in here." He handed each one down to me and I lined them up on the dirty pavement.

"Why did the grocery store throw them out?"

"I told you. The sell-by date was yesterday. They have to throw them out, even though the eggs aren't bad yet." He disappeared into the Dumpster and resurfaced a few seconds later with four unopened boxes of cereal that he handed to me.

"They just throw all this stuff out even though it's still good?" I asked.

"Yup."

"Why don't they donate it somewhere?"

"Bingo," was his answer.

"Bingo what?" I asked. He handed me a full bag of pre-washed spinach.

"Bingo, that's the question: Why don't they donate it somewhere?" He ducked down and popped back up with four loaves of perfectly good bread in his hands. "It's too much of a liability for the grocery store. If someone at a shelter got sick or hurt, the store could get sued. Here, can you reach these?" He dropped the bread into my hands.

"So you're picking the stuff out of the trash and then, what? Take it to a shelter or somewhere yourself?" I asked.

"Bingo," he said again. "Garbage is public property. I do the dirty work and take the food that's still good to a soup kitchen and a food bank over in Ash Grove. They decide whether to use it or not."

"Why don't you go Dumpster-diving in Ash Grove, then?"

He stared down at me and pushed up his glasses. "I do. The grocery stores there switch stock on Fridays, though. This store gets new shipments on Sundays and clears out the old stock. So I hit this one every Sunday afternoon before stuff gets too gross or freezes or gets too hot if it's summer. I've gotta book, though, because the garbage truck comes at five to empty the Dumpster." He checked his watch.

Hold on a sec. Luke Pavel had been Dumpster-diving for charity for months? Maybe years? How could this be the same Mr. Charming who strung me along when he already had a girlfriend?

I glared at him. "So, what do you get out of it?"

He paused with a huge, lumpy, clear plastic bag in his arms. "Me? What? Nothing." He tossed the knotted bag over the side and it landed on the ground. It was stuffed with left-over bagels and buns from the bakery section. "Why would you think I was trying to get something out of it?" he asked.

Because you're a two-faced jerk, that's why, I said to myself.

All I said out loud was, "It just seems kind of extreme. For charity."

"Isn't that the point of charity?" he said. "A hardship for you to ease someone else's struggle? I suppose you're more used to the check-writing form of charity."

"No . . ." I tried to say.

"You probably think charity only extends 'so' far." He squeezed an inch of air between his forefinger and thumb.

"That's not what I mean."

"You're all for charity, just as long as you don't have to get dirty doing it."

"NO," I said. "Stop putting words into my mouth. That's not what I meant at all. I just meant that . . . this is kind of . . . an enormous job. Especially for one person to be doing all alone."

He chuckled and tossed me a case of instant noodle soup. "You're right, it is. So climb on up and help." He examined the contents of a black garbage bag, cringed, tossed it aside, and grabbed another bag.

I opened my mouth to decline politely but instead blurted, "Why doesn't your *girlfriend* help?" It had come out too quickly for me to muffle the twang of jealousy in my voice. Lately, my brain wasn't acting faster than my feelings.

He paused again with a bottle of ketchup in each hand and was silent for a few seconds. Then his expression softened and he handed me the ketchup. "Ex-girlfriend. As of yesterday." He passed a few boxes of croutons down to me.

"Yesterday?" I said with plenty of sarcastic disbelief in my voice.

He glanced at me but kept talking. "It's been over between us for a while."

"It didn't look like it was over between you two on Monday," I said. "It didn't look like there was *anything* between you two. Including oxygen." Luke laughed. I scowled at him. I didn't think it was so hilarious.

He folded his arms on the rim of the Dumpster. "Karly and I were together for almost a year. I care about her. I didn't want to hurt her, but I felt terrible about stringing her along too. I guess I was just waiting for a reason to actually do it. To make the break."

"So why did you?" I asked.

He set his chin on his arms and stared fixedly at me. "I found a reason."

I didn't show it on my face, but inside, I turned into warm honey. Could he . . . did that . . . did he possibly mean me? Could I dare to trust my feelings for him? Or should I listen to the levelheaded reasoning that said Luke Pavel was a selfish jerk?

As if he could read my thoughts, Luke reached out his hand. "Get in here with me, Blythe. Come on. It's not as bad as you think. Trust me."

I couldn't think straight. Couldn't figure out what to do. I needed time. I muttered, "I'll get filthy."

"So?" Luke's smile was wide and inviting. I wasn't getting any suspicious signals from it. It seemed honest. I couldn't possibly be that bad a judge of character and he couldn't possibly be that good a liar. Right?

"I'm wearing linen," I said, stalling. "And two-hundred-dollar shoes." Gran had bought them for me when I visited last month. In three different spring colors.

Luke nodded like a bobble head. "Oh, sure. I under-stand," he said teasingly. He held up his hands in pretend surrender. "Of course you shouldn't help the poor if it means soiling your designer clothes." I let out a laugh. He kept roll-ing. "Or maybe you're just chicken." He flapped his elbows a few times and then beamed at me like I was the most cap-tivating thing he'd ever seen. His eyes were steady on mine. Daring me to join him. Wanting me to join him.

Should I?

I collected myself. I reminded myself to inhale. "I want to see what's inside first." I strode over to the grungy green Dumpster, where there was a series of shallow ledges up one side I could use as a ladder. I set the toe of my $200 shoe on a ledge and reached up to grab a higher one. "Just so you know," I said in a snooty voice, "I happen to be an extremely charitable person."

Luke chuckled. "Is that so?" He stretched his hand down, grasped my wrist, and pulled me up. I climbed until I was face-to-face with him over the rim of the Dumpster, perched on one of the ledges. Our eyes met, inches away from each other. We were close enough to breathe the same wedge of air. Close enough to do more than just breathe together.

"It's true," I said. I forced myself to look at the color of his hair, the curve of his collarbone, the muscles in his fore-arm. Anywhere but in his eyes, which was the only place mine stubbornly wanted to go. "In fact, I volunteer every week at a nursing home."

"Oh, really?"

Luke's grip was snug and strong around my wrist. I could feel every millimeter of where his skin touched mine. "Yes," I said. "I've been doing it for years." It was barely a whisper.

"I'm impressed," he said, and I locked eyes with him again. He held my gaze for a few seconds, then glanced at our hands. "Have you got a good hold?"

I snapped back to life and gripped the rim of the Dumpster. "I'm good."

Luke released my wrist and stepped aside. Behind him were piles of cake mixes, potato chips, baked goods, sacks of flour and sugar, pasta, salad dressing, taco shells, cookies, crackers, juice boxes, pre-sliced cheese, mayonnaise, bags of rice, and more. Most of it was still sealed in unopened packages, cans, and jars.

"There's so much," I said, trying to turn my face to avoid the stink rising from the Dumpster. "Just thrown away."

"Pretty crazy, huh?"

"This shouldn't be legal," I said. "They shouldn't be allowed to trash all this food when so many people go hungry."

"No kidding." Luke took off his glasses and cleaned them on his T-shirt. He slipped them back on his face and scooped up a canister of cake frosting. "Every week, I think it's not going to shock me how much food is in here, and every week it does. People care more about covering their asses than anything else." He dropped the frosting into a half-full cardboard box beside him.

"Well, aren't you a journalist? Write about this," I said.

"Do a story and submit it to a newspaper or magazine. Make people aware and all that."

Luke picked up a bottle of apple juice and put it in the box. Then he stooped down to collect an armful of soup cans. "I have. A few times."

I waited for him to go on. He didn't. "And?" I asked.

He sighed. "And it was rejected. The feedback I've gotten is that the piece sounds too opinionated. Too angry."

I widened my eyes and feigned surprise. "What? Captain Impartiality is opinionated? Shocking."

He stood up and stepped onto a sheet of thick cardboard. "But when I take a more objective track, I feel like I'm not stressing the importance of the subject enough." He rolled a can of peas back and forth in his hands.

"Maybe you're underestimating your readers. I bet the facts would speak for themselves. Besides, you're supposed to be impartial, right?"

"Yeah." He dropped the can into the box. "I know." He straightened up, and suddenly his eyes were on mine again. "It's hard to rein in your feelings when you care about something so much, you know?" We stared at each other for a few charged seconds. Then Luke squatted down and turned his attention to stacking a pile of dry gravy packets. "You think everyone else will feel as passionately about it as you do, but they don't. It's hard to distance yourself enough without feeling like you're a cop-out." He set the neat stack of gravy packets into the box with the cans.

"So revise it," I said, flicking a dead bug off the Dumpster rim with my thumbnail. "Or write a whole new piece."

Luke snorted. "Write another piece? Sure. No problem. Do you have any idea how much time and work goes into it?"

"WELL, isn't that the point of journalism?" I said dramatically. "Hard work for you to ease someone else's struggle against ignorance?"

"Huh?" he asked.

"I suppose you're more used to the Facebook-update format of news reporting."

"What? Hey. That's not . . ."

"I mean, revealing truths and injustices only extends 'so' far." I pinched an inch of air just like he had.

He finally caught on. "Very funny," he said, half-smiling.

"You're all for being a journalist, just as long as you don't have to *work* to do it."

"YEAH. Got it." He winged a bag of mini-marshmallows hard into the box. "Message received."

He was silent for a while, and I thought I might have struck a nerve. And by struck, I mean stomped on it with a $200 pair of designer wedge heels. I decided to make a peace offering. "Okay, Luke, I'll make you a deal. I'll climb down into that disgusting pit and help you sort out the food today if you'll write another article about all this and try to get it published somewhere."

Luke shaded his eyes from the sun behind me as he peered up from where he was squatting. "You're actually going to get in here?"

"I am."

"And really help?"

"As long as you'll write the article."

He pushed himself to his feet and crossed his arms tightly on his chest. He shifted his weight. He looked up and down the alley as if the answer was about to come running up the street.

"Come on, Luke," I said. "It's a win-win for you. For me, it's a lose-lose. First I have to live through this nightmare, then I have to read about it in *Time Magazine*." When Luke heard the last part, he blushed and smiled and got all embarrassed-looking, so I tried to make him laugh by saying, "Or maybe you're just chicken," and moving my elbows up and down like he'd done to me earlier, while still holding the Dumpster in my death grip.

It worked. He laughed lightly and smiled in the direction of his shifting feet. He unfolded his arms and rubbed the fronts of his thighs vigorously. He straightened up, arched his back, shook out his arms, and sighed extra loudly so I'd know he was giving in under duress. "Okay," he said. "Deal."

"Good," I said. "I want ten pages by Tuesday. Just kidding. Now watch out." I turned and gasped one last breath of half-decent air, then I swung my leg over the side of the Dumpster and toppled inside. Luckily, I landed on a gigantic bag of expired hamburger buns.

The putrid stench inside the Dumpster almost knocked me out. It hadn't been nearly this bad above the rim, where an occasional breeze blew by. I tried breathing only through my mouth, which, I realized, was equally disgusting. Luke pulled me to my feet as I covered my nose and looked around.

"Don't even think about bailing on that article," I said nasally, "because it's unholy in here."

"I know."

"You made a deal, and I'm going to hold you to it."

His lips parted and stayed open half an inch until he spoke. "Sorry, I 'made a deal' and what?"

"I'm going to hold you to it."

He stepped closer and turned his ear toward me. "Pardon?"

"I'm going to hold you to it," I repeated, getting frustrated.

He shook his head like he still couldn't hear. "You're going to do *what* to me?"

"I'M GOING TO *HOLD* YOU," I enunciated loudly. "*TO* IT."

One side of his mouth curled up. Then the other. A sly look came over his face again. "Well," he said, "I didn't realize you were that kind of girl, but okay! Sounds like fun. I guess after today I should've known that you had a trashy side." He threw his head back and chuckled to himself with great enthusiasm.

I smacked his shoulder. He pretended it hurt. "Whoa, wait a minute!" he said. "You didn't say anything about rough play. Are you into that? Like whips and chains?"

"No!" I cried, and swiped at him again, barely catching him with my fingertips.

He clutched his arm and turned away. "Ow! What's my safety word? Pancakes! Bathtub! Gorilla!"

"STOP!" I squealed, pummeling him with my girly fists. Laughing, he grabbed my wrists and held them to his chest. I tried in vain to wrench them free, which made us both crack up even more. Finally, I gave in and stopped struggling.

He didn't let go.

He held me against him, his hands on my skin, his face so close. I could feel his heart pounding against the wall of his chest. *Breathe, Blythe. Inhale. Exhale. Look at something other than his lips or his chest or his perfect blue eyes. Think about garbage.*

Garbage.

Something warm and wet began to seep through the fabric of my right shoe. I screamed and leapt into the air, jerking my foot out of the gunk. A strip of brown slime hung from my toe. "Oh my God, EW!" I flicked my foot and it shot across the Dumpster.

"Um, yeah, celery gives off a lot of liquid when it rots," Luke said.

I tried to wipe my toe sideways on the cardboard box, but that just rubbed the gunk in more. "Ugh," I said. "I'm going to vomit."

"At least now you don't have to worry about ruining your shoes," Luke said.

"It better be a good article."

"Then you'd better get to work," he teased.

I didn't know where to start sorting through the food because I didn't want to touch any of it. With the very tips of two fingers, I picked up a bag of pretzels by the corner and flung it toward the box. Except, I missed and hit Luke in the leg. Startled, he stepped on the bag, popping it open and crushing everything inside.

He shot me an amused look. "Blythe, I know it looks gross," he said, "but you're going to have to touch it."

I stuck my nose in the air and shook my head. "Too late. You already said the safety word."

Luke cracked up. He caught his breath and said, "Well played." Then he pointed behind me. "Hey, there's a can of powdered baby formula over there. The food bank always needs that. Can you reach it?"

I spotted it. "Sure."

We started sorting through the food in earnest. Every once in a while, we caught each other's eye or brushed up against each other. Nothing huge or obvious, just the occasional hand across hand or shoulder grazing shoulder. Once, when I lost my balance, I grabbed his arm and instantly flashed back to the school parking lot where I'd done the same. Just like then, it felt as if an electric circuit had suddenly closed, releasing kinetic jolts that buzzed and zoomed throughout my body. Did that happen to him too? Did he get excited when we touched? I desperately wanted to believe he did. Desperation was a scary, foreign feeling to me. I wasn't accustomed to being desperate. Probably because I'd never been in danger of not getting what I wanted.

I checked the seal on a jar of pickles and placed it in the box followed by two cans of tomato sauce. "Maybe you shouldn't write a fact-based piece," I said. "I mean, don't make things up, but instead of writing a newsy-type article filled with statistics, write a story about this." I waved a bottle of soy sauce around the Dumpster. "About how you go from store to store every week, salvaging groceries from the trash and taking them to the soup kitchen and food bank. Present it like a documentary. Interview people who work at the soup kitchen and even some of the people who eat there. Just tell a story. Not a list of facts. Readers would draw their own conclusions about it." I set a jar of Spanish olives in the box. "Like I did."

Luke pulled himself up and stared out over the pitted alley. The orange, sinking sun reflected off the lenses of his glasses and turned his face bronze. I stood up too.

He said, "You're smarter than most readers, though, Blythe."

Sparks erupted all over my skin. Heat flushed through my neck and cheeks and my pulse jumped forward. I couldn't remember a compliment affecting me like that before. Usually I fielded them easily. Not this time. I tried to distract myself by sorting good pre-wrapped blueberry muffins from ones that had gotten smashed. "Well, you're smarter than most writers, Luke, so you should be able to manage it."

He asked quietly, "You think so?"

I searched his face for any sign of falsehood or manipulation. All I saw was vulnerability and self-doubt. Exactly how I'd felt for the entire past two weeks. I grabbed the edge of the Dumpster for balance and stood in front of him. "Definitely," I said.

Luke skimmed his fingertip back and forth over a rusty patch between us on the Dumpster rim. "You know, Blythe, I'm usually pretty good at pegging people, but I've got to admit that I had you all wrong. You're nothing like I thought you were."

I let out a laugh. "Going off what? My father? And a picture of me picking my nose?"

Each time Luke's finger skipped over the rusty patch, it slid a little bit closer to where my hand rested on the rim. "Being a nose picker is pretty disgusting," he teased.

I came right back with, "You say that while standing on a mashed head of slimy, brown lettuce. Surrounded by garbage. In a Dumpster." Luke broke out laughing, so I took it a step further. "And I have the picture to prove it."

Luke inhaled sharply and his mouth fell open, but his blue eyes glinted behind his glasses. "Oh, do you?"

"Yes," I said. "So watch your step." I tried to keep a stern expression, but my face kept springing into smiles.

"Or else what?" he asked, grinning.

"Or else I'll use it."

"For what?"

"World domination."

"Ah, I see. What happens then?"

"Then I'll make you my personal slave and you'll do my bidding, including—but not limited to—bringing me all the choicest selections from your Dumpster-diving missions." I was flirting. I didn't care.

Okay, I did.

He crossed his arms and stuck out his chest, chuckling. "And what's in it for me?"

I struck a pinup pose against the side of the Dumpster with one arm in the air. "Me, of course! You'll worship me and do anything to make me happy because you're so enchanted with my dazzling beauty and flair for iambic pentameter." I dropped my arm and waited for him to laugh and deny it. To pretend I was ridiculous. But Luke didn't say a word. He didn't even blink.

He stayed silent long enough for the atmosphere between us to shift. I couldn't figure out in which direction, though. I froze. Not so much froze as struggled with deciding what I should make my body do, even though my cheeks were blazing away on their own. I didn't dare risk a lady look. That would be phony. And I didn't want to shut him down. Just in case.

Just in case.

Luke edged closer and started brushing his fingertip briskly over the rust spot again. "So Blythe, let me get this straight . . ." He watched his finger slide back and forth. "Are you saying that I'll get to be part of your evil plan for world domination?"

He studied his finger intensely. Too intensely. So I studied him. I saw blood rise in his cheeks. Saw his breathing quicken. His hand tremble.

Was this real?

I said quietly, "If you want to be. Yes."

His finger slid all the way to my hand and stopped, touching me as softly as a shadow but lighting up every nerve in my body. He trailed his fingertip along the length of my index finger. "And do you want me to be?" he asked. His voice was deep, like a whisper and a growl all at once.

I drew a tight sinew of air into my lungs and whispered, "Yes."

Luke's finger went still. So did the rest of him, except

for his chest rising and falling in short, uneven breaths. My own breathing was jagged. My pulse rang through me like a kettledrum. I was on fire and ice cold at the same time.

"Good," Luke said, still fixated on our fingers. "That's what I want too." After one breath longer, Luke's hand glossed across mine and wrapped around it tightly.

I could've lived my entire life in that moment. I could've spent eternity swimming inside the feeling of Luke touching me like that. It took all of my strength to tear my eyes off our hands and look Luke in the face. Because I needed to see him, and I needed to know if he saw me. If he wanted me.

His focus trailed up the length of my arm and rested at the hollow of my throat. Each breath seemed to bring him barely closer. He lifted his face, and I got my answer at last.

First, Luke's eyes met mine.

Then his lips did.

CHAPTER 17

SOMETHING RUMBLED NEARBY, AND WE SPLIT APART, startled. "Dammit," he said, almost more to himself than to me. "The garbage truck. Come on." He took my hand. "This guy hates me. He says he'll dump me with the trash if I'm ever in this thing again when he gets here." I clambered out, my hands still trembling, and Luke passed me all the food we'd collected. I kept one eye on the truck as it stopped at another Dumpster along the way, then barreled down the alley toward us. Luke grabbed a few more boxes of pasta and jumped out just as the truck roared up. The driver glared at us as he swerved to align his vehicle with the Dumpster.

I gave the driver a sweet wave—which he didn't return—before helping Luke load the groceries into the back of his pickup truck. He slammed the gate shut, and we leaned against it, watching our Dumpster get tipped into the back of the garbage truck. There was still so much food we hadn't gotten to.

"At least the landfill rats will eat well tonight," Luke said.

"I wish we had more time," I said.

"We got twice as much as I normally do, thanks to you. Want to help out again next week?"

Was that a date? Did he just ask me out on a garbage-picking date? "Obviously," I said. "As if I'd let you keep all this fun to yourself."

He grimaced at my gunk-covered wedges. "Next time, maybe don't wear two-hundred-dollar shoes."

"Nonsense," I said. "A lady always Dumpster-dives in designer heels. That's how all the Meriton girls do it." I was drawing out the conversation. I wanted us to linger there. I wanted to fend off the inevitable moment when we had to separate.

"Ha," he said. "The day I see a Meriton girl Dumpster-diving is the day I eat slimy brown lettuce."

"Well, that day is today, because I was ankle-deep in there."

Luke looked at me and said, "You're not a Meriton girl."

It felt like a compliment.

"What am I then?" I asked. I had to make myself breathe.

Luke rubbed a smudge off my cheek and let his thumb rest there for a few seconds. "You're Blythe."

When Luke said my name, it felt like my muscles slipped off my bones and puddled on the road like jelly. At first I thought it was just because he was touching me, but that wasn't it. The thing that turned me to jelly was the realization that Luke truly did see me. He not only *wanted* to see me; he *saw* me.

Up to that moment, I think I'd lost track of who I was. Was I the new girl? Was I the principal's kid? Was I the booger girl? Was I a bad girl? Was I the same person I'd been at Meriton?

I had tipped off balance, and when Luke said my name, it was as if he'd steadied me and reminded me who I really was.

A spiking electric charge was fixed between Luke's eyes and mine, pulling us in. Drawing us closer together.

The garbage truck let out a long, blaring honk, and we leapt apart automatically.

The driver started ranting and pointing at my car, which was still in the middle of the alley where I'd stopped. The guy couldn't get through, and he wasn't happy about it.

There was no time for a decent goodbye. I kind of said, "I'd better . . ." and Luke sort of mumbled, " . . . should get going," and we just backed away from each other. We waved, and I jogged over to my car. I jumped in the front seat and cranked the engine. I glanced on the passenger seat and saw that my iPhone was full of texts and voice mail messages. Then I remembered.

Tara and the girls. I'd forgotten all about them. I was supposed to have met them at the mall an hour ago.

Crap.

I called Tara right away, but it went straight to voice mail. I sent her a bunch of texts, but she didn't respond. I knew Tara well enough to understand that this meant she was mad. I raced over to the mall and checked everywhere, but she was gone. I drove over to her house, but no one was home. I felt horrible.

Kind of, anyway.

Besides having zero regret about spending the afternoon with Luke, deep down I was kind of relieved to have forgotten about Tara. That probably made me a terrible person and lousy friend, but it was the truth. Hanging out with her was getting odd. It seemed like neither one of us wanted to hear about the other's life and problems. She didn't get what I was going through over at Ash Grove, and I was sick of hearing the dirt on everyone back at Meriton. So I wasn't exactly distraught about not meeting her. But I was bummed that I'd let her down. When Tara was mad at someone, she'd just cut the person out. I wasn't sure how long I could go without a best friend. I sent her an apology e-mail on top of my texts and voice mail messages.

When I got home, I hid my ruined shoes under the passenger seat with my spoiled history textbook and sneaked into the house barefoot. My capris and top were filthy too, but they were dry-clean only, so I couldn't do any covert laundry. I dashed upstairs and stripped down before anyone could see me. I shoved the clothes into a shoe box at the back of my closet until I had a chance to take them to the cleaners. I jumped in the shower and scrubbed the Dumpster funk off me.

I put on some clean sweats and skipped downstairs. The only person there was Dad, huddled over some paperwork at his desk in the family room. "Where are Mom and Zach?" I asked.

Dad jumped when I spoke. "Blythe! Oh. I didn't hear you come in."

Luckily, he hadn't seen me either.

He went back to scribbling. "Mom took Zach to get . . . clothes . . . or . . . a . . . baseball mitt . . . helmet? Something."

I intended only to *think*, "Wow, pay attention much, Dad?

You don't even know where your wife and son are," except that it poured out of my mouth instead. My mouth had been going wild lately. Like a ventriloquist's evil doll.

Dad shot me a classic Principal Mac scowl. "Pardon me, young lady?"

I threw my head back and forced peals of laughter out of my gullet. Then I grinned like a circus clown and exclaimed, "I'm just kidding!"

Dad's face softened. He turned back to his papers. "You'd better be." He clucked, then chuckled.

Sixth rule of lying: If you say something that brings you trouble, pretend *that* was actually the lie. Lie and say you were joking before, and aren't you funny? It's a quick escape from a sticky situation. It's the liar's trapdoor.

"Whatcha workin' on?" I chirped. I was probably taking the fake-good-girl role a little far, but I was new at this.

Dad didn't even notice. "A letter to the school board," he said without looking up. "Part of my application for super-intendent."

Lovely.

"Are there plans for dinner?" I asked.

Dad waved his pen in the general direction of the kitchen. "It's fend for yourself again. Sorry. I was supposed to bar-becue a brisket, but . . ." He bent over his paper again and never finished his sentence.

I grabbed a bowl of cereal and hid in my room for the rest of the evening. I'd had enough one-on-one with Dad, thank you very much. What was the point anyway, when one was lying and the other one was ignoring?

Later that night, just before I crawled into bed, I checked my in-box one more time to see if Tara had e-mailed me. She hadn't. But Luke had. I clicked madly to open it. Inside was a single quote:

My kind Blythe,
I can no other answer make but thanks,
And thanks, and ever thanks.

I Googled the quote. *Twelfth Night*, act 3, scene 3. Shake-speare again, with my name inserted. I couldn't believe how perfect Luke was. No, not perfect. Because he wasn't perfect. But might be perfect for me.

My plans to avoid guys until I got to Bryn Mawr suddenly seemed naive and unrealistic. Cruel, even. How unfair to deny me this opportunity for happiness. Besides, what did I know about relationships? Nothing. Shouldn't I get some ex-perience with them? Who's to say my dream guy couldn't be someone I met pre-college, anyway? Why did I even come up with that dumb rule in the first place?

The answer was, because I'd never met someone like Luke. A guy who spun me in so many directions yet drew me to him at the same time. Whose deep blue eyes seemed to pierce through me and see my most closely held secrets, and I didn't mind. I wanted him to know me, everything about me. And I wanted to know everything about him. Flaws and all.

Luke and I already knew we both were flawed. We'd each proven it more than once. But that was okay. We didn't have to be perfect. Take our first kiss. How gross does it seem to have your first kiss in a filthy back-alley Dumpster? But I'm telling you, at that moment, it was the most perfect spot on earth. Nothing in the world extended beyond the perimeter of our bodies.

My heart started pounding just thinking about it.

There was no way I could possibly fall asleep.

I paid for my late-night daydreaming by sleeping through my alarm the next morning. I woke up with less than fifteen minutes to get all the way to Ash Grove by the first bell. I yanked on some old black sweats and pulled my matted hair into a messy bun. I didn't have time for makeup. I'd have to try to slip into the girls' bathroom at school the first chance I got. The problem was, I totally forgot to bring my makeup. I was headed into a full-on day of ugly. I didn't want Luke to see me like that. I'd been so happy about not needing to be perfect with him, but a girl needs her dignity. So as much as it killed me, I hid from him that morning.

The only people who didn't seem fazed by my homeless-chic look were Cy and Jenna. In fact, Cy complimented me on it at lunch.

"I dig the suicidal vibe you've got going, Blythe. Much better than the sexless Barbie look."

"Sexless?" I repeated. "I usually look sexless?"

Jenna gave Cy a sharp elbow. He stammered, "W-Well, yeah, but . . . in a sexy way. Like . . . you know . . . innocent or something. Like a sexy schoolgirl."

"You are so full of crap," I said.

Cy looked down at the cafeteria table. "Yeah, I totally

am." He brightened up and pointed to me. "My point is, you look like a real human being today, not a pod person."

Jenna shook her head in disbelief. "You are so not making her feel any better, Cy. Just shut your piehole."

He lifted her chin and leaned toward her. "Why don't you shut it for me?"

Jenna kissed him hard and sloppy.

"You two really need an NC-17 rating tattooed to your foreheads." I stabbed at my yogurt. They didn't stop. "I'm trying to eat here," I said. Finally, they dragged themselves apart. Cy wiped his mouth with the back of his hand. Gross. I snatched a napkin from the dispenser and held it out to him. "At least use this." Cy took the napkin and tossed it over his shoulder. I rolled my eyes and ate my yogurt.

"You should let me do your makeup," Jenna said. "Want some eyeliner?"

I scrutinized the thick black smears around Jenna's and Cy's eyes with the heavy black lashes and the pale skin underneath. "Sure," I said. "Why not?" I was desperate for makeup. I scooted over and Jenna hoisted her black messenger bag onto the bench. It was covered with stickers and buttons for bands or ironic advertisements or anarchist slogans. She must've been collecting them forever.

She dug inside the bag and pulled out a small black case. She unzipped it and dumped a dozen eyeliners, mascaras, and lip glosses onto the table. They all were expensive, designer-brand cosmetics. I plucked up one of the liquid liners and stuck it in her face. "Jenna! This one eyeliner is like thirty bucks!"

She blushed, but Cy said, "Didn't she tell you she was, like, mega-wealthy?"

"Uh, NO," I said. I smiled and circled the mascara in front of her. "Kind of undermines your whole meth addict look, you know."

Jenna snatched the eyeliner and motioned for me to lean forward. "Tough shit. This stuff works way better." She pulled the skin at the corner of my eye and began applying. "Besides, I stole all of this from my mother's makeup kit. Look up."

I trained my eyes on the ceiling. "Oh, I see. So stealing the makeup cancels out the fact that you're rich and privileged enough to afford it?"

"Exactly," she said. "Okay, stop talking or I'm going to accidentally blind you."

I sat stone still while Jenna worked her designer cosmetic magic. Ten minutes later, she had transformed me into a genuine bad girl. Blythe McKenna: social outcast and teenage delinquent.

I checked my reflection in the mirror of her $25 pressed powder. I looked more like the evil queen than Snow White, but I have to say, it wasn't bad. Jenna's technique was flawless. "Jenna, you're like a makeup wizard," I said. "Unbelievable. My eyelashes look amazing."

"Yeah. The trick is to scrape most of the mascara off the brush, then work the bristles into the roots of the lashes and draw it up," she said.

"God, you girls and your girly-girl talk," Cy said. "Let me know if you're going to start comparing your periods so I can shoot myself first."

Jenna tossed each piece of makeup one at a time back into the case. "You'd better watch your mouth, Cy Mason, or I won't do your eyes or cut your hair and you'll look just like your dork cousin Larry."

Cy held up his hands in surrender. "Never mind. Forget what I said. I'd actually love to hear all about your periods. Are your cramps bad? Do you like tampons?"

Luckily, the bell rang.

I thanked Jenna and got my things together. We filed out of the cafeteria, and I kept my eye out for Luke since I sometimes ran into him here. I thought I caught sight of him back in the crowd, but if he saw me, he didn't recognize me. Most people didn't. I was suddenly anonymous, and I liked it.

Jenna's makeup job stayed so perfect all day that I almost forgot I was wearing it. I was reminded out in the parking lot after school when I found Luke waiting beside my car. When he saw me, he backed away and braced himself against my trunk. "I don't know who you are, but I can't let you steal this car," he said. "Please don't shank me."

I stuck my chest out, swaggered up to him, and said, "Then you'd better back up off my ride, beyatch." Luke feigned terror and slid away from my car. I took his place, leaning against my trunk. "That's more like it," I said.

He laughed, then came over and leaned beside me. We watched cars pulling out of the parking spots like a mouth losing teeth. I glanced down the row parked across from us and noticed a hot-pink Volkswagen Beetle. The license plate read: B-U-T QUEEN.

"Oh my God!" I squealed. "*Q!* A *Q* license plate. Look!"

I dug frantically in my messenger bag for my iPhone. "That pink Bug! The plate says *Butt Queen*! Why would anyone pick that for their vanity plate? I don't care. It's the last letter I need."

Luke spun around to check out the car. "I . . . uh . . . I think it says *Beauty Queen*."

My phone was hiding between the pages of a notebook. I grabbed it and turned it on. *"Beauty Queen?"* I shook my phone as if that would make it start up faster. "That plate clearly says *Butt Queen*. How could the owner not see that?"

"She probably did, after the fact," Luke mumbled.

"God, I hope she doesn't come out before I get the picture." I loaded the camera.

"Why don't you let me take it?" Luke's hand shot out to me. "Here, I'll take it. Let me!"

I looked at him like he was deranged and headed for the Bug. He trailed behind me, trying to snag my sleeve or the strap of my bag. "Come on," he said, "I'll do it for you."

I waved him off and crouched down behind the car. Just as I aimed the camera, a female voice shouted, "You bastards need to stay the hell away from my car!"

I snapped the picture and stood up, ready to toss some lame apology to the owner, who was jogging over. I didn't quite get to it. The owner was Karly.

Luke was at my side in a shot.

CHAPTER 18

"LUKE?" KARLY CRIED. "WHAT ARE YOU DOING?" SHE glared at me. "And why are you with *her*?"

Luke placed his hand on my lower back and steered me away. "Nothing, Karly. Go home."

"That's what you left me for?" she screamed. "I wasn't good enough, so you had to find some snotty little bitch from Meriton? Ha! At least I don't pick my nose!"

Luke's hand slipped off my back as he wheeled around. His long legs brought him up to Karly in about five steps. He leaned into her personal space and said, "She's not a snotty little bitch. I broke up with you because I wasn't in love with you. And you do pick your nose. I've seen it. Many times."

As Luke strode back to me, I watched Karly's gaping mouth open and close like a fish's on a hook. Luke's hand landed on the same spot on my lower back and we walked away. "Sorry about that," he said quietly.

"It's not your fault."

"She's hurt."

"Obviously," I said. "Now I see why you wanted to be the one taking the picture."

"She's had like fifty juniors following her car around for the clue. She's embarrassed because she hates that plate."

"That's how you knew it was supposed to be *Beauty Queen*," I said. We got to my car and I unlocked it.

Luke nodded. "Yeah. She didn't notice the other way to read the lettering when she bought it. She wasn't supposed to get it in the first place, but she went behind her dad's back, and now he won't let her change it."

"Ouch." I dropped my bag on the backseat. I glanced over at Karly, but her car was gone.

"Anyway . . ." Luke shoved his hands in the front pockets of his jeans and shifted his weight back and forth. "I was wondering if you wanted to grab a coffee or something."

Damn.

Damn. Damn. Damn.

"I wish I could," I said. "But I have to go volunteer. At the nursing home. I told you yesterday, remember?"

"So you weren't making that up just to impress me?" he teased. He tipped one shoulder toward me as though he was reaching out, but his hands stayed rooted in his pockets.

"Very funny," I said. I was riveted to my car door. It was like Luke and I were suddenly two of the same magnetic poles and we couldn't force ourselves together, no matter how much we wanted to.

"You can come with me if you need proof," I joked. "Although, I believe you have a certain article to write."

Luke pushed up his glasses and then slid his hand right back in his pocket. "Yeah, yeah. And an underground scavenger hunt to run. So that was your last plate for the clue?"

"Yup." I fiddled with a loose thread on the cuff of my hoodie so my hands had something to do. "Clue number four is mission accomplished."

"You're going to love clue number five," he said.

I eyed him sideways. "Oh, no. Is it bad?"

Luke smirked. "Let's just say it'll thin out the field of contestants. Although, you might have an advantage. Then again, it could be extra challenging for you to do."

"That sounds bad," I said.

"You'll see." He winked. "Just remember, I had nothing to do with the clues. They were made up a while ago." He hooked his fingers through mine, gave them a small squeeze, and said, "I should let you get going." He backed away until our hands pulled apart. I smiled and flashed a wave good-bye. He turned and walked off. We didn't kiss.

I was so distracted at Shady Acres that I accidentally put Ms. Eulalie's Jean Naté After Bath Splash on Ms. Franny. She wouldn't stop barking about it until one of the nurse's aides came to give her a sponge bath. I cut out early so she'd have her privacy. Plus, I wanted to get home quickly, to get the fifth clue. I uploaded all twenty-six license plate pictures onto the Revolting Phoenix, careful not to delete my picture of Luke. Not because I needed it for anything; just because he looked adorable and that was the only picture I had of him.

Congratulations! You have successfully uploaded a valid picture of item #4.

Here is your clue to item #5:

Meriton and Ash Grove have been rival schools for years.
At sports events, our mascots lead opposing crowds in
cheers.
The Meriton Blue Stallion is the object of your mission.
BUT! The costume must be in a rated X position.

My forehead hit the keyboard. Now I understood what
Luke had meant. Either I had an advantage because of my
connections with Meriton or this clue was going to be especially hard for me because Meriton used to be my school. God,
if this was only the fifth clue, how bad was ten going to be?

There was a knock at my door, and I flipped my laptop
closed. "Yeah?" I called.

Mom poked her head through the door. Her eyes bugged
at the sight of my makeup. "What's on your face? Never mind.
Listen, I have to go meet Dad over at Marjorie's office to deal
with the inspection report. It might take a while, so there's a
frozen lasagna in the oven for dinner, okay?"

"What's up with the report?" I asked. The home inspector had come on Saturday and spent three hours going over
every inch of our house. It took him two days to write up the
twenty-four-page inspection report.

Mom sighed and leaned against my door frame. "The
buyers are asking for all sorts of concessions—money that
they want back at closing to cover repairs that the house
apparently needs." She rolled her eyes. "According to the
inspector, anyway."

"How much are they asking for?"

Mom puffed out her cheeks and exhaled. "Ninety-five hundred dollars."

"What? That's almost the entire amount they added on during the bidding war! They're allowed to just ask for it back?"

"If the report says that the repairs will cost that much, then yes."

"Oh my God, that's such a scam. Can we say no?"

She nodded. "But then the buyers can back out of the deal if they want, and we have to start all over again." Her pallor was dull and pasty, like plaster. She was barely even wearing any makeup.

I leaned back in my desk chair. "Isn't all this killing you?" I asked.

Mom stared blankly out my window. "Yes. No. Some ways."

"Then why did you agree to any of it?"

She took a moment to answer me. Probably because she was deciding whether to give me the same old answer or an honest reason. "Because it's the right choice for our family. And it's important to Dad."

Same old answer.

"Please," I said. "The only thing important to Dad is impressing people."

Mom's eyes snapped to me. "That is absolutely untrue," she said firmly. "This family is your father's top priority." More compulsory parent-speak.

"Ha," I said. "What a joke."

Her eyebrows knitted together and she scowled. "Why is that a joke?"

I spun my chair around to face her full-on. "Because he's hiding behind us! He's using his family to justify his own ambition."

She reared back. "We ARE the reason for his ambition."

"No, we're not!"

"Oh, really? What else is then, Blythe? What else do you think it is?"

I should have stopped myself. I should have said, "Whatever," and shut my mouth. But I didn't. "It's his insecurity! His own insecurity is driving his ambition, not love!"

Mom threw her arms wide and stepped toward me. "And so what? If that were true, so what? Nobody's perfect, Blythe, including your father. If there's a hole in him that needs fixing, we're going to help him fix it."

"But it's such garbage!" I said. "Instead of fixing it, why can't you just convince him that he doesn't have to do this stupid alpha-male crap?"

"I've been trying to for twenty years!" she yelled. "It doesn't work! He has to physically *get* there! He has to get to a place where he feels good enough. That's the only way he can stop. The only way he can make peace with himself."

"For what?" I cried. "What's he done that was so bad? Nothing! He has nothing to make up for!"

"You don't understand!" Mom screamed. Suddenly, she halted. She lowered her arms and drew herself upright. She took a cleansing breath and then shuttered the conversation. "There are things between your father and me that don't concern you, Blythe. I know this move is hard for you, but you must trust that Dad and I know what we're doing." She glanced at her gold and diamond watch. "Now, I have to run. I set the timer for the lasagna. Feed Zach too, please." She sent me a dry, emotionless air kiss and disappeared.

My cell phone rang. It was Tara.

CHAPTER 19

I DIDN'T EVEN SAY HELLO. I JUMPED RIGHT IN WITH:

"Are you still mad at me, T? I'm still sorry."

"I'm over it. But you'd better have a good reason for blowing us off." Her voice was amicable and sounded absolutely fantastic to my ears.

"Does making out with a guy count?" I said.

"WHAT? Wait. Which guy?"

"Luke Pavel. He's a senior."

"Isn't he the one you mentioned in the coffee shop?"

"Yup."

"I thought you didn't like him."

"I like him now. A lot. You'll never guess where he kissed me."

"Uh, it better have been on the lips, or there's gonna be some trouble."

"No! I mean you'll never guess where we were."

"In your car?"

"No."

"Under the bleachers? How 1965 would that be?"

"Nope."

"In your parents' bed?"

"Ew! No."

"In the stacks at the library?"

"No. I'm telling you; you're never going to guess."

"In your dad's office."

"No. Listen . . ."

"Oh!" She gasped. "In detention? Did you have your own personal *Breakfast Club*?"

"No. Tara, stop. You'll never . . ."

"In a dirty gas station bathroom?"

"Tara, SHUT UP. You will NEVER EVER guess."

"Then why are we having this conversation?"

"Oh my God. Forget we made up. Let's go back to not talking."

She started snickering.

"You're evil," I said.

"I know. Someone has to be. So get to the smooch details already. God, why are you stalling?"

We talked on the phone for over an hour. Normality achieved. She had a dentist appointment after school the next day, so we made plans to meet for coffee on Wednesday and to go to the Meriton basketball game on Friday night. I immediately started scheming a way to get the Blue Stallion picture. I couldn't tell Tara about the clue. Even if the Senior Scramble hadn't been under a strict code of secrecy, news of this particular clue wouldn't go over too well at Meriton. Especially if it came from me. Nope. I'd have to do it on my own. I'd go to the game, get in, get out, upload the picture, and be done. I knew Tara would help me if she could, so I figured out a way for her to be my accomplice without even knowing it.

The week ticked by. The highlights were that Luke and I chatted online a lot and hung out briefly after school a few times. We just couldn't get our schedules to mesh very well. No kissing to report, but there were some "almost" moments. Something always happened to spoil it. *Spoil* is actually the wrong word, because every time we couldn't kiss, it made the magnetic tension between us even stronger. I wanted so badly to bring him to the Meriton game Friday night, but there was no way I could handle that kind of distraction, and get the picture, and hang with Tara, and see all my old friends again. So Luke and I made rock-solid plans for Saturday night. Rock solid.

On the home front, the negotiations with the buyers hit a snag over the inspection report, and closing got pushed back a week. So my April Fools' Day was wide open. I was actually kind of bummed, because I figured closer proximity to Ash Grove would equal closer proximity to Luke. Even so, I was grateful for the extra time in my perfect pink bedroom.

In BFF news, Tara and I had met at the Daily Grind on Wednesday. Cerise, Veronica, and Melissa were there, and it was like we never missed a beat. We talked about school, gossip, and guys. I told them about Luke. Melissa had gone out a few times with a guy in her Spanish class. Tara reported significant progress with her crush, James Forsberg, a senior and the captain of the basketball team. I marked that down in my mental notebook because I thought it might come in handy Friday night. That afternoon at the Daily Grind was the first time since stepping foot in Ash Grove High School that I felt like one of the popular girls. I couldn't wait to see them all again at the game.

An hour before tip-off on Friday night, I was getting ready for the game. I couldn't decide between a trapeze top with leggings or a tiered mini with layered tanks. The whole time, Zach kept nagging me to take him with me to the game. "Come on, Blythe. My old friends are going to be there too," he said with just a tinge of a whine.

"Then get them to take you." It wasn't very charitable of me to say that, but he'd been pestering me for two hours straight. When Zach sets his mind on something, he won't let go until he gets what he wants. He'll make a great salesman one day. Or a hostage negotiator.

"I won't bug you," he said. "I won't get in your space. I won't talk to your friends. I'll totally disappear."

"Oh, sure. Mom and Dad would love that."

"So don't tell them. Jeez, I'm almost thirteen. I can handle a high school basketball game. I don't need a babysitter."

"I'd still be responsible for you."

Zach stretched himself across the clothes strewn on my bed and tried a new tactic. "Think about Mom and Dad. One more night . . . alone in the house. You know they'd appreciate it."

If Mom and Dad hadn't been so on edge lately, I would've thought this argument was a stretch, even for Zach. But the fact was, he had a point. I yanked a silk top out from under his butt. "Get off my clothes! See? You can't even lie on a bed responsibly."

Zach bounded to his feet. "I'm off! Look! I'm off. I'll do whatever you say tonight. Unless I'm not cool with it. But even then, I'll strongly consider your opinion."

I made the mistake of laughing, and Zach knew he had me. I sighed and said, "Fine." He clapped, jumped in a circle, and raced out of my room. I shouted after him, "I'm leaving in exactly twenty-three minutes whether you're in the car or not!" I hoped this wasn't a huge mistake. I also hoped Mom and Dad didn't waste the night arguing.

Zach was waiting in the car for me, so I let him pick the music for the drive. When we got to Meriton, I told him to meet me no later than twenty minutes after the final buzzer, and he took off to find his friends. I spotted Tara and waved. On my way to her, people right and left came up to me to say hi or give me a hug. Jenny Pritzkey raced over and threw her arms around me. "I'm so glad to see you!" she squealed. "It's not the same without you here. I wish you were back!"

Being there was the total inverse of my first walk into Ash Grove.

Tara and I found seats just behind the bench so she could stare at the back of James Forsberg's head for the five whole seconds he wasn't out on the court. I had a good view of the Blue Stallion mascot pumping up the crowd. There was pre-game music blaring, and he was doing the robot beside one of the refs. I couldn't remember the name of the guy inside the costume. In fact, I don't think I ever bothered to learn it.

Meriton was playing East Valley, yet during the game I noticed a bunch of Ash Grove juniors scattered around the gym. They must've been there to get their hands on the mascot costume. I should've seen that coming. Luckily, most of them were gone by the second half. Either they ambushed the Blue Stallion during halftime or they gave up and crawled home.

The score was tied up, but James Forsberg sank a three-pointer at the final buzzer. The crowd erupted. Tara was freaking out, screaming for James. The Blue Stallion some-how did a back handspring, which had to be difficult with a horse head. The team shook hands with East Valley and jogged into the locker room, high-fiving each other and every-one they passed. Time to set my plan in motion.

"James's going to be in a good mood tonight," I said to Tara over the noise of the crowd.

"No doubt," she said. "God, he was so hot out there."

"You know what?" I said.

"What?"

"I think you should wait outside the locker room and jump him when he comes out."

Tara gaped at me. "What?"

"Why not?" I cried. "You said yourself things were going in that direction anyway, right?"

"Yeah, I guess." She ran her hand through the short points of her razor-cut hair and glanced toward the locker room.

Meriton had a kind of honor code. The captain of any sports team was the last to leave the locker room. Like the captain of a sinking ship being the last one off. So I knew that once James left, the locker room would be empty. Did I mention that they keep the Blue Stallion costume in the locker room? That was a little tidbit of information that no one else at Ash Grove knew about, but everyone at Meriton did.

All I needed to do was find something to distract James when he came out of the locker room so he wouldn't see me slip inside before the door shut and locked behind him. Tara was going to be my distraction. At the same time, she was finally going to take her shot with James. They were perfect for each other. I knew it, and she knew it, and it was time to give her a nudge. Or a shove.

"So make it happen!" I said to her. "Since when do you wait around for something? God, it's not like he's going to punch you and run away. He likes you. You like him."

She laughed and shouted, "Ugh, you are such a pain in the ass!" She wasn't really mad. "Why do I listen to you?"

"Because you know I'm right," I said. "Come on." I grabbed her hand and dragged her through the crowd to the spot where the players exited the locker room. I needed to be near the door, but Tara didn't like it so close.

"Not right outside the door!" she said, retreating a few feet. "I don't want to look like some crazy, desperate stalker. What am I supposed to say? You were kidding about me jumping him, right? I'll talk to him. I'm not jumping him." She tugged on the V-neck of her top so that more of her cleavage showed.

Talking wouldn't be quite as distracting as grabbing James and planting her face on his, but I didn't want to push Tara any more than I had. She could easily change her mind and bolt. I'd have to make the best of the situation. I checked my watch. I had to meet Zach at the gym door in fifteen minutes. When were these guys going to leave? Five minutes later, the players finally started streaming out of the locker room, showered and fully dressed in the shirts and ties they were required to wear to home games. I hadn't accounted for showers. I checked my watch again. Nine minutes. A couple of girls from my old French class walked up and started babbling and gabbing to Tara and me. Another variable I hadn't planned on! If these two ditzy femmes were still hanging around when James came out, I'd have to abort. They'd notice me going into the locker room for sure.

"Pardon?" I asked. One of them had asked me a question. "Um, yeah, I miss Meriton. It's way better here." Who were these girls anyway? I didn't remember them. Thank God they splintered off before James came out. I checked the time. Crap, four minutes until I had to meet Zach. If James didn't come out in the next sixty seconds, there'd be no way I could make it.

As if on cue, James opened the locker room door and stepped out. He spotted Tara immediately, as if I wasn't even there. "Tara," he said right away. "Hey. What's up?"

It was all the encouragement Tara needed. She stepped over to him, ran her hand up his arm, and started complimenting him on the game. I stuck my foot in the door and waited. When Tara and James's heads inclined toward each other so they could say some more private things, I slipped inside without notice.

Wow, I had been wrong about Meriton not having any kind of smell, because the boys' locker room definitely had one. And it wasn't pleasant. I searched around quickly for the mascot costume and found it in a jumbo locker in the corner. I also found out that it smelled even worse than the locker room. There was no way to wash it, so there must've been years of sweat and guy funk and other nastiness embedded in this blue horse. I hauled it out, trying to touch it as little as possible. I could only think of one X-rated position, which was to lie the horse on his back and make one of his hooves . . . well . . . pleasure himself. I know it sounds bad, but take my word, it looked much worse. The head had even tipped back a bit so it seemed like it was arching its back with ecstasy.

I took a quick picture along with a couple of extra shots to be sure and then hauled the stench-soaked costume back to the jumbo locker. Once it was safely inside, I dashed to the locker room door, opened it a crack to make sure the coast was clear, and then sneaked out. Tara and James were nowhere in sight, which was great. I'd have to call Tara in the morning to get details, but right now I was late for meeting Zach.

"Where have you been, young lady?" he said in his best Principal McKenna voice as I jogged up to him. "You're thirty-seven seconds late. Detention for a week."

I had to stop and catch my breath. Subterfuge was exhausting. "Hey, you didn't happen to see Tara go by, did you?" I asked.

"Yeah," he said, hitching his thumb behind him. "She walked out of here with the team captain. Jealous?"

"Ha!" I said. "As if."

I wasn't jealous. I had my Senior Scramble picture. Tara could keep her captain.

CHAPTER 20

"HOW CAN SO MANY PEOPLE BE AHEAD OF ME?" I cried. "You have to tell me!"

Luke sipped his soda, smiled, and shook his head. "Nope."

I had spent most of my date with Luke grilling him about the shock I got when I uploaded my Blue Stallion picture—thinking I was in the lead—and saw that over a dozen people were already on to the next clue.

"There's no way so many could have gotten the mascot picture before I did," I said. "They had to be cheating. Photoshop or something."

"No Photoshop," Luke said. "No cheating. All the pictures were legit." He was enjoying this way too much.

"You're enjoying this way too much."

Luke leaned back, laced his arms behind his head, and said, "Actually, I'm enjoying it exactly the right amount."

I threw a French fry at his glasses, but he lobbed it back to me, laughing.

"Tell me!" I cried.

"I'll tell you this much," Luke said. "The mascot was doing some pretty nasty, raunchy things in the pictures."

I'd barely been able to get the bulky costume laid out flat on the locker room floor. How did they . . . ?

"Wait!" I cried. "Somebody was wearing the costume in those pictures? How is that possible? There's no way thirteen people could have stolen the costume, put it on, taken a picture, and returned it without being seen."

"I never said they did," Luke said pointedly.

My mind spun. There was only one answer. "Oh my God, are you saying that it was the actual Blue Stallion mascot guy in the pictures?"

Luke winked at me. He popped a French fry in his mouth and grinned.

"No! How . . . ? Why would he do that?"

Luke shrugged. "Maybe people found a way to . . . *persuade* him."

Loud music with a heavy bass beat pulsated through the restaurant and made it hard for me to puzzle out what Luke meant. At last, I got it. I dropped my face into my hands. "Ugh! They PAID him! During halftime!" I smacked the table with both hands. "Why didn't I think of that? Do you have any idea what machinations I went through to get that picture? I'm so stupid."

Luke scooped up my hands with his. "No, you're not. You're honest. Your picture was definitely the most genuine. Although, it was by far the least X-rated. Maybe PG-13 at the outside."

"Well, I worked with what I had," I said. "The horse was obviously exhausted by the time I got to him since he spent the entire halftime intermission doing porn."

Luke laughed so loud that the people in the booth next to us stared. I blushed, even though I wasn't embarrassed at all, because making Luke laugh felt like the greatest victory in the world.

"So did you get the sixth clue?" he asked.

"Yeah, but I have definite suspicions about it." I narrowed my eyes and scanned Luke's face for any hint of information about the clue. It had read:

Welcome to the halfway point! We have a treat for you.
You've earned a little rest stop with a super-easy clue.
Find a sign with lettering that you can rearrange.
Take before and after pictures of your funny change.

"It's too easy," I said. "Something's up."

Luke took a long sip of iced tea while I eyed him. Finally, he said, "It says that it's a rest stop." His voice and demeanor were overly innocent. Was he sending me a message? Or was he messing with me?

"Mmm-hmm," I said, just like Ms. Eulalie. "I remain suspicious."

"I guess you'll just have to solve the clue and find out," he said, swirling his straw around his glass with diabolical glee.

We'd been picking at our near-empty plates for half an hour, and the waitress was getting cranky. Luke paid the check, a gesture that would cheerfully meet with Ms. Eulalie's and Ms. Franny's approval. Of course, they'd be horrified that Luke hadn't picked me up for the date. He'd offered to, but it made no sense for him to schlep all the way out to Meriton and back to Ash Grove twice in one night. I insisted we just meet at the restaurant. Applebee's wasn't exactly the country club, but after you've spent a day in a Dumpster with someone, everything looks five star.

"Are you ready to go?" Luke asked.

No, I thought.

"Sure," I said. We laid our napkins on the table and stood up in perfect synchrony. When we realized it, we laughed simultaneously. Crazy.

We left the restaurant, and Luke walked me to my car. A warm, damp breeze tumbled around us. The high sounds of the peepers and other spring frogs rang out in the distance. I deeply inhaled the fresh night air. "Ahhh," I sighed. "I'm so glad March is finally over."

We got to my car and leaned against it, side by side. Luke stared up at the stars. "So . . . any chance for another Dumpster date tomorrow?" he asked.

"Totally," I answered. I'd go anywhere with him. "Wait! No!" I let my head thud back against the roof of my car. "I promised Tara and my other girlfriends that we'd hit the mall tomorrow afternoon. I can't skip out on them again after last week, even though I'd much rather pick garbage with you." It surprised me to say that. I adored my friends. Tara and I had been inseparable my whole life. Yet what I'd said was true.

Luke nudged me with his shoulder and smiled. "It's cool," he said. "We'll get together again. Soon."

I rolled sideways to face him. He turned to me. The

polarity that had held us apart was gone. Now, the only force between us was one that pulled us together.

A lock of hair blew across my face, and Luke tucked it behind my ear. His hand paused as his thumb caressed my jaw. He didn't say a word.

He just drew my face to his and softly kissed me.

CHAPTER 21

THE REAL REASON THE GIRLS AND I WERE HANGING out Sunday afternoon was so Tara and I could compare guy stories. I wanted to hear every detail of what happened with James after the basketball game, and I couldn't wait to tell her all about my date with Luke.

It was impossible to get anywhere with our stories because Veronica and Cerise were talking non-stop about their summer plans. Melissa could only stay an hour, and Veronica and Cerise had homework to do, so they bailed, leaving Tara and me alone at last. We made the rounds of the mall stores as we recounted our dates.

"So wait," I said as Tara and I sifted through the summer dresses in Forever 21. "James didn't try anything else? Not even over the shirt or anything?"

Tara shrugged one shoulder. "He grabbed my ass while we were making out. But yeah, other than that he was pretty tame. He didn't even take off his tie. What about this one?" She held up a tribal print spaghetti strap dress.

I crinkled up my nose. "Nah. This?" An emerald halter dress. Tara shook her head. I slipped the hanger back on the rack. "Maybe he's gay . . . ?"

Tara smirked. "No, he's definitely not gay." She chuckled to herself. "That much I could feel . . . I mean, tell."

I didn't press for intimate details.

I checked in the mirror beside us to see which of two colors looked best against my skin. "Okay," I said, "so James is the captain of an athletic team, he's in the top two percent of the class, he likes wearing ties, and he's a gentleman. Don't take this the wrong way, T, but he's like the total opposite of you."

"I know!" She beamed at me like a kid at Disney World. "Isn't it perfect? Opposites attract!" She was giddy. Tara—the girl who once ran into Jay-Z at the airport and didn't even break a sweat—Tara was giddy over James Forsberg.

"That really only applies to magnets. You know that, right? It's not a philosophical compass for your life."

Tara grabbed an animal print crop top from the next rack over, then unbuttoned her tie waist top and stripped down to her bra right there in the store. "But we'd make a smokin' hot couple. God, I hope he asks me to prom." She pulled the crop top over her head and shimmied into it. "When's Ash Grove's prom?"

I shrugged. "No idea. End of April? Beginning of May? A few people are talking about it." I checked the price of a baby doll dress.

Tara pulled the sleeves down off the shoulder and posed for me. "What do you think? Does it look slutty?"

"I don't think so, no."

Tara pouted. "Then forget it." She peeled it off and tossed it onto the rack. She slipped into her tie waist top and started doing up the buttons. I hung up the crop top for her.

"So what about you and Luke?" she said. "Are you opposites? I bet you don't exactly come from the same tax bracket. Is he smart? Nerdy? What? Ooh, you should try this on. Take off your shirt."

I laughed and snatched the peasant top from her. "I'll use the dressing room, thank you. Hold my purse." I also grabbed two sizes of a one-shoulder sundress I liked. I didn't trust the sizes on the tags.

Tara followed me to the dressing room area and plopped down on the upholstered bench outside the dressing room doors. I went into an empty room and started to change.

"I don't even know what Luke looks like. Is he hot?" Tara shouted to me.

I blushed, even though there was no one but my reflection to see me. "I guess so," I said. Of course he was hot, but you don't go shouting that out in the middle of a clothing store.

"Do you have a picture of him? I want to see."

I had only one picture of Luke, and it was on my iPhone. "Check the pictures on my phone," I said. "There's one of him in . . . um . . . the big green . . . bin."

"You mean the Dumpster?" Tara called louder than necessary.

I closed my eyes and took a cleansing breath. "Just find it," I said weakly.

Tara was quiet for a minute, so I figured she was zooming in on Luke's face to gauge his hotness level. I heard her call, "Uh, Blythe, what's this picture?"

"I told you!" I said in a loud whisper through the crack of the door. "It was for charity!"

"No, not that one," she said. "I mean the one with the Blue Stallion costume."

Oh, God. I never deleted the extra shots!

"It's nothing!" I yelled. I was down to only my panties because the sundress had a bra built in. I grabbed it and held it over my chest as I bolted out of the dressing room. "It's garbage. Here, let me delete it!" I tried to grab my phone, but Tara held it out of my reach.

"When did you take this?" she asked, relishing the sight of me dancing around her in my underwear as she kept the phone away from me. I noticed that everyone in the store could see me nearly naked, so I raced back into the dressing room. I didn't see any other option than to spill to Tara about the underground Senior Scramble.

I poked my head out and whispered, "It's for the Ash Grove scavenger hunt. It's back on, but it's a total secret, so you can't tell anyone about it, okay? Everybody could get in huge trouble. Like suspended." I pulled my head back inside and scrambled to strap on my bra. The hooks wouldn't catch.

"This picture was for some scavenger hunt at Ash Grove?"

"Yeah."

Tara gasped. "How could you do that to your own school? Wait, when did you take this?"

"Friday night," I said. "While you were talking to James after the game."

Tara was silent.

I said, "We had to get a picture of the Meriton Blue Stallion in a compromising position." My bra finally hooked. I grabbed my yoga pants and hopped around on one foot as I tried to pull them on. "I sneaked into the guys' locker room and took it."

"Hold up," Tara said. "Is that why you were pushing me so hard to jump James when he came out of the locker room?" Her voice was suddenly somber. "So you could sneak in to get this picture?"

I stuck my head out the door. "No. I mean, sort of. Maybe yes, but it was like a two-birds, one-stone kind of deal." She was still staring at the picture on my phone. A salesclerk gave me the evil eye, so I ducked back inside and talked through the crack in the door. "I wanted the picture; you wanted James. It all worked out, right?"

Tara sat motionless. "It could just as easily have gone the other way," she said.

"What do you mean?" I squirmed as I tried to put my top on, but it got all twisted. I peeled it off again.

"It totally could have backfired, Blythe," she cried. "What if James thought I was a freak? What if he figured I must be a desperate loser? You didn't know for sure how he'd react. But you made me do it anyway. I can't believe you totally used me like that. For a stupid picture!"

At last, I wriggled into my top. I slid my feet into my sandals, grabbed the sundresses and peasant top, and flew out of the dressing room. Tara tossed my phone onto the bench cushion beside her and crossed her arms, staring straight ahead.

"T, I didn't use you!" I shoved the garments into the store clerk's arms and snatched up my phone. I frantically scrolled to the extra stallion pictures and deleted them, as if that somehow would delete Tara's memory.

She wheeled around to me. "Answer me this: could you have gotten this picture without having me distract James?"

It had been the only scenario I could come up with. Or at least, it was the first one. I hadn't really thought any further than that. "I don't know. Probably not."

"And would you have suggested I throw myself at James if you *didn't* have to get this picture?"

I shrugged. "Maybe. I'm not sure."

Tara glared at me. "You wouldn't have, and you know it. So basically, you were using me." She stood up and snugged the knot of her tie waist top. "All you were thinking about was your own agenda. Which is all you ever think—and talk—about lately." Her hand circled in the air. "It's all about Blythe and her drama."

"That's not tr—"

"The irony is"—she swept up her purse and hooked it over her arm—"that I totally would've helped you if you'd just asked."

I tried to explain. "We aren't supposed to tell anyone about the scavenger hunt so the administration doesn't find out."

Tara nodded slowly. "I see. In other words, you didn't trust me. Damn, Blythe." She started to walk away from me. After three steps, she turned and said, "Who the hell are you now?" She didn't wait for my answer. She was gone.

I spent the next hour nursing a caramel macchiato in the food court. I was so ashamed about the way I'd treated Tara that I didn't even want to do the Senior Scramble anymore. Except that I'd promised Luke that my hands would be as bloody as anyone's. I couldn't quit. Besides, if I was losing friends at Meriton, then I'd better secure some at Ash Grove. Finishing—or better yet, winning—the hunt would do that, I hoped. Quitting the hunt would do the opposite. How could I go on, though, when it had turned me into such a jerk? Where did my loyalties lie: Meriton or Ash Grove?

My coffee had gone cold, so I dumped it and headed out of the mall. I didn't know what to do. I needed some kind of sign that I either should quit the Senior Scramble and beg Tara to forgive me or continue on with the scavenger hunt, like I'd promised Luke (and everyone else at Ash Grove, even if they didn't realize it).

I trudged to my car and headed for home. Halfway there, I got my sign. Literally. I was sitting at a stoplight when I noticed one of those A-frame placards with changeable letters tucked off to the side of a convenience store. It read:

R U CRAVING
A HOT DOG?
WE HAVE ALL-BEEF FRANKS
AND TURKEY WIENERS!
GRAB ONE AND GO!

I mean, really . . . wieners? How could that not be a sign? I instantly knew how to change the lettering, too. Part of it, anyway. I swerved into the parking lot and pulled over to the sign so that I was shielding it as much as possible. I took a few minutes to figure out the exact wording on a notepad. I checked around for witnesses, snagged my phone, and got out. I took a "before picture," and after a few minutes of frantic letter-swapping, the sign read:

CRAVING A HOT WIENER?
GRAB FRANKS WANG!
EVERY DUDE A-OK
THE ANAL BURN FEELS GOOD!

I snapped the picture, and my choice was made. I was a junior at Ash Grove High School and a contestant in the Senior Scramble. I jumped in my car and took off. I didn't even change the sign back. I was a jerk and a delinquent and a bad girl, so I figured, why bother?

When I got home, I went right upstairs and logged on to the Revolting Phoenix. I uploaded my picture, imagining how much the seniors would laugh at my brilliant re-lettering. Imagine my shock when this message popped up:

WHOA!
Your entry is up for review. This may take a day or two.
Please check back regularly to find out the status of your entry.
We'll get back to you as quickly as we can.

What? How was that possible? My entry was perfect. Wasn't it?
I reread the clue and examined my before and after

pictures of the sign. I had done everything they'd asked. The *A-OK* was a stretch in terms of language, but the clue didn't say anything about proper spelling or syntax. What was the deal?

I called Luke on my cell. There was no answer. I left him a voice mail message saying to call me PRONTO. I didn't want to say anything about the Senior Scramble since I had no idea who might have access to his phone. I checked the time; it was 6:08. He probably was finishing up his deliveries to the soup kitchen and food bank. I expected a call any minute.

I didn't hear from Luke for the rest of the night, and I didn't get approval of my entry, either. I checked constantly, but there was no change by the time I crashed at eleven thirty. I was going to be short on beauty sleep for tomorrow.

Despite my lack of sleep, the next morning I styled my hair, did my makeup, and put on skinny jeans, an asymmetrical purple top, and strappy sandals. I was fluffed and buffed and filled with that particular confidence of knowing you look fantastic.

I blasted the radio on the way to school. I found a fantastic parking spot and pulled into it. I got out, grabbed my bag, tossed my hair, and strode into school, determined to find Luke and make him explain what was happening with my entry. If I had to flirt and charm my way to it, there'd be no problem. I was all set.

Right away, I knew something was wrong. The dirty looks were back. Narrowed eyes sneered from all sides. I heard nasty names tossed at me in low tones. Why? What happened?

Had something happened with the Senior Scramble? Maybe we'd been found out. I made a beeline for the senior hallway to find Luke and see if he knew anything. When I got there, he wasn't anywhere in sight. I zoomed through the hallways of the school, surprised at how well I knew them already. He was nowhere.

The bell rang, so I had no choice but to go to homeroom. I sat in the back corner again because it was the safest place. Even so, I heard "hypocrite" and "bitch" whispered here and there around the room. Something had seriously gone down, and I had no idea what.

I found out at lunch. I plopped down with Cy and Jenna and they didn't say a word to me. "What is going on?" I cried.

Cy raised one eyebrow. "What do you mean, 'what's going on'? You know damn well what's going on."

"No, I don't," I said firmly. "I swear!"

Jenna and Cy shared a look, and then Jenna said, "You really don't?"

"I swear I have no idea."

Jenna slid down the bench to speak quietly. "You didn't send around that picture of Luke?"

"What picture? No!" I insisted.

"There's a picture of Luke that's gone around to everyone. He's in a Dumpster picking through the garbage. But that's not the worst of it. Check out the caption." She pulled out her phone and showed me the picture.

Oh, no.

Oh, no.

The picture. My picture. The one of Luke in the Dumpster. I almost couldn't bear to read the caption. But I had to.

Watch this SENIOR SCRAMBLE to impress the ladies! But a Meriton girl would never go slumming with him, not even to win a SCAVENGER HUNT!

CHAPTER 22

NO! NO! NO! NO! NO! WHERE DID THIS COME FROM?

Not only did it humiliate Luke, it completely blew the lid off the Senior Scramble! Who could have done this? Who would hate me that much? How did they get this picture? No one even knew about it!

Then it hit me.

"Oh my God," I said to Cy and Jenna. "Tara."

"Who's Tara?" Cy asked.

"My best friend," I said, reading the caption again in horror.

"Correction," Cy said. "Ex-best friend."

Tara was the only other living person who had seen that picture of Luke. She must have sent it to herself or uploaded it to her Facebook page or something while I was in the dressing room. She was that mad about Friday night? Mad enough to do this? To purposely sabotage my entire life at Ash Grove? To humiliate someone she'd never even met? Someone I cared about? I never knew Tara could be that cruel.

"I don't know what to do," I said, barely whispering.

Cy glanced over my shoulder and hitched up his chin. "You'd better figure it out fast, because Luke's here."

I spun around to see Luke striding toward me like a

soldier. His face was rigid. My heart crumpled. I stood up and ran to him. "Luke, it wasn't me, I swear! Please, let me explain . . ."

He held up his hand to stop me in my tracks. "I've spent half the morning in the office with your father and the vice principal. I'm not interested in another lecture. Especially if you're going to lie to me."

"I'd never lie to you," I said.

He acted like he didn't even hear me. "Because I just don't think I can take it, Blythe. On the one hand, here's this gorgeous, brilliant, amazing girl who makes it impossible for me to focus on anything else. On the other hand, here's this girl I know nothing about. A girl who believes I deliberately humiliated her by—of all things—posting an unflattering picture of her. That's really the kicker. A picture? How could that be a coincidence? I mean, it begs the question: Was this your plan all along, to get revenge on me and the entire school for embarrassing you?"

"NO." I tried to grab his arms, but he stepped back from me. "I don't—"

"And if that is the case—"

"It's not!"

"If that is the case, I have to say, I'm impressed with the lengths you went to. Even to the point of spending the afternoon *in that Dumpster with me!*" He stabbed the air with his pointer finger as if the Dumpster were right next to us. "I mean, that's a hell of a revenge plan! You'd have set everything up so nicely. You could take down the Senior Scramble along with me and most of the junior and senior classes. If you were lucky, you could even get me suspended and keep me from graduating."

"None of that's true!" I cried. Why wouldn't he stop and let me explain?

"I honestly hope it's not," he said. "Because I want to believe that you had nothing to do with this. I truly do. But the fact is, you took that picture. And why else would you?"

"I was mad then, but . . ."

"Sure, I admit, it's embarrassing. I get it. Especially when you get grilled by the administration about the hidden meaning in a caption you didn't even write. I mean, that caption speaks for itself, Blythe." The hurt and disappointment in his eyes cut through me.

"It was Tara!" Tears streamed down my cheeks. "I didn't write it!"

"The other fact is, I really don't know anything about you, Blythe. I thought I did. I thought you'd shown me who you really are. But for all I know, you're an exceptional liar."

"I'm a terrible liar!" I cried. "Ask Cy and Jenna! They know! Luke, I never would have sent that picture around! I even told you I took it, back in the Dumpster! Why would I do that if I was planning to use it to get back at you? I'm not trying to get revenge on anyone for that stupid picture of me. God, I don't even care about it anymore!" I spun around to face everyone in the cafeteria. All eyes were on Luke and me. "Look, everyone!" I shouted. I shoved both index fingers up my nose. "I'm picking my nose! I'm a nose picker! Blythe McKenna is a nose picker! Everyone grab your phones and take a picture! Get a good shot!"

Nobody moved.

I dropped my hands and faced Luke. "I would rather have ten thousand humiliating pictures of me plastered all over the East Coast than have you not trust me."

His face was a stone. His arms, iron bars soldered across his chest. Still, he seemed to consider what I'd said. "What did you mean by, 'It was Tara'?" he asked.

I rushed to answer him. "She's the only person I've ever shown it to, and she's extremely mad at me right now. I didn't think *this* much, though. The only explanation I can come up with is that she sent herself the picture off my phone, added the caption, and sent it out to go viral all over Ash Grove so I'd be blamed for it. Then you'd hate me, the Senior Scramble would be discovered, and everyone else would hate me too. The person she's trying to hurt is me, Luke, not you. I'm so sorry she used you to do it." Suddenly, thick sobs rose up from deep in my body and heaved out of me. I couldn't control them. I couldn't breathe. "She's my best friend! Why would she do that?" I ground my palms into my eyes to plug the tears. I ached to have Luke wrap his arms around me. To bury my face in the hollow of his neck. To feel his breath on me.

He didn't move.

I wiped my eyes on my sleeves and searched Luke's face for a glimmer of understanding. He stared at the floor in silence. His jaw flexed and the muscles in his neck bound up and released like thick rubber bands. Finally, Luke locked eyes with me. He held them for a moment, then took two steps backward, pivoted, and stalked out of the cafeteria without another word.

I stood there completely numb until I felt a hand clamp on my shoulder. Cy was in my ear. "Dude, Luke Pavel never skips class. If he ditched to come find you, he must really be hot for your ass."

Jenna appeared on the other side of me, carrying both of our bags. "Come on, Blythe," she said. "Let's leave these drama-addict freaks here to feed."

The three of us walked out of the cafeteria. Just outside the doors we saw Vice Principal Hinkler striding toward us, looking like a sour-faced rat. "Mr. Mason and Ms. DeLuca, return to lunch. Ms. McKenna, come with me. The principal and I would like to have a few words."

Cy and Jenna stood rooted at my sides until I told them it was okay. Jenna gave my hand a squeeze, and they peeled away from me. Cy glowered at the vice principal. I could've kissed both of those wasteoid, emo, punk "bad" kids. I never knew two more genuinely good people in my life.

I trailed behind Vice Principal Hinkler not out of choice, but because she wouldn't let me walk beside her, just like Darlene. She sped up every time I tried. This woman had some serious control issues.

We got to the main office and the VP walked right past all the secretaries without acknowledging any of them. I nodded politely and they gave me sheepish smiles. Even Gladys gave me a sympathetic look from behind her kitten-festooned desk. Once inside Dad's office, Hinkler clapped the door shut and stood beside my father like a sentry.

Dad was in his chair and motioned for me to sit. "Have a seat, Blythe."

I did. And guess what? I tossed that damn lady look right out the window. I let the anger and disappointment and fear on my face ring out loud and clear.

"I never thought I'd see you, of all people, in this office under these conditions." He blew a heavy puff of air out of his cheeks. "Can you please explain this?" He slid a piece of paper toward me. I didn't have to look at it directly; I knew it was my photo of Luke.

"It's a picture I took," I said, and nothing more. Seventh rule of lying: Avoid it if at all possible.

"So you don't deny taking it?" the vice principal asked, rising up on her toes, positively titillated by my confession.

"I just told you that," I answered.

"With what? Your camera? Your phone? What?" Her voice was shrill and impatient.

"My phone."

"Did you upload it or e-mail it to anyone?" Dad asked, knotting his fingers together on his desk.

"No."

"Did someone else have access to your phone?" the VP asked.

"Sure," I said.

"Like whom?" she demanded.

"Like *who*?" I corrected her. She scowled at me. I smiled sweetly. "Well, let's see. Lots of people. My friends, my brother . . . my *parents*, of course." That made Dad straighten up in his chair and smooth his tie. He stole a glance at the vice principal, who no doubt liked to blame parents for ill-behaved children.

Dad cleared his throat. "Do you know how it managed to begin circulating among the student body?"

"No, I don't." Also true. I didn't know for sure; I had a prime suspect, but no facts.

"You have no idea who sent this harassing picture," Hinkler bleated, pointing to the paper.

I shrugged. Technically, she didn't ask a question, so I didn't feel the need to reply. I wasn't sure why I was bothering to protect Tara, especially since she didn't even go to Ash Grove. Maybe it was instinct. Maybe I didn't want to snitch. Or maybe I couldn't fully accept that she would hurt me like this. I needed to know for sure first.

My father dropped his head and waved one hand above it as if to brush away everyone's argument. He said, "Well, the point is, it got e-mailed to everyone and it's online. Since you took the picture, you're the only responsible party anyone can point to."

"As the administrator in charge of discipline," Vice Principal Hinkler said, "I'd like to remind you of our zero-tolerance policy on bullying." Her eyes flashed with delight. "It carries a mandatory penalty of expulsion." My dad held up a hand to silence the VP. She crimped her mouth shut with contemptible obedience.

"Obviously, we don't want this," he said. Judging from the bitter look on the VP's face, she disagreed. Dad went on. "So, Vice Principal Hinkler and I have come to a possible resolution." He glanced up at her smug face. Then back to me. "It's obvious from this caption that the Senior Scramble has been taking place, despite being officially banned by me."

When he said this, everything below my neck was a buzzing ball of frenzied anxiety. Above my neck, every muscle was completely relaxed and complacent. Eighth rule of lying: Keep your poker face. Never have a "tell" or a physical gesture that will give yourself away and let your opponent know you're bluffing.

"Judging from this picture, it's likely you're even involved," Dad said, "which I sincerely hope is not the case. At any rate, if you can point to any students involved or responsible for the illicit Senior Scramble, then Vice Principal Hinkler and I have agreed to reduce your punishment from expulsion to a two-week suspension."

The VP sneered, "Personally, I think it sets a dangerous precedent, but of course, I defer to Principal McKenna's judgment." She pursed her lips together sourly.

The irony of it was amusing. A month ago, when I didn't want to get anywhere near Ash Grove, I was forced to be here. Now that I wanted to stay, they were threatening to kick me out. Did they really think they could manipulate me so easily? As if they could dangle my "permanent record" in front of me like a bone for a dog and I'd dance for them?

As if I'd betray Luke and Jenna and Cy? As if I'd turn on anyone involved in the Senior Scramble?

As if I were that traitorous. As if I were that cruel. As if I were that weak.

As if.

"*I can name everyone involved,*" I lied plainly. I paused to let that tantalizing bit of misinformation soak into VP Hinkler's tiny brain and make her salivate. "But I won't. I'm not a snitch. Besides, I made the mistake of ruining the Senior Scramble once. I won't do it again."

The VP's face hardened again into sharp angles and dark chasms. "So you're taking part in it?"

Dad looked to me for the answer, and a shade of desperation fell across his face. I realized that he wasn't worried about how this would look to the school board or how this would affect his authority. Dad was worried for me. He was concerned about my security and my future. Not his own. As much as it might have crushed him, if he had asked me that question, I would have been entirely truthful. I would have confessed my role and accepted the consequences.

But it was *Finkler* who had asked the question. I looked straight in her dead eyes and said, "I didn't say that. All I said was that I could name everyone involved."

Dad puffed out his cheeks. "Well, that's a relief, at least," he mumbled. He didn't realize that I hadn't answered her question. He'd heard what he wanted to hear. Or needed to hear.

"We *will* find out," VP Hinkler growled. "And everyone involved will be suspended, you can be sure. Juniors, seniors, everyone." She leaned over and tapped the picture of Luke with one of her bony claws. "In fact, I think it's pretty clear from this picture that Luke Pavel is strongly connected to it." She narrowed her eyes at me and smiled. "Perhaps his expulsion will send a message to the rest of the insubordinate participants, and they'll drop the whole thing."

My heart stopped.

She knew. Either she figured it out from the picture, or she'd seen us in the hallways or heard rumors, but that evil witch knew Luke and I had been dating. Now she was using that against me, threatening me with Luke's expulsion in addition to my own if I didn't turn everyone in.

"Perhaps Blythe needs a little time to think," Dad said, bracing himself against his desk. "Maybe she should sleep on it."

VP Hinkler clenched her yellow, uneven teeth. "Fine," she said. Her tone said the opposite.

Dad rubbed the tops of his knees and stood up. "All right, Blythe. You have until tomorrow morning to determine your course of action. Please report here first thing, before homeroom." He checked his watch. "You may return to class now."

Suddenly, he was Principal McKenna again and I was nothing more than a random anonymous student. Someone he wouldn't see until the next day, not someone he shared a bathroom and a refrigerator and a HOME with.

It was time for the lady look, because I had no intention of going back to class. How could I when everyone was so enraged with me? My emotions had been worn out and totally depleted from the confrontations with Dad and Luke. I didn't have anything left to use in my defense against the slurs and sneers from everyone. I needed to get out of there. So I plastered on a solid-gold lady look, walked out of the office, turned down the hall, and kept going until I was out the door.

I got in my car and burst into tears again. I had lost my

best friend, lost Luke, lost any chance of survival at Ash Grove, and shot my future plans to hell. I cranked the ignition, but I didn't know where to drive. I couldn't go home. I couldn't go to Meriton. I couldn't stay here. There was only one place left.

CHAPTER 23

THE MOMENT I WALKED INTO MS. FRANNY AND MS. Eulalie's room, I knew something was wrong. Ms. Franny screamed at me, "Get the hell out!" The skin on her face was sallow and sunken. Her finger shook as she pointed at me. She was slipping off her pillow.

"Ms. Franny, it's me, Blythe!" I rushed over to her so she could see me. Ms. Eulalie's bed was empty. She must have gone to get a bath or her hair done or something. She didn't usually schedule those things on Mondays, though. "Where's Ms. Eulalie?" I asked.

"Is that you, Blythe?" Ms. Franny asked, peering at me through the dusky slits between her sagging eyelids. "I can't . . . I can't figure anything out. Is that you?" She seemed to be staring straight through me like the answer was across the room.

I sat beside her on the edge of her bed. "It's me, Ms. Franny. It's Blythe. I've just been crying, and my makeup has run." I grabbed a tissue from the box on her nightstand and tried to wipe off my smeared mascara. "It's me." I waited for her to ask why I was crying. She didn't.

Ms. Franny slowly brought my face into focus. "Oh,

Blythe. When did you get here? You're supposed to come on Mondays." Her voice drifted off.

What was going on? "It *is* Monday, Ms. Franny. Are you okay? Where's Ms. Eulalie?"

"Gone," she said, indicating Ms. Eulalie's neatly made bed. "The old nag's finally gone." She touched her face with her frail, trembling hand like she was checking something but couldn't remember what.

I gingerly took her hand in both of mine and forced her to look at me. "What do you mean, *gone*?"

Strands of loose gray hair fell around Ms. Franny's face as she turned to Ms. Eulalie's empty bed. "A couple of nights ago she couldn't breathe. Stopped altogether. They took her to the hospital, and she never came back. That's what I mean, gone." Her line of vision slipped over to the window. "I always said I wanted my own room anyway." She squeezed her eyes shut and grimaced like she'd just been stuck in the belly with a needle. She wrenched her hand out of my grasp.

"Ms. Franny? I'll be right back, okay?" I slid off her bed and ran to find Darlene. I spotted her coming out of one of the resident rooms. She was shoving the end of a chocolate bar into her mouth. "Darlene!" I called. She glanced at me but didn't acknowledge me at all. She lumbered back to her desk and sat down. I stormed up to her desk, planted both hands on it, and leaned down to her face. "When someone calls your name," I growled, "it is impolite not to RESPOND." My swollen eyes and smeared makeup must've looked pretty scary because she reared back into her squeaking chair.

"I . . . I didn't hear you," she lied.

"What happened to Ms. Eulalie?" I demanded.

Darlene started rustling and straightening some of the disorganized papers on her cluttered desk. She kept her pudgy eyes off me. "She was taken to St. Michael's Hospital on Friday with pneumonia," she said as easily as if it were the weather. "Probably got sick when you took her outside last week."

I glowered at Darlene like I wanted to wipe her off the bottom of my shoe after stomping her into a pulp. "No, she did not," I said. "Insinuate that one more time, and I'll punch you right in the face." Where was this coming from?

All I knew was that Darlene was an obstacle between me and the truth about Ms. Eulalie, and nothing was going to prevent me from finding out what happened. "Now, tell me how she is." My gut was twisted into such a knot. Ms. Eulalie couldn't be dead. It was unacceptable.

Darlene seemed to draw a sick pleasure from my obvious concern. "It was touch and go," she sneered. "She died."

My heart fell to my stomach.

Then Darlene said, "Twice. They revived her both times. She's in intensive care."

I worked very hard to keep my voice level and empty of fear. "Will she be coming back?"

Darlene said, "From what I hear, it doesn't look good." She licked her lips and gave me a greasy smirk. I never wanted to slap someone so badly before. I'd never wanted to slap someone at all before. Now, it took all of my mother's dignity training to keep my hands on top of that desk and not around Darlene's beastly neck.

"Does Ms. Franny know?" I asked.

"Know what?" She popped a piece of gum in her mouth and chewed noisily.

"That Ms. Eulalie's NOT DEAD."

Darlene shrugged, looking apathetic. "How should I know?"

Unbelievable.

I leaned closer to her. She drew back. "You should know," I said, "because you're supposed to care about the welfare of the residents, not about how much candy you can steal from them while they're asleep, you bitch."

Darlene crossed her arms and leaned back in her chair, looking smug. "Blythe McKenna, you are officially dismissed from the volunteer program at Shady Acres. Leave your ID badge at the front desk." She raised one hand and waved at me. "Buh-bye."

I tore the badge from my shirt and tossed it at her. I turned to head back to Ms. Franny. Darlene said, "Where do you think you're going?"

I reeled around and said, "Visiting hours don't end until seven. I'm visiting my friend." I marched down the hall.

"I'm calling security!" she cried after me.

"Go ahead," I yelled over my shoulder. I had zero doubt that she would. I knew I'd only have a couple of minutes with Ms. Franny. I veered into her room and sat on her bed again. She kept staring out the window while she plucked hairs from the shaggy braid on her shoulder.

"Ms. Franny?" I whispered. She seemed startled and turned her head as though she'd just noticed me. "Ms. Franny, I can't stay today. I'm sorry. I have to go, but I just want you to know that Ms. Eulalie is still in the hospital and they hope she'll be back soon. So don't worry about her, okay?"

Ms. Franny's eyes brightened a tiny bit, but she said, "Who said I was worried?" Her face darkened again. Her jaw hardened. "I don't need that old cow." She rolled over in bed and curled up as tightly as her stiffened joints would allow. I stroked her back, feeling the sharp edges and jagged turns of her bones beneath her nightgown.

Soon there were heavy footsteps in the doorway. "Goodbye, Ms. Franny," I whispered, and slipped out of the door before the security guard had a chance to say a word.

My heart was breaking for Ms. Franny and was full of worry for Ms. Eulalie. I thought about going to the hospital to see her, but I knew they only let family visit patients in the ICU. Of course, Ms. Eulalie's husband and children were gone and the rest of her extended family lived back in Alabama, so it was likely nobody was there for her. She and Ms. Franny were pretty much all each other had, no matter how much they bickered and fought. They were closer than sisters.

Tara and I had been closer than sisters too. We'd keep track of each other all day so it seemed like we were never apart. We could communicate with just a gesture or an expression. We filled in the blanks of each other.

How could she destroy all that?

I had to know. I needed to know why Tara had done that, and I needed to know now. Immediately. Forget the fact that school hours weren't over. I couldn't get to Meriton High School fast enough.

When I got there, I walked in the main entrance, which led to the front office. I acted like I was still a student there, and since the secretaries vaguely recognized me, they didn't bat an eye when I signed a fake name into the late-student ledger. I even waved, smiled, and thanked them when they buzzed me through the inner door.

It was 1:27. Tara would be in study hall on the second floor. I scaled the stairs and navigated the familiar turns in the hallways without even thinking. I reached the room, rapped on the door, and opened it a crack. From where I stood, the teacher, Mr. Papadopoulos, could see me, but the students couldn't. Mr. Papadopoulos always liked me, so he smiled. Before he had a chance to say my name, I said, "I need Tara Henry, please," as if nothing was out of the ordinary. He called her name. I stepped back from the door so she wouldn't see me until she came out. When she shut the door and turned around, she froze and her eyes saucered. It was as good as a confession. She opened her mouth, but I didn't let her get a sound out.

"Have a little fun with Photoshop last night, T?" I said sarcastically. "And you compiled a nice mailing list of e-mails too. So much work, just to be malicious and cruel."

She looked up to the left and nibbled her pinky cuticle. I knew the move. She was feigning boredom to mask her nervousness. "It wasn't *malicious and cruel*," she imitated. "I did it for your own good."

"What?" I cried "How? By making Luke and everyone in Ash Grove hate me? AGAIN? They had just started to accept me!"

"I'm not surprised they're accepting you, because you're changing into one of them. You're like an Ash Grove clone. I can't stand by and watch them turn you into white trash. Literally! You were in a garbage Dumpster, for God's sake, Blythe, and you thought it was romantic. You know why I sent out that picture? To remind everyone at Ash Grove who you are. To remind YOU who you are. To let them know that you're better than they are, and they're ruining you. Luke Pavel is ruining you. Those Ash Grove assholes deserve to have everything ruined for them in return!"

None of that was true. Tara had spun out this ludicrous story to validate her actions and conceal the fact that she was bitter and jealous and hurt. I wasn't turning into trash. I knew that, because the people at Ash Grove weren't trash. Even if Tara believed they were, it wouldn't make a difference. She still based her excuse for why she did it on a pile of lies so thick that even she believed them. I'd seen her manipulate her parents like that a hundred times before.

It was definitely a moment for profanity.

"Bullshit," I said. "You were mad and you wanted to hurt me. That's all. Go ahead and justify it any way you want, but I know you, Tara, and I know exactly why you did this. Your face said everything when you walked out here. You weren't happy to see me. You were scared. You know you screwed me over. Now you're lying to me about it and probably lying to yourself too. Nobody at Ash Grove has ever lied to me. Not a single person. Yes, sometimes the truth hurts, but you know what? I'd rather hear the truth from my enemies than lies from my friends."

I spun around and left. I figured she'd shout after me. Call me back so she could apologize. So we could make up. Go back to before.

She didn't. Each step I took put another mile between us.

I got in the car and drove. I couldn't go home and face my mother. One look from her and I would splinter into a thousand pieces. I was already a spiderweb of fractures. The parts of my life seemed to be falling away from me, and the more I tried to hold them together, the worse the breaks became.

I needed to see Luke.

That's the only thing I was sure of. Everything else was quicksand.

School wouldn't be out for half an hour. I drove around. Somehow, I ended up at our new house. I hated that house. I'd been fooled by its promise of new beginnings. All it really stood for was the end of things I loved. My home. My friends. My future.

Luke.

The house had lied to me. Don't hide, it had said. Let them see the real you, flaws and all. Well, I had. And it cost me everything. Nobody liked what they saw. Everyone preferred perfect Blythe. Cheerful, organized, put-together Blythe. Well rounded, well dressed, and well liked. It was a package deal.

I got out of the car and stood on the landscaped paver walkway. My eyes darted from picture window to porch to eaves to roof to siding to garage to chimney and back to picture window. It was a flawless exterior. A perfect facade. Like perfect Blythe had been.

I reached down, wrestled one of the paver stones from the edge of the walk, and hurled it as hard as I could. It smashed through the front window, sending shards of glass everywhere. It felt good to watch something shatter besides me. To hear it smash. A slab of the cracked pane dangled from the frame and then sliced through the air as it fell. "How does it feel?" I jeered at the house. The gaping hole in the window marred the house's facade like a toothless mouth. I opened mine to mimic it.

The window beside the picture window was still unbroken. I bent down and wrenched another paver stone loose. It was cool and dense in my hand. "This might hurt," I sneered. I cocked back my arm, took aim at the remaining pane of glass . . .

. . . and paused.

I was talking to a house. I was trying to hurt a house. *A house can't feel,* I said to myself. What was I doing, then? Who did I think I was hurting here? My friends? My father?

I heard a loud *BLEEP* behind me. I turned and was blinded by the flashing red and blue lights of an Ash Grove police cruiser pulling in behind my car. The answer to my question instantly fell upon me like a sheet of ice water.

The person I was trying to hurt was myself.

And I had done the job.

CHAPTER 24

"DROP THE ROCK AND STEP AWAY FROM THE HOUSE," boomed a voice over a loudspeaker. A moment later, two uniformed officers exited the car simultaneously. One started talking into the radio on his shoulder. The other one spun me around and locked me in handcuffs before I could say a word.

As the officer dragged me to the cruiser, he said, "I'm placing you under arrest for trespassing, vandalism, criminal mischief, and attempted robbery. You have the right to remain silent . . ." He prattled off the rest of the Miranda rights as he stood me against the cruiser and patted me down. He opened the back door, put one hand on my head, and shoved me inside.

Two minutes later, the cop's partner and some old woman in an ugly floral apron that had to be from the seventies peered at me through the window. "That's her!" I heard the woman say. "I saw her from my kitchen window two weeks ago snooping around the house. I knew she'd be back. Probably wants to rob the place for drug money!"

So nice of you to welcome me to the neighborhood, I thought. *What a treat it will be to see your smiling face every single day.*

I went into zombie mode from there. I mean, really, who needs to remember the specifics about getting fingerprinted, photographed, and tossed into the local jail at sixteen?

I sat in that rank, filthy cell and knew one thing for sure. I was alone. Physically, socially, emotionally alone. And probably would be for a while. My dad had already been disappointed in me at school; I couldn't imagine how ashamed he'd be now. This would be a huge public embarrassment for him. What school board would appoint a superintendent with an expelled, criminal daughter? The irony was, none of this would've happened if he hadn't tried to get that position in the first place. I had to face the fact that his decision was just the starting point, though. I took over from there. I was the one who dug my heels in about going to Ash Grove. I was the one who made everyone there hate me by ruining the Senior Scramble, the yearbook, and *Buried Ashes*. I was the one who went against my dad's rules and re-launched the Senior Scramble underground. I took the picture of Luke. I smashed the window.

And I did use Tara. I had to acknowledge that truth. Maybe I hadn't seen it—or didn't want to see it—just as Tara claimed not to have seen how the viral picture of Luke would hurt me. We were so alike. It was obvious now that when I persuaded Tara to throw herself at James, I was putting my own needs before hers. Wow. That was the same charge I had leveled at Dad for the past month.

I curled up on the cold cement bench and laid my head on my arms. My mind drifted and my body shut down. I wanted to sleep, but it was impossible with the noise of the jail and the rank stink of urine and body odor permeating the walls of my cell.

About an hour later, the sound of heavy clinking and the scraping of metal brought me back to reality. I watched the cell door creep open to reveal a stern, heavyset officer. On either side of him were my parents.

I wanted to bolt upright and sprint into my mom's embrace, but I held back to gauge my parents' temperament first. Mom headed straight for me and wrapped me in her arms. "What happened, Blythe?" she said into my hair. "Why did you do that? Why would you smash a window at the house?"

I glanced at Dad since he knew part of the reason, having threatened me with expulsion earlier. Had he told Mom, though? He stared off into the corner of the jail cell, looking haggard.

"I had a rough day," I said. I didn't want to give too much information, especially about ditching school. I didn't have the strength to go over the details again anyway. I'd gone over them a hundred times in my head.

"Your father mentioned what happened in school," she said.

So she did know.

"Everyone has rough days, but they don't go around committing crimes and destroying private property!" Dad bellowed. "What on earth came over you?"

"I flipped out," I said. "I'm so sorry. I'll pay for the window."

"You're damn right you will," Dad said. "Along with

some additional repercussions. You're grounded until further notice. You may go to school and to Shady—"

"*Scott*," Mom said firmly. His eyes snapped to her. "Can we discuss this later?" she asked, although it was hardly a suggestion. "Let's get Blythe home. She's been through enough."

Dad shoved his hands in his jacket pockets and turned his back to us, but he stayed quiet.

"Does that mean I can go?" I asked.

"They dropped the charges," Mom said. "Dad showed them the agreement of sale on the new house, explaining that we were days from closing and essentially, we were the owners. You're a minor and have no previous record, so they decided to show you leniency."

"Thanks, Dad," I mumbled to his back. He nodded briskly without turning around.

Mom drew me to her and squeezed me again. "I was so worried for you," she whispered, almost more to herself than to me. "I wish you'd tell us if something is bothering you this badly. We may not be able to fix it, but at least we can be there for you so you're not going through it alone."

I glanced back and forth between them. *You're too busy*, I wanted to say. *You're too wrapped up in your own problems.* Instead, I said, "You have enough on your plate already."

"Don't be ridiculous," Mom said, petting my hair. "You're our first priority." Dad coughed. Mom kissed my head. "All right now, let's get you home."

"I'll drop you off," Dad said to her. "I'm going back to the school. I have paperwork."

Mom blinked. "Can't it wait? I think Blythe needs us right now." Dad's expression clearly said that he'd had enough of me for one day.

"It's no big deal," I said. "I'm okay. I'll be fine."

That might have been my biggest lie yet.

As soon as Dad dropped Mom and me off at home, I went straight upstairs. I had a hot, extra-sudsy shower and got in my pajamas. It wasn't even dinnertime, but I didn't care. I wasn't going anywhere.

The next thing I did was call Luke. He didn't pick up. Over the next hour, I left three voice mail messages, but I didn't bother leaving four. It was useless. Obviously he wasn't going to call back. I needed to do something to show him that I was sincere and that I was sorry.

I pulled out my enormous anthology of Shakespearean plays and sonnets. There was a particular sonnet I was looking for. I flipped through the pages in a robotic rhythm until I found it. I read through it several times to make sure it said what I remembered. It was an apology between two people who had hurt each other in similar ways. It was an admission of thoughtlessness and guilt and a plea for mutual forgiveness.

I typed it into an e-mail for Luke.

from blythespirit@gmail.com

to: lpavel@hotmail.com

subject: I'm so sorry

For you:

"That you were once unkind befriends me now,
And for that sorrow which I then did feel
Needs must I under my transgression bow,
Unless my nerves were brass or hammer'd steel.
For if you were by my unkindness shaken,
As I by yours, you've pass'd a hell of time;
And I, a tyrant, have no leisure taken
To weigh how once I suffer'd in your crime.
O, that our night of woe might have remember'd
My deepest sense, how hard true sorrow hits,
And soon to you as you to me, then tender'd
The humble salve which wounded bosoms fits!
 But that your trespass now becomes a fee;
 Mine ransoms yours, and yours must ransom me."

—Blythe (and William S.)
Only with you, I was always true.

I hit Send.

I knew I probably wouldn't get a response. It wouldn't surprise me if Luke never spoke to me again. At least I'd said the things I wanted to say to him at lunch. All I could do was hope he'd believe me. And possibly forgive me.

Next, I logged on to the Revolting Phoenix to see if there was any notice about the breach in secrecy. There was. It said that the administration had no concrete evidence of the Senior Scramble, so everyone should sit tight because more would be known tomorrow. I guess word had gone around that I had until morning to spill the names. Good old Gladys.

I clicked over to check the status of my entry. It was still pending approval. I doubted approval would ever come now. I was pretty sure that no matter what happened tomorrow, I'd be exiled from the scavenger hunt. I couldn't win it anyway. Cy and Jenna were already on the tenth and final clue. Good for them. If anyone deserved to win a delinquent contest, they did. I hoped the rumor about the prize was true.

Mom called me for dinner, even though I had told her I wasn't hungry. I logged off the website, deleted my browsing history, and trudged downstairs for meatloaf I didn't want.

Dad didn't come home for dinner. In a way, I was relieved. In a way, I felt guilty. Family dinners had always been important to Dad, yet I'd driven him away from one. At least Zach was enjoying it. He kept sneaking winks and sly grins at me. He figured that my arrest would get him major coolness points with his new Ash Grove buddies. I'd hoped to keep my jail experience out of the general public rumor mill, but apparently, the cops had come to school and told Dad about my arrest in front of Gladys and the secretaries and everyone else who happened to be in the front office. He was sure everyone from the custodian to the school board knew about my arrest. Mom had relayed all of this information to me over the meatloaf.

After I had dissected my food for about thirty minutes, Mom excused me and I retreated to my room.

Sometime after midnight, my appetite showed up. I crawled out of bed and crept down to the kitchen. I made myself a peanut butter sandwich and went to carry it upstairs when something in the family room caught my eye. It was the silhouette of someone sitting in the dark. There was only one person it could be. "Dad?" I said. "Is that you?"

"Honey," he said. "Why are you up so late?" He'd never sounded so dejected. I never thought I'd be the one to make him that way.

"I was hungry," I said.

"Oh."

Silence.

I stepped into the darkened room. "Dad? I'm sorry. About everything. The house, school . . . and especially about pretty much ruining your shot at superintendent. I've messed up so many things, but I never meant to screw that up. I swear."

Dad let out a deep long sigh that seemed to echo out of some hidden place inside him. "I don't care about that, Blythe. All I care about is you and your future. I'm worried that I've messed that up for you. I just . . . I never dreamed that things could get this out of hand."

"Me either," I said. "One thing just kept leading to another. I didn't know how far was too far. Until I got there."

"I just don't understand why you did any of it, though. Breaking rules, lying, vandalizing the new house . . . It's like you were somebody else. Why did you do those things?"

The first lines from the sonnet directly after the one I sent Luke popped into my head. *"'Tis better to be vile than vile esteemed,"* I quoted, *"when not to be receives reproach of being."*

Dad nodded slowly in the dim room. He said softly, *"And they that level at my abuses reckon up their own."* Here he was, still that high school English teacher my mother brought home to her parents. The words seemed to mean something more to him. "How true," he mumbled to himself. "How true."

He was silent again. I was afraid to speak.

"Everything's my fault, Blythe. Not yours," he said. "I've been so focused on getting that job that I didn't see how it was negatively affecting you. Or if I did see it, I excused it away. I never should have pulled you out of Meriton. You were on a good track there. You were so rock solid that I convinced myself you'd transition to Ash Grove without a hiccup." He shook his head. He held one hand above the other and pressed them together, lacing his spread fingers. "I've been trying to force your future success to mesh into the fabric of mine." He dropped his hands. "So selfish. It should be the other way around."

"But Dad, you're doing it for the family. You want a better life for us. That's what you said."

"That's what I told myself too. Very convincingly. I guess it's true, but not in the way you think. It doesn't have to do with social status or being able to buy expensive clothes and cars, or even paying for Bryn Mawr. It has to do with how you and Zach will live your lives. I don't want you and your brother to have to make concessions when you get older. I don't want you to have to settle for less in life and then feel like you have to defend or explain or excuse the choices you've made. Or had to make."

He shook his head and looked at the shadowed floor between his feet. "I've watched your mom do that for twenty years. I hear her defending me to your grandparents—and I know she's doing it because she loves me—but, God, it kills me. It kills me. Because she shouldn't have to do it at all. That's not what I want for her. I want her to be proud of her life and her choice in a husband. I want to be good enough so that there's no need for explanation or defense. I want to give her back the lifestyle she sacrificed when she married me. The one she's lived without, all these years. I owe it to her. And she deserves it."

"Dad, you don't owe Mom anything. There's no way she'd ever say you owe her."

"She denies it, but it's there. The debt is still there."

The way he said that reminded me of the last two lines of the sonnet I had sent Luke. Most textbooks translate them as roughly, "I hurt you, but you hurt me first, so now we're even."

I had a different interpretation, especially of the very last two words. They're not "ransom mine," they're "ransom me." Deliver me from the punishment for my sin.

To me, that last couplet meant, "We each screwed up and hurt the other. Let's say that your screwup was a debt you owed me. Well, my screwup now releases you of that debt. Consider the slate clean. There is nothing for me to forgive anymore. But I still need your forgiveness because that's the only way I can stop punishing myself."

As far as Mom and Dad were concerned, her short-comings might cancel out his shortcomings, but until Dad believed that Mom truly forgave him for those shortcomings and accepted him completely—flaws and all—he'd never be able to stop punishing himself for making her sacrifice so much in order to be with him.

It was insane. She'd done that the day she fell in love with him.

"Did you ever think that maybe she saw it as a fair trade?" I said. "Or even a better deal for her? She got to swap a dull, predictable, passionless life like her parents' for a fun, spontaneous, love-filled life with you. Money matters most to people who don't have it, Dad. She wasn't interested in money. You brought things to the table that nobody else could give her. Nobody. Including Gran and Granddad. Those are the things she deserves—the things only you can provide for her. She owes you a debt too, Dad."

Dad went, *"Psssh,"* and waved the idea away. A few seconds later, he sniffed and rubbed the back of his shirtsleeve across his nose. He swiped his thumb under one eye. Then the other.

I had to lighten the moment because if I didn't, I would disintegrate in tears at this man—no, he was only a guy—just this guy so in love with a girl that he was desperate to give her the world and spent his entire life trying to do it. How could I not cry? But I couldn't cry. It would make Dad cry more, and he deserved his dignity.

"Well, she definitely can be a huge pain in the neck sometimes," I joked. "You should get points for putting up with that, at least."

Dad let out one halfhearted laugh. "I know she's not perfect . . ."

"And she knows you're not perfect either, Dad, but she's

cool with it. She wants the whole package. So, come on. Yank the stick out of your butt, and get over yourself."

Dad inhaled sharply. He scoffed in jest, "Is that how you and your friends talk to each other?"

"Nah," I said. "We say, 'yank the stick out of your *ass.*'"

Dad snorted and chuckled. "Well, those must be some pretty good friends, then."

Yeah, they *were*, I almost said.

I kissed him good night before I went upstairs. He didn't ask me about the next morning, and I was glad. Because it meant that for those few minutes in the dark, he was Dad. Just my dad.

Principal Mac was nowhere to be found.

He didn't live here anyway.

Upstairs I tried to sleep, but Tara kept creeping into my thoughts. We had hurt each other. Betrayed each other. Was it possible one offense could cancel out the other? If she forgave me, could I forgive her? Could things ever go back to normal between us?

Did I want them to?

I decided not to decide that night. My brain was a wreck. I did feel the need to apologize for my part, though. I'd see what happened from there. That was as far ahead as I could plan. I debated whether to text her or e-mail. I was too exhausted for a conversation, so I opted for e-mail. It ended up sounding just like what Dad had said to me.

from: blythespirit@gmail.com

to: tarabletrouble@gmail.com

subject: Friday

You were right. I did use you. I was so focused on getting the picture that I didn't see it. Or if I did see it, I excused it away. I'm sorry.

I didn't sign it. I hadn't signed an e-mail to Tara in my life, so it seemed phony to do it now. I hit Send, shut down my laptop, switched off my light, and even turned off my phone. If Luke had wanted to respond, he would have by then. I was too exhausted to deal with anyone else. I laid my head on my pillow and put an end to that horrible day. Not that I was looking forward to the next one.

CHAPTER 25

THE MORNING SUNLIGHT TORE INTO MY ROOM LIKE an obnoxious cartoon sun trumpeting a jubilant day full of bright promise and excitement. The day I was facing was anything but jubilant. Foreboding was more accurate. I felt an ominous sense of impending change. There'd be no more fantasizing about Bryn Mawr and a handsome Haverford husband and a stunning home and a life of perfection. That whole dream seemed incredibly boring now, so it wasn't too hard to let go.

I got dressed in the same pencil skirt outfit I'd worn the first day of school. I like circular things, and it seemed fitting to wear these clothes on what would inevitably be my last day at Ash Grove.

I was ready to pull the rip cord on the agreement Luke and I had made that first week of school. If we got found out, I'd take the fall for the Senior Scramble. It'd been non-negotiable, and I was ready. On the way to school, I rehearsed my speech in my head. The picture of Luke was mine, and I took it with the intention of bullying him. Luke had nothing to do with the Senior Scramble, no matter what the caption said. I organized the underground Senior Scramble. I was solely responsible, and I would not divulge anyone's name, no matter what.

When I walked through the school doors, people all around turned and stared at me just like on my first day. Today was different, though. Today, everyone was silent. The looks on their faces weren't ones of disgust or ridicule. They were looks of trepidation, worry, and fear. They probably were scared I was going to turn them in for being in the scavenger hunt. I wanted to reassure them that I wouldn't, but I couldn't stop. I needed to get to the office. They'd find out soon enough anyway.

The crowd parted down the middle as I walked through. I'd never felt so alone in a sea of people. When I saw Jenna with her black-ringed eyes and Neapolitan hair coming toward me, I couldn't help but break out into a small smile. "Hi, Jenna," I said. "I'm so glad to see you, you have no idea. Where's Cy?"

"He's outside having a smoke," she said quietly, drawing me over to a bank of lockers inside a little alcove. "That's why I wanted to sneak in here to find you. Listen, he would never say anything, but you know the vice principal?"

"Yeah," I said.

"Cy got in trouble last month, and when he saw her, she said that it was his official 'strike two.' God, I hate her."

I nodded. "I hear ya."

"So here's the thing, if he gets one more strike, they're gonna kick him out of school. That's what she said, anyway. I just was wondering . . . I mean, everyone knows what happened yesterday, thanks to Mrs. Bolger. We know that they're making you name people in the Senior Scramble or they'll expel you for bullying or some such crap. So, I was just wondering if you could . . . not mention Cy. Otherwise he'll be expelled. He'd kill me if he knew I was asking you this, but you know . . . I had to. It's Cy."

I rubbed the sides of Jenna's arms and firmly squeezed them. "Jenna. Don't worry. I'm not naming any names. I'd stick needles in my eyes first. Hinkler's going to expel me or suspend me or whatever anyway. And you're totally nuts if you think I'd ever turn Cy or you in. Or anybody else. It's not happening, so don't worry."

I swear I saw Jenna tear up a bit. She smiled and thanked me more than once. Keeping Cy safe was all she needed in order to be happy. Cy's happiness was Jenna's happiness. I couldn't help but feel jealous of what she and Cy had. They loved each other so much, and I loved them both. They were an absolutely perfect couple of oddballs.

Less than two minutes later, I was standing outside the main office, taking a second to brace myself for what was coming. Finally, I opened the door and all the secretaries looked up at me simultaneously. I glanced at Dad's office door. It was closed. "Are they in there?" I asked Gladys. She nodded. I took a deep breath and put on the last lady look I ever intended to use. I was done with pretending things were okay when they weren't, but I couldn't let that witch of a vice principal think she'd rattled me.

I strode over to Dad's door, rapped twice, and turned the knob. I pushed open the door and nearly fell over when I saw who was inside.

Luke.

He held out his hand to motion for me to stop. "Blythe," he said, "you don't need to come in here."

I pushed his hand aside and stepped past him. "What's going on? Dad?"

Dad sat at his desk rubbing the palms of his hands together like he was trying to make fire. The VP stood next to him again. I think she enjoyed being higher than him in the room. It was she who answered my question. "Mr. Pavel has just confessed to running the prohibited Senior Scramble. He says he acted alone and won't name any of the participants. Of course, he will be suspended. For two months. Such a shame that he'll miss graduation. I suppose he can finish over the summer. Or next fall."

My eyes locked with Luke's. I held them, but I spoke to Dad. "He's lying," I said. "He had nothing to do with the Senior Scramble. It was all me."

Luke stood up, his expression imploring me to stop talking. "NO. It was my idea. Blythe is completely innocent."

"I am not!" I argued. "It was my fault!" I was growing desperate. I needed to stop him. I turned my back to Dad and the VP and whispered to Luke, "Why are you doing this?" Then even quieter, "We had a deal!"

Luke reached up and tucked a strand of my hair behind my ear like he had in the parking lot after our date. "I'm breaking the deal," he said. His voice was like spicy warm caramel. I could swim in the sound of it. Dive into it. Drown in it.

He had forgiven me.

I leaned in to Luke's ear.

"What are you whispering?" the VP cawed. My long hair had blocked their view.

I kissed Luke lightly on the cheek and whispered, "I won't let you do this," and then I spun around to face my father. "Dad, if you've ever trusted me, please trust me now. I know it seems impossible, but it was all my idea to bring back the Senior Scramble because I was the one who got it banned in the first place. Can't you see that?"

"Luke has already shown us the website," Dad said. "He couldn't know about it if he wasn't involved."

I slammed my palms down on the desk and shouted at my father, "It wasn't him! Don't you see that Luke is just trying to protect me?"

Dad's eyebrows lifted with surprise. He opened his mouth slightly and glanced at Luke. Then back to me. Then back to Luke. His eyes flashed and I knew he understood. Even more, he seemed to approve.

"Well, there's a simple solution to all this," Vice Principal Hinkler whinnied. "We can suspend you both. Unless that picture of Mr. Pavel from yesterday truly had nothing to do with the scavenger hunt, in which case Ms. McKenna faces expulsion for bullying."

"That's absurd," Luke interjected. "I have no problem with that picture. It can't be called bullying if I wasn't bullied. As a matter of fact," he said to the scowling VP, his voice and face brightening like someone had thrown a switch, "I happen to love that picture." He inched closer to me and hooked his pinky in mine. "It reminds me of my most favorite day ever."

My heart dissolved into soft, glittering dust. I struggled to take a full breath of the suddenly thick air. The walls drew close around us, and it felt like Luke and I were alone in that office and nothing could ever be wrong. Or if something was, it didn't matter.

All that mattered was that Luke's most favorite day ever had been with me.

"So I guess it'll have to be suspension for both of us," Luke chirped. We stood side by side facing my dad and the vice principal. I unhooked my pinky and entwined all of my fingers in his. When Luke closed his hand around mine, all my worry and fear of what was about to happen to us suddenly evaporated. I didn't care anymore what my future might be. No more planning everything ahead of time step by step to make sure it turned out right down the line. From now on, I was going to live my life, not wait for it.

Vice Principal Hinkler was nearly twitching with rage. Obviously, she had hoped to expel someone today. Maybe even break some legs or chop off a finger or two. "Fine," she snarled through her needle-thin lips. Dad raised a finger as though he might object, but she ignored him. "If that's what you want, then that's what you'll—"

The intercom on Dad's desk blared. Gladys's voice came through saying, "Principal Mac, could you come to the front, please?"

"Not now, Gladys," Dad responded. "I'm in the middle of something here." He opened his mouth to speak to us, but Gladys interrupted again.

"I think you should come to the front, Principal McKenna,"

she said. "There's a situation out here that requires your attention. Immediately."

The four of us in the office exchanged puzzled looks. Dad pushed himself back from his desk, stood up, and led us out of the room. Two steps through the door, he stopped short and we nearly collided into him. When he inched forward, we could see why he'd halted.

The entire junior class had crowded into the front office, spilling through the double doors and out into the hallway. Behind them, several teachers flitted around, fruitlessly trying to corral the mass. The throng hummed with chatter and energy. Up at the very front of the group, just behind the counter, stood Cy and Jenna.

Cy held up his hands and motioned for everyone to be quiet. "Principal Mac," he said, "my fellow juniors and I"—he turned and scanned the crowd, and then turned back to Dad—"and some seniors too"—chuckles ping-ponged around—"are here to surrender ourselves. We've all been involved in an illegal, immoral, and degenerate underground competition known as the Senior Scramble. We know that our confessions will get us suspended, as your policy clearly dictates"—some "oohs" shot up here and there—"but there's no way in hell we're going to let the booger girl—or the Dumpster dork—take the fall for the rest of us." Swells of clapping built up and rose as he spoke. "If you're suspending them, you might as well suspend us all. So let's get going on the paperwork, because this is gonna be a long day!"

Cheers and applause erupted behind Cy. Fists pumped

in the air and whistles flew through the room. People everywhere shouted and jumped.

Luke whispered in my ear, "Half of those people aren't
even doing the hunt."

A totally goofy smile bloomed on my face. Even people
not doing the hunt were there? Unbelievable. "They're all
here for us?" I asked.

"No." Luke shook his head. "They're all here for you."

"What?"

Luke's sideways smile was as goofy as mine. "Nobody
knew I was coming in to confess this morning. I didn't tell
anyone. Cy saw me standing here and must have figured it
out. All these people are here for you, Blythe."

I went numb.

Then I started to float.

I floated up to the ceiling and through the clouds and out
into the universe, which was the only place huge enough to
contain how full I felt with gratitude and affection.

They were here for me.

The booger girl.

The principal's kid.

Social outcast and teenage delinquent.

kate4eva.

Blythe.

Me.

I reeled myself back down into the office and immediately
started to cry. Luke wrapped his arm around my shoulders
and snuggled me. I nuzzled his neck and let my tears soak
into his cotton shirt.

"FINE!" screeched Vice Principal Hinkler. It cut through the noise of the crowd like a razor blade. "YOU ARE ALL SUSPENDED! FORM A LINE AND WE WILL PROCESS YOU WITH DUE—"

"MEREDITH!" Dad roared at her. "That is quite ENOUGH!" She froze with her hateful words still hanging in her angry mouth. Dad craned his neck toward her. "I know I charged you with overseeing student discipline, but I think you would agree that suspending the entire junior class and much of the senior class is . . ."

What was he going to say? That it was unrealistic? Inconvenient? Or some other wimpy thing?

" . . . absolutely *out of the question.*"

The place exploded again. Everyone started chanting, "PRINCIPAL MAC! PRINCIPAL MAC! PRINCIPAL MAC!"

While Vice Principal Hinkler stormed off and Dad motioned halfheartedly for people to settle down, Luke took my hand and pulled me over to the far corner of the room. "Blythe," he said, taking both of my hands, "I'm sorry about yesterday in the cafeteria. With the picture."

"I never should've taken it."

He waved me off. "I never cared about the picture. I just cared about what I thought you might have done with it. Obviously, I was wrong."

"I was telling you the truth," I whispered desperately.

"I know you were," he said. "I knew it then too, but I forced myself to question it. I'm a stupid journalist. You know. After last night when I got your e-mail, I couldn't question it anymore. I never will again, Blythe. I promise.

And I'm sorry." Luke kissed me quickly without letting go of my hands.

Dad had sent everyone back to class, and the office was emptying out. When he spotted Luke and me with our hands clasped, he snapped his fingers and pointed at us like a bad lounge singer. "You two should . . . um . . . you can get to class, then. Yup. You're dismissed."

It was a toss-up over who was blushing more, Dad or me.

Luke and I filed out of the office and into the crowd of students dispersing through the hallways. When we finally had to part, Luke whispered in his low, smoky voice, "Meet me right after school. By your car. Okay?"

I'd go anywhere for him. "Absolutely."

Over the course of the day, word spread that Dad had decided to officially reinstate the Senior Scramble. Cy had successfully argued that it was technically out of the school's jurisdiction. It was going forward, whether the administration liked it or not, so they might as well sanction it. Cy would make a fantastic attorney one day.

When the final bell rang at last, I raced out to my car. Luke wasn't there, but a note was pinned under my windshield wiper. I snatched it up. It was a single printed page that said in large black lettering, CHECK YOUR E-MAIL.

Huh?

Okay, fine. I fished out my phone, turned it on, and pulled up my e-mail account. At the top of the in-box was an e-mail sent directly from The Revolting Phoenix administrators' account. I opened it.

This is a courtesy message from the Revolting Phoenix online forum. Your profile has been updated. Please check back with the forum as soon as possible. Thank you.

What? The Senior Scramble had been official for less than a few hours and already the admins felt liberated enough to be sending e-mails around? Wow, that was fast. Did Luke know about this? Where was he, anyway? The parking lot was emptying out quickly.

I logged on to the Revolting Phoenix and a message popped up right away.

Congratulations! Your picture of item #6 has now been approved.
Here is your clue to item #7:

First, return to school and find the ragged Eagle's beak.
It will point you to the destination that you seek.
But the object of this clue is only there TODAY.
Don't delay a moment more, start hunting right away.

I was glad my sign picture was finally approved, but what was with this clue? What did it mean? My only guess was that it referred to the Ash Grove Fighting Eagles, since *Eagle* was capitalized. There were Fighting Eagle pictures and statues all over school. Which was the ragged one?

I waited another fifteen minutes. It was clear Luke wasn't coming out. The exit door hadn't opened in over ten minutes, and the last cars had pulled out of the parking lot. I called him but got his voice mail. I texted him, but there was no reply. Where was he? What should I do?

Hold on. Instead of Luke, the note was here at my car and it had led me directly to this clue. Was the clue connected with Luke's disappearance? It said that I should start hunting right away. Was I really supposed to follow it? Now? Should I give it a shot?

I waited two more minutes and then I decided to go for it. I locked my bag in the car but kept my phone with me in case Luke called. I went back inside and swung by the gym first since it was close. I knew there was an eagle statue in the vestibule outside the gym doors. When I got there, it was pretty obvious that this wasn't the ragged eagle. It was in pristine condition, gleaming with layers and layers of varnish.

I needed to find a shabby eagle. A worn-out eagle. One with paint chipped off, maybe. One where a lot of people would touch it as they went by. There was one in the main lobby of the school. That was a high-traffic area for sure. I raced through the halls, surprised that I knew them so well. I got to the lobby and examined the statue. The paint had worn off on several edges, so I checked to see where the beak pointed. It was a solid concrete wall. There was nothing there. This couldn't be the right eagle. I needed a ragged one.

Ragged. What was ragged?

Fabric was ragged. Were there any Fighting Eagles made of fabric? I had never seen a stuffed-animal Fighting Eagle in the time I'd been there. What about an eagle picture on fabric? Like a pennant.

Or a flag!

I knew exactly where to go. I sped around through the maze of halls and turned into the cafeteria one. Down at the hallway's dead end hung the huge Ash Grove Fighting Eagles flag I had seen just after starting school here. I looked closely at the flag, and sure enough, the green and yellow fabric was frayed and threadbare in many spots. Where was the eagle's beak pointing?

CHAPTER 26

THE BEAK WAS POINTING TO MY RIGHT, BUT THERE was nowhere to go. The dead end surrounded me on three sides with solid walls. I checked under the flag, but there was nothing. What could it be pointing at? Other than me, the only thing here was a rusty metal folding chair leaning up against the wall to my right. The direction the beak pointed. I couldn't imagine how a folding chair could be the answer to the clue, but I checked it out. I unfolded the chair and gasped when I found another note, this one taped to the seat. I opened it and read the verse at the top.

> You have almost solved the clue, so hang on to your hopes.
> But first there is a hunt for large manila envelopes.
> Open each, and go the way the arrow tells you to.
> Reach the end, and you will have the answer to your clue.

Also on the paper was a bold black arrow pointing straight up. Up must mean forward, I guessed, because forward was the only direction I could go to get out of this hallway. I jogged to the end and saw a manila envelope on the ground exactly where the halls intersected. It hadn't been there here five minutes ago when I passed this spot. Where had it come from? I snatched it up and opened it. Inside was a sheet of paper that said, MAY, in the same large, black font as in the note on my car. *Okay,* I thought. *Something about the month of May, perhaps?*

Below the word was an arrow pointing left. I turned and started walking. I could see another manila envelope on the floor way ahead, so I ran to it. Inside was another sheet of paper. It said, I, with an arrow pointing left again, down the hallway beside me. Off I went.

I passed two hallways before I saw the third envelope on the floor in front of the main office. It said, TAKE, and the arrow pointed through the office doors. The secretaries and staff were still milling around inside. I tucked the papers and envelopes under my arm and timidly opened the office door. I glanced around the area in front of the counter. I tried to peek inconspicuously under the waiting chairs and in the wastebasket.

I heard a quick whistle and looked up. Gladys beckoned me over to the counter. Without saying a word, she slid a manila envelope across the countertop to me. "Do you know who sent me this?" I asked. Her answer was wink and a grin before she trundled back to her kitty cat desk. I slid my finger under the envelope flap and opened it. The word was YOU.

MAY I TAKE YOU . . . ? What did that mean? Were these words in a sentence? Were they even in the right order?

Would I have to figure it out like a puzzle in the newspaper? Oh, no! Was there punctuation missing? Because, "*May I take you* seriously?" is much different than, "*May I take you* to be my wedded wife" or "*May I? Take*—*you* are welcome to it. Please help yourself." Not to mention the all caps! AGH!

I wasn't going to get the answer standing here in the office. I looked at the arrow pointing to the right. But I was turned around now, facing the counter. Did it mean to turn right from where I was standing or turn right as I exited the office? Which way?

I heard another high whistle. Gladys again. She hitched her head to her right and gave me another wink. She meant that I should turn right, out of the office. Good old Gladys, always keeping tabs on everyone else's business. I smiled, waved thank you to her, and left.

May I take you . . . May I take you . . . May I take you . . . *someplace.* That was the most logical conclusion. But where? And by whom? Was this just going to take me to another string of clues? God, I hoped not!

I spotted a manila envelope tucked between the sliding glass panes in the display case outside the auditorium. I slid it out and tore off the flap.

The word: **TO**.

The arrow: pointing right, into the auditorium.

May I take you to . . . what? To China? To paradise? To court? I pushed through the wooden double doors to the auditorium. Why would I be brought here? Was the sentence going to be *May I take you to your seat?* Ugh! So frustrating.

(But so fun!)

I trotted down the center aisle. In the very front row of seats, next to the aisle, was a chair with an envelope lying on it. I grabbed it. *RIP* went the top.

Word: THE.

May I take you to the . . . The what? The moon? The beach? The outer ring of Saturn? The edge of a cliff so I can push you off?

I checked the arrow. It went right, then zigzagged up, then went left, then down, almost in a square. HUH? I looked around. I didn't see any other envelopes nearby. What could it mean? The only thing I could do was follow it. I turned right and walked as far as the side wall of the auditorium; to my right was another aisle. To my left was . . .

Stairs! Stairs up onto the stage!

I raced up the stairs and onto the stage until I hit the curtain. I turned left and started crossing the stage. I stopped in my tracks halfway because to my left on the stage, directly down front and center, stood a movable podium. On it lay a manila envelope. I tiptoed quickly to the podium and plopped my stack of six envelopes and papers on top. I grabbed the seventh envelope and tore into it like it was a Christmas present and I was a six-year-old.

My heart stopped when I read the word.

PROM.

MAY I TAKE YOU TO THE PROM.

Ohmygod! Please let this be from Luke! Please! Please! I scanned the auditorium. The entire place was empty. Every seat. Every aisle. Where was he? Wait, was this even the last word? Maybe this wasn't the last word! There was no question mark, after all. Plus, there was another arrow. It pointed up, then it curved over and pointed down like a U-turn sign.

I had to turn around.

I spun on my heels to see Luke in a rumpled tuxedo from the costume shop, holding one last sheet of paper that said, PLEASE?

Punctuation plus etiquette. Was this guy for me or what?

I squealed like a pageant queen and jumped into his arms. I pressed my mouth to his, and he held me up off the ground as we kissed. I might as well have been out in space.

He set me back down on earth and said, "I guess that's a yes, then?"

"Uh, yeah," I said. "That's a yes. How did you do all this? When?"

"I started planning it last week. That's why your sign entry was held for 'review.' I needed to make sure that the next clue you got was mine. Just so you know, your sign entry was brilliant. The best by a mile. Everyone loved it."

"I used all the letters! And the punctuation marks!"

"I know!" He mirrored my enthusiasm. "Yeah, so originally, I had planned to do all this yesterday, but . . . yesterday was kind of a disaster."

I pinched an inch of air. "Just a little bit."

"Today was much better."

"Much, much," I agreed.

"I'll send you the real clue number seven for the Senior Scramble later."

"Don't bother," I said.

"You're not quitting now, are you?" he asked.

"First of all, Cy and Jenna are going to win. They're tearing it up. Second, I don't need that scavenger hunt because I just won my own."

"Technically, it was more of a treasure hunt," he said.

I nodded. "You're absolutely right. It was definitely for treasure. And I found the treasure. I won the prize."

He touched his forehead to mine. "Yes, you did," he whispered.

I'd won the best prize of all.

I'd won Luke.

I lifted my face and kissed him again right there, center stage, in the silent theater, with no one but us and echoes of lines from Shakespeare. My phone rang in my pocket, but I ignored it. My hands were busy running through Luke's hair as we kissed.

And kissed.

We finally pried ourselves apart after the third time my phone ding-donged to let me know there was a voice mail message. Luke laughed and said, "I know you want to get it. Just get it."

I slid my phone out of my pocket as Luke nuzzled the nape of my neck. I selected the new message and held the phone to my ear. A cheerless nasal voice said:

Hello, I'm calling for Blythe McKenna. This is Nurse Darlene from Shady Acres Nursing Home. Blythe, Ms. Calhoun has requested that I call you and tell you that she needs you here as

soon as possible. Please return this call or come to Shady Acres
during visiting hours.

My heart instantly shrank from a hot-air balloon to a nut.
I was afraid that Darlene's message meant only one thing:
Ms. Eulalie was dead.

"Luke," I heard myself barely whisper. "Can you come
somewhere with me?"

Luke drove me to Shady Acres. When we got out of his
pickup truck, the sun was bright and I could smell the early
lilacs blooming in the garden. I closed my eyes and hoped
with every cell in my body that this was a good sign and not
a lesson from the universe about contradiction and irony.

Luke took my hand as we walked through the front
doors. When I stopped to sign us in as visitors, the woman
at the desk frowned at me and then became absorbed in her
book. We turned the corner and passed Darlene's desk. It
was empty. I was glad. I didn't want any delays on my way
to see Ms. Franny. The quiet in the hallway was unsettling.
I struggled to listen for any sound coming from the ladies'
room, laughter, arguing, anything. There was only silence.

I paused at the door to their room before Luke and I
went inside. I closed my eyes and steeled myself for what
I was surely about to learn: Ms. Eulalie was dead and Ms.
Franny was in pieces.

I inhaled. I exhaled. I inhaled again.

Luke firmed his grip on my hand.

We went inside.

A tongue depressor flew past my face and clattered into a clean bedpan on the bureau.

"Bull's-eye!" Ms. Franny threw her hands in the air.

"Whoo-hoo!" Ms. Eulalie yelled, clapping. "That's five in a row for me!"

She was alive. Alive!

And apparently, a great shot with a tongue depressor.

"Hi, ladies," I said timidly. Luke flashed a quick wave as well.

"Baby girl!" Ms. Eulalie cried. "Come on over here and give me some sugar. I missed you so."

I ran and flung my arms around Ms. Eulalie's soft round shoulders. She smelled like Jean Naté After Bath Splash, and it was even better than the lilacs to me. "I missed you too," I said.

Ms. Franny pointed a tongue depressor at Luke. "So who's the beanpole with the x-ray specs?"

Luke took half a step into the room. "My name's Luke Pavel, ma'am."

"Mmm-hmm," Ms. Eulalie said extra loudly. She winked at me.

"Well, you've got yourself one long set of legs there, boy," Ms. Franny said. "Use 'em to get in here."

Luke blushed and smiled at the linoleum floor. He stepped over to Ms. Franny and extended his hand. "It's a pleasure to meet you, Ms. Calhoun. Blythe has told me many complimentary things about you."

"Ha!" Ms. Eulalie yelped. "Then baby girl lied to you, boy." Ms. Franny tossed her tongue depressor at Ms. Eulalie but missed, I'm pretty sure, on purpose. Ms. Eulalie grace-fully held her hand out to Luke like she was royalty. Which, to me, she was. "Eulalie Cornelia Stallworth Jones. Stallworth was my maiden name. You can't throw a five-pound rock in Alabama without hitting a Stallworth or their kin."

Luke took her hand gently and shook it. "Nice to meet you, Ms. Jones."

She waved her free hand at him. "Oh, you just go on and call me Ms. Eulalie. Everyone else does." She narrowed her eyes at Ms. Franny. "Except one."

"I'm so happy you're okay, Ms. Eulalie," I said. "I was really worried."

"I knew," Ms. Franny belted. "That's why I had Nurse Ratched call you. I didn't want you stewing for a week about whether or not Ukulele had croaked yet."

I smiled at her. "I was worried about you too, Ms. Franny."

She went, *"Psssh!* I was fine. No need to worry about me."

I leaned close to Ms. Eulalie. "She was a basket case," I whispered. "She's a total mess without you."

"I can hear you!" Ms. Franny cried. "I'm old, not deaf, and I was not a basket case or a mess. I was . . . I had a stomach-ache. I was medicated."

I made the cuckoo sign with my finger circling beside my head. Ms. Eulalie giggled, and Ms. Franny flung another tongue depressor at us. I picked it up. "What are you doing with these?"

"Playing HORSE," Ms. Franny said. "Ukulele's whipping my butt, if you can believe it."

"Believe it, 'cause it's true!" Ms. Eulalie crowed. "That

is, when she don't cheat by making noise when I throw." Ms. Eulalie plucked the tongue depressor from my hand and flipped it across the room. It pegged Ms. Franny on the shoulder, and she pretended to fall over dead with her tongue hanging out.

Luke cracked up so loudly that one of the orderlies poked his head in. That might have been the moment the ladies decided that Luke was all right with them.

"You young folk should get out and take in the day the Lord has given you." Ms. Eulalie held out her arms to me and I hugged her again for a long time.

"I can't stay anyway," I said. "I don't know if Darlene told you, but I got fired from volunteering."

"Mmm-hmm, she told us," Ms. Eulalie said.

"Couldn't wait to tell us, in fact," Ms. Franny said. "But we let her know how we felt about the situation."

"That we did!" Ms. Eulalie echoed, and they cackled together. Luke looked back and forth between them and wouldn't stop grinning.

I went over and wrapped my arms around Ms. Franny too and promised both of them that I'd be back to visit soon. Luke promised to come with me.

As we left, Ms. Eulalie called, "Go make hay while the sun shines!"

Once we were out the door, we heard Ms. Franny say to Ms. Eulalie, "You do know that saying means to go fornicate while you're still young, right?"

"Oh!" Ms. Eulalie gasped. "No, it don't! It don't mean that! Tell me it don't mean that!"

"And I thought I was the one with the dirty mind."

"Oh, sweet Jesus, please forgive me."

Luke hooked his arm around my waist and drew me against his body. "I see why they're so special to you. They're certainly more entertaining than Dumpster-diving."

I nudged him sideways with my hips. "Only a little."

Darlene was at her desk down at the end of the hallway.

I grabbed Luke's arm. "I have to talk to that woman really quick, okay? You go on out. I'll be there in a minute."

"No prob," he said.

"And Luke?" I said. "Thanks for coming with me."

"Of course." He landed a kiss on my cheek. "I'll be outside."

I walked to Darlene's desk. She was peering intensely at a chart through reading glasses on a chain around her neck. She took off the glasses when I said hello. "You're here," she said flatly.

"Yes."

She hitched her head toward the ladies' room. "Seen 'em yet?"

"Yes. Thank you so much for calling me. I was really worried. I appreciate you doing that."

She nodded once and put her glasses back on.

"Darlene?" I said.

She took the glasses off again and looked at me impatiently.

"I want to apologize for being rude to you yesterday," I said. "I was having an exceptionally bad day. I took it out on you, and I'm sorry."

Darlene's mouth scrunched to the side. She let her glasses

hang down. "Are things better today?" she asked, almost sounding interested.

I laughed and glanced toward where Luke had gone. "Some stuff, yes. Some's still a total mess." Darlene raised her eyebrows and half-smiled. I said, "That's why I was so happy to see Ms. Eulalie back. It meant a lot to me. So thanks."

"You're welcome." Darlene slid her glasses back on and went back to her chart. "And Blythe?" she said without looking up. "You may return to your position next week."

"But I thought . . ."

"Those two griping grannies threatened to forget their adult diapers if I didn't let you volunteer again," she said. She smiled at the chart, but I saw it. "Anyone who can keep those battle-axes happy and off my back for a few hours is fine by me."

I suddenly sensed what Darlene had to go through with her job. How she had to work long hours with failing bodies and fading minds. How she had to keep staff in line and still not melt down herself. How she had to play the bad guy and put up with residents disliking her because unpleasant things had to be done and Darlene was the one who did them.

"Thanks, Darlene," I said. "Let me know if I can do anything else to help out."

"Will do," she said. She flipped the page and went on reading.

I left to find Luke.

He was in the garden, bent over one of the lilac bushes with his nose buried deep in a clump of purple blossoms. I walked to him so quietly that I was nearly beside him and he still hadn't seen me. I watched him silently as he smelled cluster after cluster of flowers. Around us, the garden was in its first breath of fullness. Leaves had unfurled, colors peeked out, and each plant was plump and glossy and ready to erupt into the abundance of spring. The garden was on the very cusp of beginning. It was poised to flourish.

Just like Luke and me.

Why had I ever cared about happy endings?

Happy beginnings were so much better.

Many thanks go to my family for encouraging me, to my editor for guiding me, and to my agent for believing in me. I wouldn't have this book without any of you.